In an era of corporate journalism, the media industry is willing to experiment with the irrational and the perverse. Youngsters across news channels are fed on the diet of crime, sleaze and entertainment, their baptism complete only when they have touched the new high of grounding a news story at the altar of TRP.

Newsroom LIVE attempts to capture the shenanigans of the newsroom and its illicit relationship with power corridors and corporate sharks.

PRABHAT SHUNGLU began as a reporter with *The Statesman* and later worked for *The Pioneer* and *The Times of India*, before switching to electronic media with *BiTV*. He has reported extensively from the conflict zones of Kargil (1999), Afghanistan (2001-2002) and Iraq (2003), on national disasters like the cyclone in Orissa (2000) and the Gujarat earthquake (2001), on national and provincial elections, and interviewed several political personalities, including the Prime Minister of India.

He has worked with *Aaj Tak, Star News, IBN7, Rajya Sabha TV* and *News Express*.

The author's first book, *Yahan Mukhaute Bikte Hain*, a collection of essays on politics and contemporary issues was published to critical acclaim in 2010. Prabhat studied at St Joseph's College, Allahabad and graduated in Commerce from Allahabad University. *Newsroom LIVE* is his second book and his first work of fiction.

NEWSROOM LIVE

PRABHAT SHUNGLU

OM

Om Books International

First published in 2012 by

OM

Om Books International

Corporate & Editorial Office
A-12, Sector 64, Noida 201 301
Uttar Pradesh, India
Phone: +91 120 477 4100
Email: editorial@ombooks.com
Website: www.ombooksinternational.com

Sales Office
4379/4B, Prakash House, Ansari Road
Darya Ganj, New Delhi 110 002, India
Phone: +91 11 2326 3363, 2326 5303
Fax: +91 11 2327 8091
Email: sales@ombooks.com
Website: www.ombooks.com

ISBN: 978-93-80069-30-2

Printed in India

10 9 8 7 6 5 4 3 2 1

To my Amma
who gave me the courage to fight against all odds…

Mat Kaho Aakash Mein Kohra Ghana Hai,
Yeh Kisi Ki Vyaktigat Aalochna Hai.

—Dushyant Kumar

Contents

Part I

TRP

Golu, the *hathi*

Uday was fast asleep until a call from Binny rudely woke him up. "An elephant has fallen down a ditch! You have to cover that LIVE!"

"Why me?"

"Because the boss wants you to cover it."

"But I got back late last night."

"That is all right! " she said. "It is in the Pushta area, close to your home. Why don't you hop into a taxi and rush to the spot. I am sending the crew and the OB."

"But, ma'am…"

"Try to understand Uday. Don't waste time. Just rush!" Binny quipped. "I am sending in the OB van", she added before hanging up.

He sat up on the bed staring vacantly out of the window. This is ridiculous, he thought. What would people back in his hometown, Siwan think? Uday Verma, son of Dhirendra and Sushma, who doggedly argued with his parents against answering civil services exam and instead went in for a diploma in journalism after graduating in political science, was last seen reporting about an elephant that had fallen into a ditch. For Almighty's sake!

He tossed away the blanket and walked groggily towards the bathroom. Chances were good that he would spend a terrible time on the pot. The early morning thought of 'Psycho' could send even the healthiest metabolism for a toss. But, last night's whisky with soda in the 'car-o-bar' saved the day for him. As he stepped into the shower, the cold water soothed his nerves and he decided to indulge in a bit longer. The elephant was unlikely to climb out of the ditch before the media jamboree exacted its TRP moments, he thought.

In the midst of it all, Binny's words struck him like a Thames of groans. "Let's create a drama!"

"*Bhonsdi ke, sab paagal hain,*" he mumbled.

Uday was livid as he went down the stairs to the waiting cab. He barely got in when his mobile rang. Again. It was Psycho. "Hope you have been briefed by Binny. Two things... every little detail about the elephant...want the mahout LIVE!"

Uday managed a feeble "Yes, sir", before the line got disconnected.

As the cab negotiated the Patparganj Mother Dairy manufacturing unit, Uday pulled out his mobile and dialled Dadu. "Hello, Dadu, how are you?"

"Hel...o!"

"You must watch me today," Uday cut him short. "I will present the biggest breaking news of my career." Uday's voice assumed a self-deprecatory tone. "An elephant has fallen into a *nallah* along the banks of the Yamuna."

"Elephant? Breaking news? I thought an earthquake has brought down the Qutub Minar. These days news channels are too much!" Dadu was direct and Uday loved him for that. "By the way, your amma and papa have boarded the train. Hope you will receive them at the railway station in the evening," Dadu dropped a gentle reminder for his grandson.

"Will do! But I have important things to do right now. The fate of the nation hinges on my performance. Will catch up with you later." Uday hung up.

Golu was struggling to breathe. The *nallah* had all but dried up, leaving behind a slush of black marshy waste. He had fallen into it the previous night after he had broken the chain with which his mahout had secured him to a tree, and run amok. He bellowed in rage and fear, struggling to get out of the slush pool as the onlookers watched in horror. Uday's heart went out to the trapped mammal. "We are going to take your phone-in in two minutes." It was Binny. "We have already flashed the news and slugged it: *Hathi Gira, Shahar Hila.*"

The crowd gathered around Uday and the OB van as if they were there with medical help, and an ambulance in tow.

While his cameraperson looked for a perfect parking place for the camera angle, Uday went looking for the mahout. Someone from the crowd pointed to the man wearing a multicoloured turban and sporting ear studs. Uday lunged at him.

Ram Asrey was a prize catch. Being first on the spot threw up its moments of glory. Other channels would arrive shortly, and then Uday would have to share Ram Asrey with them. But it seemed Ram Asrey's moment had not arrived yet. Pervez frantically paced up to Uday and said, "The dish atop the OB van refuses to go up. Minor snag. Our engineer Keshav says he will set it right in a jiffy."

The OB van only added to Uday's irritation. Psycho would be mad if the spot LIVE did not hit the 8 am bulletin. Today, Uday could afford no bloopers. He ran up to Keshav. "I want the exact time the dish will go up. Why can't we take the van up close? I think there is scope." Uday screamed at the OB van driver.

"Impossible! We cannot go any further in. Not without risking the van, sir." The driver sounded firm and unambiguous.

The metalled road tapered off into a narrow mud track that soon became a steep decline along the Pushta area, leading to a huge drain. A cluster of *jhuggis*, set up by politicians aware of their vote banks, stood bordering the drain. The *jhuggi*-dwellers were a lucky lot. The Yamuna which remained dry throughout the year, with its stream narrowing down to almost the diameter of Delhi's ubiquitous *nallahs*, would swell during the monsoons. The floodwater pushed back by Haryana would further threaten to inundate the *jhuggi* clusters closer to the banks. For three complete months, the *jhuggi*-dwellers would be uprooted, with no help from those politicians who had 'settled' them to begin with. But last monsoon, they were better off as the Delhi government had arranged for timely rehabilitation and provided the necessary help, all thanks to the FPI youth leader, Sidhartha Sawhney, who had visited them just as the Yamuna threatened to devour their clusters and lives.

When the waters receded, the *jhuggi*-dwellers rebuilt their houses with such resolve as though these would never sweep away again.

The elephant and mahout and his family lived on the outskirts of this *jhuggi* cluster, alongside the road connecting to ITO bridge. Golu was a gentle elephant and had never disturbed the neighbourhood peace. But last night, he threw a tantrum, smashed his chain, and ran to his doom. His plight moved the residents, especially since Golu never harmed anyone. Not even last night when he was on, a mad run.

"It is not possible to go beyond this point," Pervez said looking at the deep, thick slush that was ready to suck him in.

"Try it once man… I don't want you to give up without trying." Uday said impatiently.

The driver shouted back from behind the wheel, "Sirji, not possible now."

Pervez tried to reason with Uday. "Yaar come on, we shall endanger our own communication system if we stretch beyond this point."

"I just got a call from Binny. She said Psycho was on his way to office. Just imagine him breathing instructions down our neck." Pervez smiled at a grumpy Uday, and went back to setting up the camera.

Amid this confusion, Ram Asrey managed to give Uday the slip. After a moment of panic, Uday spotted him. Pushing bystanders away, he made his way to Ram Asrey and pulled him aside. "Bhaiyya, one interview for TV… *Seedha Prasaran*… It's LIVE Ram Asrey bhai…"

Ram Asrey did not give a damn. Golu's health worried him more than the camera plonking right in the middle of the messy surroundings. Time was running out and there was no help in sight. He had told the police. At once, two beat constables came but they were equally clueless about the next move.

Uday was now connected to the Production Control Room (PCR). He was LIVE, breaking the biggest news of his career.

"Yes, this cry of pain is Golu's, that unfortunate elephant. Listen to it carefully. He is dying. *Golu mar raha hai*… Someone has to help him…" Suddenly he heard a crackle on his earphone.

"Get closer. Where is the mahout?" Psycho barked from his safety net.

Uday continued LIVE."Golu's caretaker and mahout Ram Asrey will soon join us. In fact, he is right here." Pervez quickly zoomed out from Golu and panned to Ram Asrey as Uday fired his first question to him.

"How old is Golu?"

"He is twenty-two."

"How long have you been together?"

"I reared his mother. But she passed away when Golu was five."

"What happened to her?"

"She died of a mysterious disease."

"And where is Golu's father?"

"He passed away last year. He had grown too old."

"You mean he is an orphan?" ('Create a drama', Binny's words rung back again.)

"No, he is not an orphan. Like his mother, he, too, is a part of my extended family." Ram Asrey insisted.

"This is double tragedy. This orphan has no one from his immediate family. And Ram Asrey is the only one left from his extended family. And he is fighting death." Uday knew he was mouthing rubbish."And why do you think he behaved the way he did last night?"

"I don't know."

"You should know… Was he upset?"

"No, nothing unusual. Last week, he attended a large congregation of his community in Rajasthan. After that, he took part in the wedding of Maharaj Shreedhar Rathore's great granddaughter to that *gora* sa'ab from London. We travelled to Udaipur for that. He appeared unflustered with all the resplendent outfits we had made him wear on the special occasion," Ram Asrey recounted Golu's engagements in detail.

"What did he eat?"

"He had plenty of *ganna* on our way back from Shahdara," said Ram Asrey.

"Was the *ganna* edible?"

"I ate it too."

A voice crackled on Uday's earphone again, "Drama, drama...!" That was Ernesto. And suddenly another voice overlapped, this one stinging him in his ears. "Find out about his marital status." This one stumped Uday. He could distinctly make out Psycho's shrill voice.

"You said he is twenty-two years old. Is he married?" Uday was direct with the mahout.

But Ram Asrey hadn't bargained for this one. "Sir, what do you mean?"

"Is he married, or still a bachelor?" Uday asked stressing on each word with the right pause.

"Yes. He had developed a liking for Chameli in our neighbourhood. So I got him married to her three years ago."

"Where is she?"

"Chameli is now with my brother in Orissa. She delivered a baby there months ago. We call her Champa," said Ram Asrey. "She is part of a large family of tuskers my brother and I own," he added.

"Could Golu have felt incomplete without his better half?" Uday lobbed another question at Ram Asrey.

"No, he had other cows in the neighbourhood to look forward to. But why are you asking me all this, bhai sa'ab? What do I tell you?"

"Tell me one more thing Ram Asreyji, is Golu a much sought after elephant?"

"Well, he is."

"How is he different from his peers? Is he the strongest?"

"Indeed. But will that help get him out?" lamented Ram Asrey. He was getting increasingly fidgety. Time was running out for his dear Golu, and there was no help in sight. Four to five ambulance-like vans were parked bumper-to-bumper on the road at a distance. On closer look, they turned out to be OB vans. Reporters and TV crew were streaming in.

"Ram Asreyji, some animal-lovers and wildlife experts are watching Golu's plight. We might get some help. Well, hold on. We have a question from Mr Saxena from Kanpur. Ram Asreyji, Mr Saxena says since elephants are fond of water, how often do you bathe Golu? Do you keep him well-groomed?"

"He is like a son to me. I am concerned about his health just as I am about mine or my family's. Now will you please excuse me..." Ram Asrey struggled to get out of the frame and called out for Dulare, his friend. "*Arrey, ye bhonsdi ke TV wale hamra Golu ka maar deheyen.*" The gun-microphone picked up Ram Asrey's gravitas loud and clear, the camera caught the lip movement, the OB relayed it and the PCR in office switched it on LIVE.

As the evening wore on, floodlights were mounted on wooden poles nearby so rescue operations could be carried out, unhindered. Word had spread that the crane was on its way. By now Golu's body lay inert in the *nallah*. Only his trunk moved. The crowd was slowly giving up.

Time was running out for Uday. He had to pick up his parents from the railway station. But since the elephant saga was the main agenda on prime-time, Anushka, who was on the night shift was called in earlier to take over the baton.

Ram Asrey could not resist Anushka's charms as she tucked him into the frame. Anushka's earphone crackled. She was told that Prithvi would grill Ram Asrey straight out of the newsroom. "Ram Asreyji, let me ask you straight out, Golu turned violent because you separated him from his partner; from her Chameli?" Ram Asrey looked a bit befuddled, so Anushka repeated Prithvi's question.

"I don't know what you mean by that. He is just like any other normal elephant—only that he is a bit errant."

"But obviously, you have denied him his partner?"

"Well, his current predicament has nothing to do with Chameli."

Anushka heard another crackle on her earphone. "Ram Asrey is lying," it was Prithvi on the screen now. "I have a pug and I know that. I have named him Ghunghroo—he is just like my family. He yearns for freedom to indulge in his basic instincts. And I encourage his indulgence. It seems Ram Asrey carefully chose to ignore Golu's rush of testosterone." Psycho pronounced those words with a sexologist's conviction.

"Why should I lie to you, madam? Golu is like a son to me. I am concerned about his health and I carefully watch his behaviour. He has been like any other normal elephant."

"This is the most barbaric form of domestic violence," Prithvi barked on air.

The line suddenly snapped. Back in the newsroom, Prithvi was ready to explode. Shazia's voice boomed on his earphone: "Sir, the connection snapped. I have asked the assignment to connect Anushka again."

"You guys are hopeless."

"But sir, how can I help it if the phone connection gets snapped? That's for the assignment desk to handle."

"No point arguing. And Binny, I want two top psychologists on the line. We have to grill this Ram Asrey chap."

"A psychologist is already in. He just needs to be wired up," Binny informed as she casually sank into her chair. As the bulletin slipped into a commercial break, Prithvi turned around in his chair and issued another set of instructions. "This is getting bigger. Need the who's who of Delhi on line."

"Give me a moment and you will have the minister on the line. I am lining up the rest. Don't worry." Binny's words must have worked like balm on Prithvi's frayed nerves as he swivelled in his chair to face the camera once again.

"Ma'am, Pandit Giriraj Maharaj should be here any moment." Farhat informed Binny. "And I have lined up a couple of other astrologers on phone too," she added.

Bhoomi and Muskan darted a quick look at Farhat and smiled before resuming their work on their terminals.

He got back to his apartment and switched on the TV set to get updates on Golu. Psycho was in the studio surrounded by a panel of experts, animal lovers and psychologists and, of course, Pandit Somdev Brahmatmaj, the channel's resident astrologer. Pandit Brahmatmaj sported a bold, red tilak on his forehead that had three distinct vertical creases betraying the worldly worries that engaged his mind all the time. Certainly, Golu was one such.

"His *shukra* appears to retrograde. That is why he got separated from his lover. *Rahu* is not well placed either, in his chart. That is why, he fell into the ditch." Pandit Brahmatmaj proudly pronounced from the studio.

Suddenly, Pandit Brahmatmaj dug into his kurta pocket, took out a conch shell and blew it hard. "He shall live to see another day. His Jupiter is the strongest. And no power on this earth can prove me wrong," declared Pandit Brahmatmaj LIVE on DNN.

Seconds after his pronouncement, a message got pasted on the DNN screen in big, bold letters in red:

GOLU WILL SURVIVE.

–Pandit Brahmatmaj

Uday recalled Binny's unbroken string of instructions and how he had set about carrying them out. He felt ashamed for diligently carrying out Prithvi's ridiculous instructions earlier in the day. He remembered the cynical look on Ram Asrey's face when he asked him about Golu's date of birth. That was the last instruction from Binny before he handed over the baton to Anushka.

Many more astrologers, card readers and parrot *baba*s were contacted. All the updates ran at the bottom of the screen in bold capitals:

SHANI, RAHU, KETU GOLU KE SAATH,
AMANGAL ASAMBHAV.

–Nariyal Baba

GOLU *JEETEGA*.

–Acharya Kapil

NO POWER CAN HARM GOLU.

–Pandit Nagmani

For once, Uday wished all their prophesies would come true. He couldn't bear to see Golu's trauma any longer.

DNN's on-the-hour poll survey proved Psycho right. Eight-five per cent of people echoed channel's concerns: viewers were unanimous that Golu's basic instincts were suppressed and that the mahout should be given adequate punishment for Golu's trials and tribulations.

"The fuckers can rig the polls to reach their own conclusions." Uday could not help swearing at the pie chart on the screen as he picked up the broom to sweep the floor in a single fast forward motion. Then he headed straight for the kitchen. Used and unwashed utensils laid in a heap in the sink. Weeks had gone by since he had last cleaned his refrigerator. He had to hurry up or else nobody could save him from amma's wrath. The train was running on schedule and would arrive in half an hour. After doing up a quick job at the sink and the refrigerator, he darted into the bathroom for a quick shower. As he readied to step out, he cast a glance at the TV screen, and froze in his tracks. Everything appeared to be running in slow motion. He could see an object going up and then coming down. The visuals were running in a loop. He could hear a loud, collective shriek as the object fell on the ground. Uday sank to the floor. He could not believe what he was seeing, not even the big, bold messages that were flashed across the screen. Frantically, he switched channels. Vishphot and Angaar were showing the same visuals. Angaar had even circled the subject red. He switched back to DNN. *'Golu Crane Se Gira'.*

"This can't be. How could they do this to me?" he thought. He could hear Anushka's voice in the background, an octave higher than a shriek laced with panic. "Can't say whether Golu will live to see another day." Anushka's words rang in his ear.

"Live for me, Golu! This was my story, not Anushka's." Uday wanted to rush back to the spot, snatch the microphone from Anushka and go LIVE right then. Even at the cost of being dubbed a rogue son. He dialled his father's number. "Office emergency," he would tell him. Instead, he heard the irritatingly familiar recorded message: "The number you have dialled is either switched off or out of coverage area". Another thud echoed in the room. The phone was thrown to the bed with a fielder's force. How he wished the train to get delayed for a few hours. Golu's situation could suddenly take a turn for the worse. And Pandit Somdev Brahmatmaj could not have been more off the mark about Golu.

Golu is Dead

Uday's demeanour suggested that the arrival of his parents was a huge pile on. Amma could make out that her son, was not in his element. Uday could sense that she was trying to read his face. Sent on a guilt trip, he immediately picked up her khadi *jhola*. The coolie lugged the heavier *jholas* as Uday walked ahead of his parents, the cell phone glued to his right ear. No sooner had he got into the taxi and gave instructions to the driver than, he got the call he had perversely expected. "Golu is dead."

Uday felt crushed. No matter he slogged the entire day without stepping out even for a meal, Anushka would walk away with the laurels for the story. Golu's death would surely make prime time headlines. And in the newsroom the next day, she will strut around like a queen.

These newsrooms mould youngsters, right from the start. Camps, led by power centres, take a recruit into their fold. Launch pads take shape owing to subtle manoeuvres. Stories are created and played up. Extra footage is given to the greenhorn until one morning, when this rookie finds his mailbox flooded with congratulatory messages: starting with a two-liner from the immediate superior, invariably a camp follower of a greater God, endorsed by the greater God, and a still greater God, and so on. Then the creator, destroyer and preserver of the newsroom sign it off, "Congrats. Keep at it!" Messages start pouring in from bureaus across India—the baptism is over.

Uday's launch was no different. But Psycho and Hemendra realised that this rocket would find his own orbit, not the one they destined for him. So they took extra care to launch the next rookie, and it was bang on. Anushka earned brownie points from the bosses instantaneously. The next year's appraisal was a no-brainer. While Uday got the regular 12 per cent hike, Anushka received a 40 per cent increment plus, a promotion as a bonus. Psycho claimed that she was his most sensational discovery. More sensations were to follow. At the year's prestigious awards ceremony, instituted by the news portal, *Mediawar.com* and co-sponsored by the DNN, Anushka landed the 'Young Professional of the Year Award' for her story 'Ghunghroo—a day in the life of a pug.'

The award was, the culmination of the love she lavished on Psycho's pet. After the award, she even thought of adopting Ghunghroo. Psycho declined the offer with a smile, saying she should rather adopt the owner.

All along the half hour taxi drive, Uday was lost in deep thought. It was as if he was sharing the taxi with complete strangers.

"You didn't like that we are here?" Uday's mother could be curt if she wanted to. His father saved the situation for him. "Come on Sushma... Something must be troubling Munna. Will speak to him later. Come, let's settle down first," he said.

They had dinner on the floor of the living room in candle light. Uday had little space in his 10 by 14 living room to furnish it with a dining table set. Even the presence of the best teak-wood table, would not deter his mother from sitting on the floor and eating her dinner. The dinner was laid out on the bedsheet and a few old newspapers on the floor. Uday was irritated because of constant power cut in his area, but he ensured he plied his parents with second helping of boiled rice, *chokha* (a mix of boiled mashed potato, onion, green chillies, laced in mustard oil) and hot *arhar dal*. The *chokha* made him forget office. Only for a while, though.

He wanted to throw his arms around his mother in a tight hug for two reasons: one, to say sorry for having spoiled her mood and second, to congratulate her for preparing such a sumptuous meal. But he could not muster the wits to do that when he observed the harsh expressions on his mother's face that sat etched in steel. He hurried with the dinner plates to the kitchen sink.

He had laid out the mattresses for his parents in the living room. His bedroom was too cramped with his spoils. He retired to his room, blew off the candles and before long, was fast asleep.

Dreams

The Dream # 1: Binny

Uday woke up with a start. That was one hell of a nightmare. He was sweating profusely as he sat up on the bed. He looked up, but he could not see the white ceiling, only darkness. In the dark grey silence, he could hear the ba-ba-BOOM of his heart. He could not spot the fan, but realised it had gone dead. The air blast of the running desert cooler suddenly fell silent. Bow down to thee, pesky intrusions! He realised the power had conked out. There was no back up and the inverter struggled to breathe. But why did he wake up with a sudden start? Was he sweating because of the power failure? Some questions are best left unanswered. He looked for his mobile phone to check the mobile clock. It was quarter past four. He was barely able to breathe. A big ferocious cat, with its thick hair, sharp claws and trendy eye make-up had been clawing his heart out, his right leg severed. He was still breathing even as that hulk of a beast relished his other leg.

Before he could pick himself up for the counter, he woke up. Almost as a reflex, Uday groped for his important body organs. He found both his legs intact and the parcel of the same body that held his hands and tummy and his face together. He ran his sweaty fingers across his thick mop of hair, trying to feel the touch of a wound or a laceration. He suddenly jumped out of the bed, hearing the roar of a lion. His heart skipped a few heartbeats. Where was he? A dream within a dream? Inception explained. He could hear the animal roar. He could hear the echo in that pitch-dark room. Where could he disappear?

Uday tried to recollect the nightmare. A vast expanse of a stadium, unfolded before him. What was Uday doing at the stadium?

He was brought to the stadium in a cage, like a circus lion… He had gone down the ravine, looking for a story when a gang of menacing men caught him. They appeared to be talking in a language, which, Uday had not heard before. Not even his perfunctory knowledge about the tribes of the world after having seen unlimited stories on The Discovery Channel, helped him figure out the tribe's mumbo-jumbo. They had long and sharp spears and sported a headgear made of bird feathers. Two men took hold of him, before the others blindfolded him. He was taken away to a place unknown and undiscovered. He pleaded with them that he had no intention to harm them and that he was not a spy for all that they were suspecting him to be. His thoughts were wavering between the dream and the newsroom and Binny ma'am's special spying assignment.

Uday always tried to find ways to be in Binny's good books. The clout she held among the bosses was too much to be ignored by any youngster like him, he thought. For him, she was his stepping stone to success. But she had not entrusted him with any major spying responsibility yet, he knew though, she would go to any length to find out what Raman was up to after his morning shifts.

Before he got married six months ago, Raman shared his DDA flat with Uday. Though Raman was happily married now, and moved out with his wife in a separate house, it was quite impossible for Binny to banish him out of her thoughts. Raman had once confessed to him last year that he had invited Binny over to their flat, while Uday was away, vacationing with his parents in Mussoorie. "Come on, you were already engaged then, weren't you?"

"So…?"

"Did you two do anything?"

"We ate. Got drunk. Waited. And waited. And left."

"Oh, I got my answer."

"Look, Uday, it was consensual. She was an equal partner."

"Oh yes, how can I forget your egalitarian, women-are-the-pillars-of-the-society bullshit. So what did you do to allow her an equal space? You allowed her to ride you? Come on. Say that."

"Look, Uday, you are crossing the limit." Raman mocked with anger, but was equally eager to confess everything to Uday. "I mean, I was in no position to refuse her."

"Bravo… Bravo… I know exactly the position you were in," chuckled Uday. "Now I know why bum-chic-bum loves to molly-coodle me. She thinks I know her darkest secret."

"Oh come on, maybe she is pining for your love and affection now that, I am a happily married man."

"I hope you guys did not use my bed."

"Well, I can't say for sure."

"What do you mean you are not sure? You must tell me the truth. Did you use my bed?" Uday was getting restless and edgy.

"Well, Uday, you know, she accidentally spilled water on my bed."

"How could you? And, you did not have the decency to get the bedsheet laundered before I returned?"

"We did it in the kitchen!" It was Raman's turn to chuckle as Uday seemed scrawny, almost undernourished, anorexic lad after hearing that. Turning away from him, he darted across the living room and plonked next to the wall facing the TV. "Did you wrap up your willy?" Raman acted as though he had not heard Uday.

"Come on, now don't pretend. Did you wrap up your tool," Uday's excitement was spilling over.

"Well, I wanted to use it but she insisted otherwise. She likes them as water bombs."

"Goodness grief! Our hero believes in raw sex."

"Well, she said it was a safe period."

"And she believed you were a safe bet?" A sense of nervous excitement overtook Uday. "We got wild with passion. Nothing could come between us, that day," Raman bragged.

"Bravo, love guru… Bravo!" Uday clapped in derision.

"You know Uday."

"What?"

"There are only two kinds of battles you face in life. Ek haq ki, aur doosri fuck ki. And I don't want to lose the second battle." Raman said it straight-facedly. Uday could now recall Raman's dalliances with at least, two other female colleagues. Not to count his last roaring encounter with the housemaid's daughter, who would come to cook food for them whenever her mother stayed away from work. A teenager and also a mother, she fell for Raman's charms. Uday stumbled upon their secret relationship only by accident, when he found empty boxes of a brand, known for manufacturing female undergarments in the kitchen dustbin. Raman valiantly accepted he got them as presents for Madhu—the maid's daughter.

Uday tried to recollect the number of days he had been away from Delhi on official reporting assignments, when Raman used to share the flat with him. He lost the count and gave up. It dawned upon Uday that what a perfect 'chootiya' he had been, not to sense the passionate dalliances his roommate was involved in, while he was away grazing the waste.

The Dream # 2: The Gladiator

But who were those guys? Why would they tie him up blindfolding him? What was their intention? Uday saw himself trapped in a cage. Like the one they would use to wheel a lion, in a circus ring.

He was being transported somewhere. He could hear a female speaking a semblance of English, giving instructions. He could hear her voice booming closer to the cage now: "Take him to the stadium." The princess, it seemed, was keen on a spectacle of blood and gore after a long, long time.

The stadium was reverberating with wild cheers of spectators, waiting in anticipation of a great game. What do the spectators expect him to do? And what have they taken him for? His hands went cold with sweat. His lips had gone dry and he was barely able to speak. He muttered something. The sound ricocheted from the upper lip before dying out in the cave of his mouth. He was too terrified by the spectacle.

Suddenly, a pair of hands pushed in from the grill and in one sudden jerk, the blindfold was removed. The princess was sitting on a large throne, below the jewel adorned canopy that overlooked the motley group of spectators in the stadium. Attendants in animal hide were fanning her with peacock feathers. A mysterious smile flashed across her face as she met the gaze of the man, trapped in the cage.

Uday tried hard to recognise her, but could not, having once seen her on The Discovery Channel. He was almost convinced the channel was shooting an entirely new episode: 'Human Civilisation And Beyond', with Uday as the case study.

She sat upright on the throne, thrusting her diamond-studded cups, its radius an inch wider than the largest cup on offer at the Café Cofi Korner, holding her twins in a tight hug, pressing out the flesh around the oriole in a seductive display of a woman most desired. "What is Tiya doing here? Has she got me here as a slave? That should be fun," he thought.

The princess smiled back, soaking in the pride of her tribe members to have got such a lovely catch. Suddenly the crowd let out a frenzied roar. Another cage, bigger than the one he was trapped in, was wheeled into the stadium from the far end of the gate to the right of where the princesses sat. Another hapless person like him, he thought. The cage sat on a wagon-wheel pulled by two giant men, bald and their oil-massaged body glistening due to sweat. The wagon wheel trundled right up to the middle of that vast stadium—to be exhibited before the queen when a heart-rending roar filled the air, drawing an equally lusty cheer from the crowd.

The two bald men then brought the lion's cage in direct line with that of Uday's. The two locked eyeballs. The lion appeared angry and furiously mumbled some incoherent one liners.

Lifting his right paw out of that iron grill as if eager to take on his challenger, the lion made clear his intention. Uday could hear the lion say: "You killed my man. You are a dead man."

"Oh my god! Are my sensory instincts in place? How can I understand the language of an animal? I killed his man. I am the honourable son of my honourable father who could not even bring himself to killing a 'machchar'." Even the houseflies he captured with

one circular jab in the air while reading newspaper in the morning, he would cradle them between the thumb and the middle finger, rub their puny bodies and let go of them. It was as if by conspiracy that the flies would hover around him, eager to give up their bodies for a free massage.

The crowd roared again as the lion lifted his paw and let out a deafening roar.

They were going to set the lesser mortal free before the beast. Like a lamb before a hungry lion, Uday was too paralysed with fear to be able to break into a run.

He could already visualise the beast feasting on his flesh. And after having devoured Uday, he would let out a loud burp. That was the side effect of having Uday Verma's flesh. There is no way he can resist drinking Verma family's blood and not acquire contagious absurdities.

Uday was passed on this unique trait in his genes by his father. Every time his father got up from the dinner table, he would let out loud burps. It would come in piecemeal for the next half-hour. Uday hated his father for this. But as he grew up and stepped into adolescence, he realised his digestive system would always find a reason to help release a load of hot air. Uday would wonder at the theory of genetic codification. Some traits are passed on from a generation to generation, without design. His younger brother, Hriday, had taken after his father cent per cent. He too was a burpoholic.

The lion was roaming free. He ran up to Uday's cage and sank his teeth into it as if, daring the entrapped victim to come out. Uday recoiled in fear. As the Lion withdrew, he heard him say that again, "You killed my man, you are a dead man." The crowd's cacophonous cheer lent an awful intensity to the roar of the lion. "I am going to die any moment. The lion is going to eat me up. They are going to throw me to the beast. I am going to die." He was getting hysteric. He did not want to die. Not until he has taken a sweet revenge on Anushka. He cursed himself for not shepherding through the Golu story and therefore allowing Anushka the space and the accolades on the coverage following Golu's death. Oh wait, he thought. Suddenly, the reality struck him. The woman on the throne cannot be Tiya. It has to be Anushka. She has a vengeful mind. She hates him. She is jealous of him. She has finally trapped him. It cannot be anyone but that whore, he thought. Anushka, the whore. Anushka, the whore.

Her attendant whispered something into her ear as she looked across the arena, at the two black men. As if on cue, one of the two men passed on the gladiator armour to Uday. Uday could see the lion taking a pre-victory lap of the arena as the crowd lustily cheered.

"Kill him! Kill him! Kill, kill, kill..." The lion stopped before the throne, tilted his tail up, and respectfully saluted the princess. Then he threw a glance from across the far end at his victim, "It's payback time, my prey." Uday could hear the lion mumble under his breath.

Was the lion out to revenge Golu's death? Lions and elephants have a mutual respect for each other. They would not come in each other's way. But do they have a bonding strong enough to revenge on each other's killing? He never saw any such case study on The Discovery Channel. But who knows? "You think I killed Golu? The fact is that the whore sitting on the throne killed him," Uday tried to negotiate, but he knew that the angry lion would not listen to him. Uday resigned himself to his fate.

The gladiator was ready for the battle of death. The lion made one last dash towards his victim Uday, and stopped a few feet away raising a cloud of dust. The beast seemed a veteran of many such battles. Uday convulsed with fear.

"You killed my man. You are a dead man," the lion repeated with kingly authority.

Uday looked one last time at the princess. He wanted to beg her for mercy, tell her he would never entertain thoughts about her as a whore, will always support her and would never touch an animal story, not even with a barge pole. But the princess sat on the throne unmoved. "Kill him, kill him..." The cry went up in air as the crowd stood up in one last spurt of excitement.

The Dream # 3: Leg Piece

The lion's roar brought him back to the arena. The beast was standing in front of him, baring a set of skin shearing and skull cracking jaws. Uday met his gaze and tried to manoeuvre the foil, but he could not lift it high enough. Uday pleaded with him one last time, "I did not kill anyone. How can you say I killed your man? I have killed nobody in my life. I am a poor guy. Just a simple reporter! Please spare me!"The lion jumped aiming for his throat. Uday could hear Snowball jump out of the animal farm and say: 'War is war. The only good human being is a dead one.'

The foil fell away. The lion had his throat in his jaws, like they show it on The Discovery Channel. The lion catching its prey by the neck, sinking its fangs deep into prey's throat and draining his poor body off all the blood. He heard one last roar before falling unconscious. The lion held his victim in that freeze frame for some time before the body limped in his jaws. After ensuring the victim was dead, the lion dropped it on the ground, took a short victory lap around the stadium and came back to feast on his kill. He paused, looked heavenwards and said in a loud baritone: "Dear Golu, I kept my promise. I took my revenge. Rest in peace, bro." As Uday's soul left his body, it could see the lion chomping away on the body. It noticed the lion's penchant for leg-pieces. After relishing his meal, the big, ferocious cat turned around to dart one last look at the canopy and the row of spectators who were now on their feet and were cheering him wildly.

He paced up and down and then paused suddenly to sniff the ground around him. He sat there in a yoga posture before letting out a loud burp.

The Dream # 4: The Uday and The Golu

Uday's soul was an errant one. As it wandered in space, it wondered whether Uday's colleagues and friends would at all mourn his death. Will Binny cry buckets? How would Psycho react? Will he ever say he lost a good reporter? It looked down from the skies and saw a condolence meeting in progress, in the DNN newsroom. It couldn't help but hear the din, before deciding to partake in the revelry aka condolence meeting, even though it were to remain invisible. "It's going to be lots of fun", thought Uday's soul as it descended in one big skydive.

Psycho itched to speak first and chose English as his medium from an ever-expanding array of communication languages to choose from. With all his the's at the wrong places, the s's and z's murdered at the altar of 'j', he was sure of using language rules unknown to others.

"The Uday wauj a very nice person. He wauj the very good reporter aalso. I lost the two peepul today. Sorry...one wauj the animal. The Golu and the Uday. I cannot see the animal dying like this. You know how the Golu died in front of aavar eyej. He was LIVE on our channel when he died."

Uday's soul could hear Muskan whispering into Raman's ears, "Actually we were on a commercial break, when he fell off the crane. Psycho screamed at all of us right there, as if we conspired against Golu and helped drop him from the crane during the break."

Uday's soul got back to Prithvi's speech. "It wauj the first LIVE death aaf the animal that was the Golu. I say that with the proud, that we were the first in the history of the televejun newj to show the elephaant, the Golu dying after the phalling."

"I even suggested Sudhanshu sir to drop the commercial and go LIVE, but he told me to shut up. Bencho...!" Binny whispered.

"It made common sense that you dropped that goddamned undergarment commercial for a mega twist in the news story, which we were doing LIVE since morning." Ritwik nodded an affirmative reply and tapped her head affectionately.

Uday's soul tried to strain his ears to what Psycho was saying. "And you know, just as I was joking with the Uday about hij girlfriends, Golu also died becauj thoj peepul had taken away hij lover from him... I tell you guyj, the Golu and the Uday waaj like twins. I loved both of them. I still do. Both died because they did not get what they wanted. U guyj noticed the way the Golu was lying aan the ground? His privates were sowing... I mean sorry girls...you know I am very straightpharward and blunt... That ij a whery conclujeev proof that the Golu was denied hij conjugal rights... You know what I mean? That ij why the Golu ran away.

"We were able to egg-jhaktly pinpoint the real cauj of the Golu's death. This ij the aggresun we need. You are the best. I salute you guyj!"

Uday's soul now saw Ernesto whispering into Raman's ears. It tiptoed closer. "Marx argued that the capitalist bourgeoisie mercilessly exploited the proletariat. The bourgeoisie do not realise that capitalism contains seeds of its own destruction. After all, the wealth of the bourgeoisie depends on the work of the proletariat; by mercilessly suppressing Golu, Ram Asrey has written his own death warrant."

Raman looked at Ernesto with disdain. "My friend Uday has died young. God was cruel." Raman shot back.

"What has God to do with this? This was all Ram Asrey's fault. That is how the bourgeoisie exploit the working class. I am telling you, Ram Asrey must have set the lion on Uday," said Ernesto.

Uday's soul could see Raman ingenuously weaning himself away from Ernesto, melting into the crowd before reappearing again next to Binny, who seemed amused at something Haldi had just said. Haldi held a multicoloured pocket-comb in his hand. The bearded wonder ran it on his moustache for the third time, giving equal time to either parting.

"I am sad today, becauj we all know how excited the Uday was about getting married one day. Poor guy! Uday cast his eyes down his pants. He could feel the wet patch. Wet with his own pee. While his manhood is still feeling sticky and disgusting after resting feebly against his wet balls, feared to submission by the mammoth hulk and his heart-rending roar, I offer my condolences to both families. Even animals are humans..."

"And some humans are animals too," Farhat whispered into Muskan's ears.

"...even they have emosuns, like us... You should know how my the cute Ghunghroo behavej when I go back home... I can't even think of him aj an animal... Yes he treats me like hij own father... I can feel hij pain... I feel pain when he hurts hij body or when he ij sick... I feel the pain when he criej if the doctor givej him anti-rabiej injeksun... I can feel the pain of the Golu's family... My heart goej out for hij family..."

Prithvi aka Psycho had again triumphed with his crap. Uday's soul could see Pushkar 'poet' sir, Sabir 'proud Allahabadi' sir busy on their mobile handsets. Standing right behind them were Ranvir 'ace anchor' sir and Baba 'immediate boss' sir. Uday's soul crept close to Pushkar and sneaked a peek at his mobile. 'My heart goej out for the Psycho's family. Plj accept my condolencej'. Pushkar added 'The Gang' in the recipient list and pressed 'send'.

"Bloody rascals! This is hippopotamus tears," Thethar mumbled, throwing a curse at Prithvi. Muskan was within earshot. "Crocodile tears, Thethar sir. Crocodiles tears."

"Yes, yes. Whatever! This place is going to the dogs. Now, it's beyond redemption." Thethar continued in the same vein.

Rajkishore sir, known to be a great hand at scripts, stood at the back of the crowd. It seemed his body was present, but his mind was in a different zone. He shuffled from one leg on to another, even as he played with his mobile. Uday's soul could notice an expression of sadness resting tautly on his face. It was difficult to fathom, however, whether Uday's death was the reason. Days had passed in the newsroom, but he still hadn't changed his expression. He was confined to the expression of those sentiments since time immemorial. It was now the turn of Hemendra aka crotch-scratcher and Psycho's supari-man to take to the floor. "Uday was a nice boy. There must be some connection between Uday and Golu. The way they both died... Strange, both died a tortuous death...and perished the same night."

Karuna looked dressed for the occasion in her black suit. She perennially wore an expression of a woman wronged. Adept at inventing tragedies, she would shed copious tears at the drop of a hat. Prithvi never got tired praising her 'velvet' voice, but it was Hemendra who fell for her histrionics. Amidst the newsroom din, Hemendra's cabin would turn into a 'don't-disturb-zone' if Karuna was spotted inside. Outside Hemendra's cabin, she was referred to in hushed tones as Mata Karuneshwari. Tears rolled down her cheeks, smudging her puffy make up as Hemendra held forth on Uday and Golu in his inimitable pose—his right hand casually rubbing his crotch.

"Oh, how I would miss Uday and the great work he put in to see Golu alive..."

Hemendra could lie through his teeth. He was the one who started that mail business, late night, reserving much praises for Anushka over Uday.

And Prithvi poured his affection on his 'most promising' reporter, who, according to him, would be DNN's answer to Christiane Amanpour.

Uday's soul could see Pushkar fire another sms missile to 'The Gang'. This time a couplet from Dushyant:

> *'Aap Bachkar Chal Sakein, Aisi Koi Soorat Nahi,*
> *Rehguzar Ghere Huye Murde, Kharhe Hain Beshumar.'*

'Dushyant ki jai ho!' Sabir keyed his reply before sending to Pushkar and the rest of 'The Gang' members... Ranvir couldn't help replying with a short and crisp 'Hahahahahaha...gud 1.' Baba smiled as he opened the inbox, but chose not to reply.

Uday's soul saw its own obituary running on DNN. It shared screen space with Golu. Golu to the left, while the right side of the screen had a freeze frame of Uday, holding a gun-microphone with the DNN mic-id. The bold red under his image read: 1981–2006. It also opened Uday's official mailbox. It was overflowing with congratulatory and condolence messages by colleagues across bureaus, all in the past tense.'Golu has taken the channel to new heights,' wrote Milind from Bhopal.

'Thanks to you, Prithvi sir, we are the number one aggression channel,' said the Bangalore greenhorn, Sudhakar Rao.

'Down with that mahout… He was indulging in love jehad… We will not tolerate injustice,' read Shahzad's mail from Srinagar.

'Thanks Uday (may his soul Rest in Peace), thanks Anushka. But Prithvi sir, you showed us the way… Your LIVE grilling of the mahout tilted the scales against him…' Anirban from Kolkata bureau was unambiguous in his praise for Prithvi.

'Uday and Anushka made me cry for Golu,' wrote Jayanthi from Chennai bureau.

Unmaad from Lucknow bureau quoted, 'Chacha Ghalib in fond memory of Golu, "Ye ishq nahin asaan bus itna samajh lijye…ek aag ka darya hai aur doob ke jaana hai…"'

'The world shall never forget the sacrifices made by Golu and Uday. Golu-Uday amar rahe!' A one-liner landed from Chandigarh desk said it all.

But Uday's eyes groped for somebody special. A sober condolence waited from Satyendra Mahto from Surya Nagar: 'The channel has lost a promising young journalist. I have lost a brother.'

Baba Prasanmukh

Press your right nostril with your thumb and breathe in from your left. Do that as slowly as you can,' Baba Prasanmukh's voice came wafting through the humid morning air. Amma was an early riser. She would watch Baba Prasanmukh perform *pranayam* every day, like a teenager who would never miss a single film of their Bollywood icon.

It was ten past six in the morning as Uday strolled out to the balcony. The morning sun blazed outside, dazzling him for a moment. It was an excruciatingly hot summer as mercury broke all the previous records. He came back to his room and sat on the bed. The snatches from the nightmare came rushing back. He felt the lion was still lurking around in his room and would jump off from the cupboard, straight up into him if he weren't alert.He smiled at his own thoughts while trying to subdue his fear.

Uday could hear his mother call out for him. "Guddu, you must give 15-20 minutes to *pranayam* everyday. You live in a polluted city. *Pranayam* helps you clear the system."

He could hear her deep breaths over Baba Prasannmukh's voiceover. Uday watched the guru and the disciple in perfect synchrony; the almost perfect postures, closed eyes, right thumbs pressed against right nostrils, chests puffed up, breathing in and breathing out, and the zeal and zest to exercise for 15 minutes every day. She had been practising *pranayam* for some time now, particularly after Colitis started giving her sleepless nights. Papa was the most deserving candidate for the disease, but, strangely, amma got it. Papa, who was fit as a fiddle, especially for a man of his age, was out for his mandatory morning walk. Uday picked up the morning newspapers, lying in a heap at his doorstep and immediately turned over to the city page of the English daily he preferred over others. '*Govt. red tapism takes the life of a tusker*' read one of the articles. '*The Killer Crane*' ran another headline in an English daily which also published a series of photos of Golu. Another newspaper reported series of events through the graphic timeline: '*1. Golu lying in the ditch at 9 am, 3 pm, and 5 pm. 2. Golu being lifted by the crane at 8 pm. 3. Golu is dropped (the last TV grab of Golu being dropped from the crane) at 10.20 pm.*'

While vernacular newspapers cashed in on the drama around Golu's death, the English language dailies were all unanimous in stating that he could have been saved. The NCR Times was a tad more precise: '*Govt. cranes Golu to death.*'

Uday had a great urge to switch on DNN. As soon as his mother un-rolled the mattress, he grabbed the remote lying atop his Samsung and sank back into a cane chair. '*Golu longed for his beloved. He gave up life for Chameli. He had fire in his belly. The mahout is the culprit.*' Uday pinched himself. Was he watching the same organisation's channel where he worked? "I never said all those things during my LIVE! Beloved? Gave up life? Fire in the belly?" Uday was trying to make sense out of these baseless conclusions.

"Why are those breaking news flashes looking so familiar as if I have seen them before?" He was switching on the TV for news after the 9 pm debate last evening. Constant power-cuts after he came back with his parents kept him away from TV. He ate his dinner in candle light and then crashed immediately.

Uday jumped out of his chair as if he were sitting on a throne of nails, "Shit man! This can't be!" The mystery gradually began to sink in. *The dream!* It was in his dreams and he saw it all. He saw Psycho. He dreamt of the condolence meeting. He dreamt of Psycho's appalling speech. *Golu was not allowed to do it. The domestic violence. The love jehad etc etc.* Psycho's words now rang clearly in his ears as he sat watching the Diamond News Network.

He ran his eyes over a collage of still frames on the TV screen. The last frame opened into a video clip showing Golu falling 30-feet to his death. But the frame that immediately caught his attention was the one in which Golu lay on the edge of the ditch after being dropped from the crane and the area between his hind legs was circled red. Red. RED?

The red circle was the latest tool used by the news channels to mark or highlight an area of importance. It has been simply used to enhance the drama around the visuals. Did Golu get a fatal wound on his private part? Is that why they mosaiced the encircled space, to cover his shame? In a fit of anger, he picked up his mobile and dialled Binny. "So, that was Prithvi's Pulitzer moment. *Hahn*...! Such a brilliant piece of investigation...!" Uday heard Binny's giggles and noticed a sudden shift in her manner of speech. "Prithvi said Golu was international stuff. He is strange, yaar. Last month, Satyendra had filed a fantastic investigative piece on how poachers were indiscriminately killing elephants in Jumbo National Park. You know what Prithvi said? 'What's new about poaching? Get me LIVE footage of a tiger or a lion being shot. And I promise I will put it on prime time'. I felt so bad for Satyendra."

"Yeah, Satyendra bhai had called me to watch out for his latest investigative *dhamaka*," said Uday.

"We could have played up the story and nailed the guys who are now after Satyendra's life," said Binny. "He went deep into the National Park, and filmed the poachers' hideout with tons of elephant tusks and blackbuck horns. That was one hell of a real undercover operation. But Prithvi put the story on hold. And look at the amount of drama he is creating over Golu."

"How can he do this with Satyendra bhai's story?" Uday shot back as he idolised Satyendra.

"Now don't tell this to anyone. Satyendra has gone underground. I mean he is getting death threats from the mafia."

"WHATTT? Is he safe?"

"The police are on the job. We are also under pressure to run the story."

"He should be recalled to the headquarters and be made in charge of the investigative cell," said Uday. "Let's pray for Satyendra's safety," said Binny.

Uday always thought Binny was a clever woman who knew which side to butter. She had a terrific rapport with all the bosses. Sharing with them dirtiest of jokes on short messages was a common sight. In fact, Uday always suspected her of playing the perfect informer for Prithvi, and yet there were times when her attitude foxed him completely. This was one of those moments. Binny had stepped into her thirties and if stories were to be believed, she had rejected a string of proposals from suitable men. That, however, did not extinguish her desire to be lusted after. Not that her figure was nobody else's business; she was a girl of a rather average height and a bulky frame. Her fetish for wearing body-hugging clothes only enhanced her bulges and allowed that extra sparkle to the eyes of colleagues. Uday's thoughts veered around Binny's before coming back to the telephonic conversation.

"But there must be a limit to the kind of nonsense we peddle," said the disheartened and vexed lad.

"*Arrey,* forget it! It's done now," Binny tried to sooth his nerves.

"There is something terribly wrong with the system, ma'am. I am sorry to say that." Uday retorted.

"Take an off! Enjoy a day with your parents," Binny giggled and the line got snapped.

Media Kills Golu

Paagalvaani.blogspot.com

Media reported on murder. It conspired against him yesterday. TV channels killed Golu. Like the grim and evil vultures that swoop down on the carcass of an animal and thirsts for blood and oil, they made a rather ugly song and dance about Golu's death. Diamond News Network (DNN) sparkled in its own conceited wisdom. The channel was convinced that Golu's basic instinct to copulate was suppressed, which caused him to commit suicide. Call it DNN's collective sense of naked voyeurism or whatever, whose morals were at stake was the bigger question. Golu's? Mahout's? Media's? Yes, you guessed it!

At least we now have an editorial policy on animals. All animals who are run over by passing vehicles on roads, voluntarily give up their lives because they are sexually starved.

Lessons drawn:

The next time your pet Labrador refuses to eat food, be sure he needs a good fuck. Go on a hunt. Find him a bitch whose vagina smells anything but a pile of rusty coins. No, do not dare to sniff her down there; you can smell it as she walks past you.

Ghunghroo

Prithvi's glass cabin was a perfect setting for a great rendezvous between the owner of the glass cabin and DNN's very own 'Christiana Amanpour' in making. The newsroom could set its clock to the consummate ease with which Anushka would slide away the glass door, slide it shut behind her, walk a couple of steps and take her seat across Prithvi's table everyday at 4 pm. This was a cue for Mehboob to enter Prithvi's cabin with two sets of teacups and saucers in the tray and Britannia's Good Day biscuits. Prithvi hated biscuits but Mehboob knew it was Anushka ma'am's favourite.

"You did a great job with the Golu story," Prithvi said in a congratulatory tone as Anushka took the first bite of Good Day.

"O thank you, sir. Thanks for reposing faith in me to cover such a historic event, sir." Anushka knew what pleased Prithvi.

"You should write a novel. You are not born for ordinary stories. I see a great writer in you." Prithvi was gradually discovering Anushka's hidden talents.

"I love writing, sir. I want to write a book on pets, sir. That's a dream, sir."

"What about this pet?"

"Which pet, sir?"

"The one sitting across from you..."

"Come on, sir!" Anushka broke into a giggle. "You are a great journalist, sir. I've always admired you as a student, sir. You are so aggressive on TV. I liked your interview with our former home minister, Charles Sobhraj."

"That was Ramakrishna Shetty." Prithvi said matter-of-factly. "Sobhraj is an international criminal and is in jail in Nepal, facing trial for crimes committed there. It's still my dream to interview him, though," he hastily added.

"Oh yes, sir, right sir... Mr Shetty. I remember you had grilled him about some *chara ghotala*," Anushka persisted with her wise ones.

"No, that was about the police recruitment scam," Prithvi appeared unperturbed, an indulgent smile playing on his lips throughout.

"Oh, sorry sir. I fail to remember the who is who. There are many ministers and no one is clean. Isn't it, sir? But you must write a book. And you write well. I read your columns. Yes, sir, the one on Mr Khan. He is really so cute, sir. I watch *aaalllll* his films."

"What about me? You don't find me cute?" Prithvi was direct now.

"Come on, sir. You are the boss."

"Is that a yes?"

"Oh... Of course, you are!" Anushka smiled and casually ran her fingers through a heavy mop of hair that fell on her bare shoulders, almost teasing the noodle strap. "But you are also my boss, sir."

Psycho looked displeased.

"Sir, please don't get angry. I admire you. But I find Shamsher Khan cuter. He is dashing. He is my favourite Bollywood hero."

"I am not dashing enough, eh? *Soch lo,* you are courting disaster by ignoring me for Shamsher." Anushka could figure out a streak of meanness in Prithvi's voice and decided she has to humour him.

Outside the glass cabin at the far end of the newsroom, Priyam raised his head from the keyboard after darting a quick look at the glass cabin. He turned around to chat with Sachin while preparing the next bulletin's rundown. "Want her... She is available... *Pyaar se degi, beta. Baat karun usse teri?* Shall I talk to her for you?"

"Come on... I have never seen you speaking with her. *Phat-ti hai tumhari.* Don't make tall claims now." Sachin teased Priyam.

"Yaar, she speaks only in English. And my English *toh* you know." Priyam could not have been more candid.

"Boss, her pouts are sexy and she also got some assets to jerk off. She is *haawtt,* man." Sachin kept looking at the computer screen as he talked with Priyam.

"She is Hemendra's girl. *Saala, leta hoga uski.* I am sure she is sleeping with him. Prithvi will only have disappointment."

"*Ubeh chootiyeh*... Have a bet! She is Psycho's *Basanti,*" said Priyam, his eyes fixed on the cabin.

"Stop staring into his cabin. He'll fire you if he spots you," warned Sachin.

"I know he does not like me. Guess I should cross my fingers and knock on wood. My bad luck... I don't have a pair of waxed legs..."

"Poor you," Sachin teased him as he turned around to get on with the rundown.

Loyalty

"I am telling you one last time. One more word and you will be out of the newsroom," Sudhanshu aka Pig was yelling at Ritwik.

"But sir..."

"I don't want any argument," Sudhanshu rattled off.

"What have I done? I am asking you to provide me an edit suite, that's that." Ritwik stuck his ground like a young Turk.

"*Nahi milega aapko abhi...jaiyye keh dijiye jisse kehna hai...*"

"But why are you shouting? And why should I go to anyone? I have come to you. You give me a solution."

"I don't have any solution."

"But sir, I have to leave early today and before that I have to get my story edited."

"You will not get the edit bay. You will have to wait."

"Sir, I can't wait endlessly."

"You will have to..."

"Sir, I told you, I have to leave early. My father has taken ill. I have to take him to the doctor."

"So what? Am I responsible for your father's sickness?"

"No sir, I never said that. I want to finish off my work and leave as early as I can, to attend on my father. That is why I am requesting you to get me an edit suite."

"You know the answer."

"Then I leave it to you. Please get this story edited whenever. I am leaving."

"Nobody is going to do your dirty work."

"Then give me the edit machine and an editor."

"I can't, and I won't. And this is office. Don't bring your personal things here."

"It's my father's sickness. Nothing can be more important than attending on my sick father right now."

"You don't have anyone else in your family to attend to your father?"

"No."

"I am sorry, you will have to wait."

"I cannot. Why can't you understand? *Kaise insaan hain aap?* My father is not well. I have to rush. Can't this simple thing enter your head?" Ritwik's voice boomed across the newsroom. Heads turned.

"I am not stopping you, but you will have to get your story edited yourself. And how dare you shout at me?"

"I am not shouting, but *kaise insaan hain aap?*" Ritwik was visibly shaking. The script almost dropped from his hand, strength slipping out of his fingers as the blood froze out of fear and nervousness at the sudden turn of events and a sudden face off with his senior. But he quickly collected his wits, turned around and walked away after slapping the script at the desk behind him.

"I can't work here. I am resigning."

Ritwik's sudden rush of adrenaline caught everyone by surprise. He was always considered a soft-spoken, well-behaved youngster. He had done well for himself and established his credentials as a gritty and investigative reporter. He never shied away from keeping long hours.

"*Kya ho raha hai yeh?* Ritwik, this is not done," Psycho came out of his cabin and yelled back at Ritwik.

"Sir, this is getting too much. Sudhanshu sir is not cooperating."

"I don't want to hear any nonsense. Is this the way you speak to your parents at home?"

Ritwik kept mum.

"How dare you raise your voice at your senior?"

"Sir, Sudhanshuji got personal. He hurt my sentiments," Ritwik fought back his tears.

"I only know that you raised your voice against him. And this will not be tolerated. This is gross indiscipline."

Hemendra flung his glass door open and walked up to Prithvi, and then as if almost on cue took over from Prithvi, "Both of you, come to my cabin right away."

A pin-drop silence descended over the newsroom. For a moment, the work stations froze. VT editors turned around to see the drama unfold. But bulldozing a subordinate, running him down, humiliating him in the presence of the entire newsroom had become the order of the day.

Inside the cabin, Psycho's supari-man was at work. "What is your problem?" Hemendra looked up at Ritwik and shot back.

"Nothing, sir."

"No, tell me."

"Nothing sir, I just requested Sudhanshu sir for the edit suite."

"And what did he say?"

"He said I can't get it."

"And then..."

"Sir, I told him I have to leave early."

"And then...?"

"Sudhanshu sir just refused to give me the edit suite."

"And then you shouted." Hemendra suddenly shot back in anger.

"No."

"Yes, of course you did," he turned to Sudhanshu. "You tell me what happened next."

"I can't allocate the edit suite just because somebody's father has taken ill. I was being professional. I only told him there were other important stories in queue for edit. I was following your instructions, sir that things will have to be prioritised. You know *Nark ka Darwaza* is our driver for 9 pm... And we were running out of time... Animesh has not delivered the graphics yet. And to make matters worse, Ritwik had the cheek to shout at me."

"I never shouted. You misbehaved," Ritwik cut short Sudhanshu, the rage still burning inside him.

Phatak...! A sound of an object slapped against a wood slab filled the cabin. The remote control's cover had come off, its batteries flew all across the room before falling on the carpet below. Hemendra was on his feet. At eye-level with the young lad.

"Mind your body language...*tumhari body language theek nahi hai*. Stop this nonsense. This is indiscipline. What do you think you are," yelled Hemendra pointing his finger angrily at Ritwik.

"But sir, please listen..."

"Shut up," Hemendra's face twisted visibly as he clenched his jaws in anger. "This is the height of unseemliness and immodesty. You decide what is more important to you. Your father or this job?"

"My father is really unwell."

"Then don't come to office."

"But sir..."

"Shut up! Who do you think you are? The company does not deserve such undisciplined soldiers. I will ensure you don't get a job outside this office."

Ritwik saw in his peripheral vision people stealing glances at the glass cabin, trying to spy on the goings-on inside it. "Please listen to me, sir," Ritwik begged for a hearing.

"Just get out..."

"This is not fair."

"You are not going to tell me what is fair and what is not," Hemendra yelled again. Turning to Sudhanshu, he instructed, "Mail me the entire sequence. You must emphasise Ritwik's insubordination. I will see what I can do. Justice will be delivered. Now both, leave my room."

"But, sir, would you please care to listen to me..."

"Did I just tell you to leave my room? Immediately." Hemendra scowled.

Ritwik almost banged the glass door behind him. He picked up his belongings from his desk and barged out of the newsroom before anyone could follow him. He took a lift down the ground floor and headed straight to Mamu's.

Thethar

Kumar Amrendra walked up to his workstation with a cute looking girl in tow, perhaps one of those interns from a media college who'd keep flocking the newsroom every month. He dumped the executive leather bag, his evergreen accessoire on the table next to the dust laden computer panel. Muskan looked up from her computer screen and pursed a smile. The subsequent manoeuvres of Kumarji etched machine like in her mind. Kumar would walk up to Binny and then introduce the new intern to her. Later, as the intern would be tagged along with a reporter on an assignment, Kumar would bid her goodbye, wishing her great success with her new role.

"Call when you need me. Best of luck!" The lines kept coming all-to-clear in Muskan's mind. But, the best was reserved for later. "*Arrey*, she is just a kid. *Bachchi hai meri*," he would say squashing doubts about his intentions; but Muskan could make out it was an answer ridden with mystery. As for herself, she kept him at more than an arm's length distance.

Muskan could now see Kumar walking up to her. She buried her face in the screen.

"These buggers will sink the channel. You take it from me." Muskan knew it was Kumarji's recantation, but pretended she was too busy with her work.

"Good morning, Kumarji," she said without leaving her eyes from the computer screen. "Good morning, Muskan."

The overnight double-murder in South Delhi had set the newsroom abuzz since early morning and inputs were still pouring in from the reporter on the spot. Muskan knew that striking up a conversation with Kumarji was like walking straight into a trap of unforeseen dangers, the most expected and unpleasant of all being at Mamu's for a cup of tea with him.

"Let us break for tea," announced Kumar, sounding like the producer working overtime on his shift.

"Please go ahead. I will join you soon." Muskan knew well she will certainly not survive the encounter, let alone preventing it from happening. She could only work on ways to delay it.

"No problem, I shall wait. Will go together."

After a while, Muskan got up from her chair and glanced around to see if anyone was watching her slip away. Binny was busy gossiping with Sudhanshu after the morning edit meeting. Jagat Singh aka Haldi was in his glass cabin. For a person just five feet eight, broad chested but perhaps a bit thin in the legs, his roundness stretched his age by a full decade. But he more than covered for his ageing body with a thick coat of salt-pepper hair that rested on his head. He had a folding pocket comb that shared the meaty space of his shirt pocket with his smart phone. So often, he would flick out the comb and let it meticulously meander through the mop, holding one side of the parting with his other hand. Then he would run the middle finger through the mop and give it a measured shake, like an immortal ancient hero having just saved the honour of a girl from a pack of marauding *goondas*.

From the far end of her seat, Muskan could see Haldi lift the dustbin from under his table and spit a long jet of *gutkha* into it. His court was in progress. "Balamganj session must be on," she mumbled. Dharmesh and Pankaj sat right across from him. Thanks to Haldi's backing, they can refuse reporting assignments to Baba. Haldi would use them only in 'challenging' assignments. Therefore, every time a reporter broke a story from the spot, Haldi would make sure Dharmesh or Pankaj went LIVE from the newsroom rather than the spot. "*You see, TV news is all about value addition. Look at me. Every time there is a big crime story, I volunteer myself for LIVE newsroom chat.*" Dharmesh-Pankaj duo would get proactive only in the evening to deck up Haldi's Tata Safari for the booze session. So every evening at 7.30 or sundown, whichever came earlier, Haldi would walk into his SUV to find the bar laid out. A line up of neatly packaged *chakhna* (a mixture of various salty fried eatables) would be resting in the back seat, his bartenders waiting for the master to take his throne and become the master of the feast. The twosome had earned back-to-back promotions in two successive years because of their services rendered at the evening car-o-bar.

Other than the usual courtiers Pankaj and Dharmesh, Nidheesh and Nitin seemed to be Haldi's latest preys. Muskan pitied them. Early in the morning, they had to go through the torture of listening to those Red and White stories of self-acclaimed bravery and spunk, repeatedly. Almost every new recruit would have to take the necessary crash course on Balamganj riots and Haldi's *fantastic* coverage of those riots, even before they got a hang, about the special science of the newsroom. Muskan, too, had been his victim several times over as a fresher. "*We travelled to the other end of the curfew-*

bound area. The IG Police happened to be my father's student. He regarded me as his own brother. He gave me the curfew pass and two police escorts as well," Muskan remembered being told. She knew everything by rote: *how* Haldi *gave a LIVE phone-in from atop the tallest building in the area* (rumour has it he gave the phone-in from the police check post, because he was too afraid to go deep in the curfew-bound area), *how it took him just one take to do his piece-to-camera* (while the cameraman counted 22), *how he interviewed a local Muslim and his Hindu neighbour who shared brotherly bonds in times of strife* (it became talk of the town not because of its topicality and texture, but because it was speculated that the families interviewed lived off the curfew-bound area), *and lastly, how he subsequently won an award for best reporting, instituted by the leading exporters of turmeric (Haldi), and presided over by a young neta in Delhi. The world of journalism had found its new L'enfant terrible—Jagat Pratap Singh.* His colleagues and peers now called him Haldi—a sobriquet he wore as a badge of honour.

This was the safe time to slip out. Haldi would not even notice. Muskan logged out, picked up her purse and confidently walked out of the newsroom.

"I heard about Ritwik. Is this the way? He is among the brightest we have. Do they want such persons to leave the company? I tell you Muskan, this place is going to the dogs," Kumar started as soon as they took the lift to the ground floor, unmindful there were other passengers sharing the lift.

He was born Kumar Amrendra, but in the newsroom he had earned himself an alias and a much deserved one at that, Thethar. The word 'Thethar' cannot be traced in Hindi or Sanskrit lexicon. It is definitely not Urdu. But Balendu Rai, the quintessential rustic leader of Bihar, and, a favourite with TV news channels would use—Thethar—to describe his staunchest opponents. It loosely meant a vacuous loudmouth who need not be taken seriously. Because whenever he opened his mouth and moved his lips, what came out was a bunch of gibberish.

Kumar Amrendra aka Thethar's work responsibility began and ended with, arranging experts and political bigwigs as guests for special shows. He believed he held the most important job in the newsroom, after the News Director and the Managing Editor.

"Who is resigning, Kumarji?" asked a squeaky, innocent tone.

"You do not know? These bastards are trying to ruin Ritwik's career."

"Ritwik? Career? Why are you talking in riddles?" Muskan feigned ignorance about all matters concerning Ritwik.

"As if you don't know about that." Thethar threw the ball in Muskan's court.

"I do not know. I was not here yesterday." Muskan knew she could carry this bluff with Thethar because it was his weekly off yesterday. Ritwik had sent a short message to Muskan on her mobile late last night to give her an update on his father's recovery. But she was more concerned about his run-in with Hemendra and what transpired between the two in Hemendra's cabin. She decided against broaching on the subject over the phone and decided to wait till Ritwik returned to office, the next day.

"These people have served him a disciplinary notice," Thethar said.

"Indiscipline?"

"I know it was Sudhanshu's fault. And Ritwik was made the scapegoat. He is one of the finest in the industry, just look at the way he is treated here."

"This is news to me, Kumarji," Muskan played along.

"Tell him he should not quit. This is not the right time. These bastards cannot have a free run. People like Prithvi and Hemendra should be sacked for DNN to progress. At least they should be sacked for misbehaving with Rati. You know how Sudhanshu misbehaved with her at the last year's office party?"

"I know every single detail of that party and how that bastard Sudhanshu misbehaved with poor Rati. I told her she must write to the HR manager to address her problems, but she was so upset and disgusted by the whole thing that she sent in her resignation the next morning." Muskan could not hold her pent up anger.

"But I don't want Ritwik to resign. He should report the matter to the CEO-cum-News Director, the Super Boss," he added.

Thethar was referring to Yashwant Thakur, who had recently launched a cluster of regional channels from Gujarat and Maharashtra in addition to DNN. He had shown promise of a media baron in the making. He was recently featured on the cover of lifestyle magazine, *Z for Zing* and was being touted as among the next big thing in the media industry.

"How will that help? Prithvi and Hemendra are Yashwant sir's handpicked men. Even you are, Kumar sir. You cannot hide the fact. Why would Yashwant sir listen to Ritwik?"

Kumar never expected Muskan to put things so bluntly. Nobody had described his relationship with Yashwant so matter-of-factly, and, everyone had at some point of time tolerated Kumar and his 'Thethorology' (his highest potency of bunkum and supercilious acts) only because of his closeness to Yashwant.

"I know that in this industry you are only as valuable to the organisation as the one supporting you, but Ritwik is a self-made man. He doesn't need no crutches. He knows how to fight his own battles." Muskan argued with Kumar like a seasoned advocate. "He strongly believes a life shorn of principles is better not lived. I admire his courage."

"Why do you say that? I am always there for him. He is like my kid brother." Kumar sounded concerned.

Muskan did not care to respond. Emotions spilled over as Muskan realised she loved Ritwik more dearly, than ever before.

Muskan called out for Nandu and gestured him for cigarettes. "*Laaya didi*..." he shot back reading Muskan's two-fingers-on-the-lips gesture bang on.

As they got up from the table and took slow and steady steps towards office, Muskan looked up, ruminating over the curls of cigarette smoke as her eyes settled at the fourth floor window.

"Hemendraji will have to pay for misbehaving with Rits," she muttered under her breath as she stubbed out her cigarette, to take the lift back to the newsroom, in long strides, unmindful that she had outpaced Thethar by a couple of yards.

Mamu Tea Stall

Mamu *ek* Navy Cut *aur ek* Secular..."

Hashim Ali on cue pulled the drawer, fished out the cigarettes from the rectangular paperboard container, and handed them over to Ritwik. The deep eyes of the old man met Ritwik's. Ritwik was back to office late next afternoon, but was in no mood to resume work. He parked his motorbike in the parking lot, outside DNN Towers, but did not take the lift to the fourth floor. Instead, he headed towards Mamu's where Muskan would join him after her shift.

"You are in a bad mood. What happened?" Mamu's deep bass voice carried genuine concern.

Ritwik knew Mamu had an uncanny ability to read faces. Mamu was a stark contrast to the characters up in the newsroom. "Did he know I had a spat with Sudhanshu and that Hemendra censured me so brutally? What if he is Hemendra's '*khabri*'?" Ritwik could see horns growing out of Mamu's head and defense growing out of his own voice.

"Nothing Mamu," Ritwik was curt as he turned around and started walking towards his favourite corner table, which had grown to accept Ritwik's mood swings.

As he released the first vortex ring of smoke, one could make out the tension bottled up inside him. His thoughts wandered back to the newsroom. He had been courting thoughts of switching his job. Would this episode be the last straw? He wondered.

"Hi Ritwik!"

He turned around to see Muskan standing at his table, smiling and waving at him.

"Hi! Come, sit."

"What's up? What was Hemendraji up to?" asked Muskan.

Muskan went to the US while still in school. She returned after her graduation with a superlative American accent in tow. She never made any attempt to speak in Hindi. On rare occasions when she did, it sounded French to those around her.

Not that it was a smooth sail for her to get on with the 'Hindi-belt' work culture of the newsroom, but she knew the work she needed to put in to continue to sound less French at the professional level. Once, there was a call on the reporter's extension on the landline. The caller asked for Dhirendra, the civic-beat reporter. Muskan, who was then new to the newsroom, answered the call and turned around to look for the reporter. She called out the name twice. From the far end, Ritwik decided to pull a fast one in chaste Hindi: "Dhirendra has gone to fetch some oil." Muskan only added her peculiar accent before she relayed it across the mouthpiece, in a mix of English and her own brand of Hindi, "He's not in office. *Woh tel lene gaye hain*." The entire newsroom broke into a hearty laugh. Muskan looked around, sheepishly, trying to figure out as to what triggered that.

Ritwik was to become her closest buddy, though. They discovered they had common tastes; both loved to read Jeffrey Archer and Roald Dahl. Ritwik found to his big surprise Muskan's near hysteric admiration for Gulzar, a lyricist he counted among all time greats in the history of Bollywood. In between shifts, they would share their tiffin in the canteen, would chitchat in the small balcony adjacent to the library post meals, sharing a proverbial smoke or encouraging some gossip. If not in office, one could spot them together at the Mamu's.

"What did Hemendraji say? Will you tell me?" Ritwik disliked when Muskan referred to Hemendra as Hemendraji, but the '*ji*' syndrome was all-pervasive in the newsroom and had got etched into her system as well.

"The same old story," Ritwik mumbled.

"Tell me *na*..." Muskan persisted.

Ritwik narrated the entire sequence frame by frame. He then leaned on the chair and lit another cigarette.

"What, you got a call from dad?"asked Muskan.

"Yeah, he was coughing like anything. For a while, I thought I have lost him. The earpiece went dead as if somebody had run out of breath. You know *na*, after mom passed away, Dad has been staying with me and Didi in turns. Dad is asthmatic. The mere thought of losing him brings me to tears."

"How is he now?" Muskan looked concerned.

"Thankfully, my younger brother returned from his classes just in time and rushed Dad to the hospital."

Nandu quietly placed two Seculars at their table before hopping on to the other one.

Muskan called for Nandu and ordered a Classic Mild.

"Theek hai didi," replied Nandu who looked crisp in his sunglasses, tight denims and oiled hair. "How do you deal with Hemendra now?" Muskan jolted Ritwik from his stupor.

"I want to quit. They treat you like a fucking war criminal, starting to hate this place..." Ritwik spoke his mind.

"Come on Rits, I do not need a report card on either of our *bencho* bosses," Muskan butted in forcefully.

Ritwik was exceedingly fond of Muskan and fell in love with her every time she would utter that cuss word—*bencho.*

"Do not be a sentimental fool. This is not the time. Be a man! Prepare yourself for a fight. But don't rush into it."

"That *muthafucka* was rude, felt like slapping him and flipping him over hard on the ground."

"Those people want you to commit a mistake so that they can hang you. Is this what you want? I hope not."

"Don't start it all over again," Ritwik said disapprovingly.

"I am not. I am just asking you to think wisely. Do not give me that resignation bullshit…not in the least! Stay back and fight." Muskan put it bluntly.

"I cannot compromise with my self-respect. P-E-R-I-O-D!" Ritwik was stuck to his guns.

"I only want to see you face the crisis with a clear head." Muskan's voice was choking with concern and well-being for Ritwik.

"You are not my mom, so keep the stupid lecture to yourself," Ritwik looked at her angrily. He took out his wallet, pulled out two ten-rupee notes and flung it on the table before banging the tea glass on the thin wad. He got up without further preliminaries and walked away.

Muskan felt that it was not the right time to drill reason in his head. He was too shaken with his run-in with Sudhanshu and Hemendra. She gave in to Ritwik's pleas, but not before exacting a promise from him that he will not reply to any official mail before consulting her.

The Great Escape

What Muskan did not know was that Ritwik had already scripted his way out of DNN. After her rendezvous with Ritwik at Mamu's the other day, she'd left for home. She shot a short message to Ritwik after reaching home, but got no reply. A while later, Ritwik got another message on his mobile from the same sender: '*avoid knee-jerk action*'.

But Ritwik had decided he would not go down on his knees. Today, he took the DNN Tower lift not to the fourth floor, but to the fifth. The floor where two studios were set up.

The other end of the floor was occupied by technical, PCR and camera colleagues.

"What happened, Ritwik? You seem to be in a hurry." Ritwik turned around to see chief cameraperson Chaddhaji ambling on a stick in his right hand. "I heard you had a spat with Hemendra and Prithvi. *Suna ditta na onnu?*" Chaddhaji always spoke to him in Punjabi. Ritwik turned back and smiled at Chaddhaji. "Not worth it," came the reply. Chaddhaji put his left arm around Ritwik. "Want to have a smoke?" he asked pulling out the Gold Flake pack from his shirt pocket. "Let us go to the balcony outside," offered the well meaning man. "*Hmm...* I am in a bit of a hurry. My father is not well and I have to leave at the earliest, can I use your work station for five minutes?" he pleaded.

"Sure. But those creases do not look good on you," Chaddhaji said in a matter of fact tone. They both entered the camera section and tucked in the far end corner of the floor. Sanyal and Sukhwinder, playing billiards on computers parked on either side of the room, with their backs to each other, stood to attention as Chaddhaji entered the camerapersons' den, with Ritwik in tow. "Keep sitting. Who is winning?" he darted a non-challant look at Sukhwinder.

"Do you think this Bengali can ever beat the Sher-e-Punjab," Sukhwinder said without even looking at Chaddhaji. Between Sukhwinder and Sanyal, the former was almost invincible when it came to computer games. Sukhwinder was poised for a second consecutive win.

"Come, take this," Chaddhaji offered his own workstation to Ritwik. "You do your work. I will go out on to the balcony for a drag."

Ritwik sat down on the terminal; anger and nervous excitement writ large on his face. He knew what he was going to write. It filled him with the thought that this could be the last e-mail he would write using the Diamond News Network IP address. After the second line, he could not see what he was writing as tears welled up in his eyes.

Dear Hemendra sir, he began typing. *After going through the e-mail, I realised it does not make any sense defending myself as you have already passed the verdict and pronounced me guilty. I tried to explain to you that since my father had suddenly taken ill, I wish I could take an early leave from office, but you were not willing to listen to my pleading. In fact, you made yourself clear that I will have to choose between my father and my job. There was never any confusion about that, sir. My parents are dear to me and will always have a priority over other things in my life. I do not know where your priorities lie, but they certainly do not seem to be with people who raised you to be what you are today. I am sorry if I hurt your feelings, but, in hindsight, this is too small a price for being a good son.*

With the unwarranted suspension of Anwar on fabricated allegation and the circumstances that pushed Rati to quit this channel, it is amply clear how seniors like you, wish to set benchmark of healthy work culture in the newsroom. Please treat this also as my resignation letter.

Ritwik Sinha

He cut-paste the text on his e-mail and marked it to Hemendra, with a copy to Prithvi and Yashwant.

And then he proceeded to add a footnote:

PS: I would really love to see you live out your threat to block my attempts at seeking employment outside DNN.

Tears that had welled up in his eyes had gone dry by the time he finished writing the e-mail. It had only helped firm up his resolve. Muskan would have loved him to dig in firmly and fight it out some other day, but Ritwik never believed in the rulebook style.

Mickey and Muskan

"You don't love me, do you? Tell me." Muskan tugged at Ritwik lovingly.

"Vodka brings out the romantic side of Mus-kaaaan, *huh?* Shall I pour you another one?" Ritwik replied with a chuckle.

"No, answer me. Do you love me?" Muskan insisted.

"What if I said no, I don't," Ritwik teased her.

"I will kill you. No, I can't... I cannot do that. I love you so dearly. But, you break my trust and you shall never see my face again." Muskan's voice assumed unprecedented sternness.

"Can we have some music, please? Do you have some latest downloads?"

"*Arrey,* I will play you the latest sensation. We must see this movie, *Life in a Metro* when it releases next month," said Muskan.

"Are you going to play 'Alvida'?" Muskan forgot Ritwik liked Kenny Rogers, but was an avid Hindi film buff too.

"No, my favourite is 'In Dino'. The soft rock number just lifts up your spirit," said an excited Muskan as she arranged the playlist.

"Ya, even I like that number."

"Wish I could have Soham sing to me one day!" Muskan lustily cheered for the singer as he crooned '*...Tu Khwaab Saja...*'

Ritwik wrapped Muskan in his arms and pressed his lips against hers, as they lay entwined in the Mickey Mouse bedspread. If Mickey had his way, he would have nudged them to switch off the room lights, but they appeared riding on the wave of ecstasy to be bothered about a compromised environment and Mickey, could only clap with glee. His valentine, Minnie, launched into a small burst of '*Yoo Hoo*' as the couple on the upper storey conjoined in a desperate bid to be one.

"Hey, stop! Answer me."

She did not have the courage to get Ritwik off her body. He was kissing her passionately; his kisses travelling all over her as she writhed in pleasure. Behind Ritwik's lean and thin body, there lay a bundle of electrifying stamina.

Muskan broke into a frenzied laughter as Ritwik grimaced like Mr Bean in The Bean Show. Ritwik was trying to ignite her testosterone levels and sex drive by being funny. The same thing happened last time, when she went into what looked like convulsive sort of trance, and in a fit of infinite excitement sank her nails deep into Ritwik's back. Muskan panicked on seeing the blood trickle uncontrollably. "You have the skin of a girl," she teased. "Without any doubt, the impact on men is to a huge extent bloody."

"You know, Meenu," that's what Ritwik called her lovingly, "you have claws of a *dayan*," he teased back. "Hey, stop... Hey, Rits...put out the lights please, will you? The computer screen is throwing up adequate light to read the devil in your eyes...but it's most desirable when I feel you with eyes closed," Muskan pleaded him again to switch off the tube rod.

Ritwik worked his legs up the wall and put off the switch in one tight skilled manoeuvre, an indoor sport he had perfected over his off and on visits at Muskan's 12 x 10 barsaati.

"Your sense of human anatomy is all mixed up. The devil resides not in my eyes but at the end of the tunnel down below," Ritwik juggled with Muskan's breasts blindfolded.

"Let's see, *bencho*!" Muskan was quick to counter challenge as she giggled invitingly. Her cuss word '*bencho*' always worked as an aphrodisiac for Ritwik. He discovered a new wave of erotic energy lashing up in a torrent inside him. He took her into a tight clasp before rolling over her and from the corner of his right eye, he could see Mickey wink at him. Ritwik did not believe in preliminaries. Muskan's patience always ran out in bed.

She particularly liked the way Ritwik would take short and quick gasps of fresh air as he lifted his head, occasionally, after having logged a milestone. "Hey stop! You did not answer my question. Do you love me?"

That was the last thing she remembered before she was sucked into a pool of ecstasy. Two climaxes and the power failure dashed their shot at another milestone. The desert cooler stopped dead and Muskan's one room barsaati baked like a hot cake. The silence triggered by power failure would have only carried their pleasure moans deep into the neighbourhood, so both resigned to the fate.

The electricity came back in ten minutes but they had already got out of the mood. Ritwik sat up, removed the blindfold and lit a cigarette. As he drew out the first smoke circle, Muskan played with the curls on his chest. She could feel Ritwik's eyes floating over her and she drew the bedspread to cover them. Muskan buried her face into his chest, savouring the musk of their joint sweat. Ritwik passed on the cigarette to her. The aroma of burning tobacco only pronounced the ambience laden with pollen grains of love.

Ritwik's resignation had been accepted and Muskan felt a sudden stab of pain at the prospect of seeing him less and less. He had not heeded to her advise to stay put and fight the evil forces at work, but she was confident Rits will land himself a better job very soon. She was happy for him. Even though Ritwik did not answer her question, she knew together they have a long and beautiful life ahead.

They both looked at each other and smiled in the radiance of spent energy.

Soham crooned passionately, *'usako chhupaakar main sabse kabhi le chaloon kahin door...'* Muskan could see Mickey clapping with glee and Minnie breaking into a small jig.

Bajrang Prasad 'Ji'

Prithvi was late for the morning meeting. In the conference room, Shahid seized the opportunity to hold forth on the day's likely trend of analysing stock market news and financial opinions. He knew he had a large swathe of attentive investors around the oval table in the room.

"Today is going to be crucial for the market. The Damani brothers hold the key to market behavior," Shahid announced.

"I am only concerned with Srivenkat Softwares and Raheja Petrochemicals," said Hemendra.

"My hunch is that they are going to get hit today," said Shahid with the confidence of a broker on the Dalal Street.

"Look who's here," Binny screamed in excitement upon seeing Prithvi. He sprinted in and sank into his chair for the morning edit meeting. "So, when did you return from Ahsanganj?"

"Came late last night. We missed the early evening flight because Bajrang Prasadji arrived late for the interview."

"How did the interview go...?"

"Oh, great! Bajrang Prasadji is a nice person."

"You bet! I am fed up with people who keep talking crap about him," said Hemendra tearing his eyes away from Money

LIVE channel. "Sir, you are right! My uncle, who is posted there as a forest officer, says Mr Prasad is a strict and able administrator. Talks about his communal image is all bunkum," Amitabh butted in out of turn.

"Hang on," Jagat Singh Haldi gestured with the wave of his hand. After realising he could barely speak with his mouth full of *gutkha*, he flicked his comb back into its case and into his shirt pocket, stretched out his leg under the oval table to grope for the dustbin, lifted the plastic bin, bent down under the table and salivated a long jet of *gutkha* into it, yawned elaborately and leaned back ready with dignified analysis. "An IPS officer told me last year how Bajrang Prasad issued a carte blanche to eliminate criminals. Over 30 hardcore criminals have been shot dead in the encounter with the state police in the last 10 months itself. Bajrangji does not believe in negotiations, he believes in action," he said.

Pushkar was sitting at the other corner of the oval table. Behind Rajkishore and out of the line of sight of Prithvi, his eyes groped for Sabir's. Sabir looked at him furtively from over his paper teacup. Both locked their gaze for a split second, endorsing a joint disapproval of the way things were being discussed in the morning editorial meeting, but decided to remain silent on the issue.

"I think his name has got him bad publicity than it deserves. I was awestruck by his hospitality. He treated me to veritable regional cuisine," said Prithvi.

"Mmmm... Mouthwatering..." Binny knew how to indulge Prithvi.

"He personally plied me with *halvasan* and *ghevar*. And the *shreekhand* was penultimate."

"Oh how I love *shreekhand*... Hemendra, did you ever try it?"

"Madam, I have a sweet tooth. I have tasted every regional flavour, but nothing can beat *shreekhand*. You should have got it packed for us, boss." It was Hemendra's turn to indulge Prithvi.

"He sure is a messiah of the masses," Prithvi butted in. "You won't believe the stupendous development he has undertaken in the state. An officer in the CM secretariat showed statistics that bowled me over. In the last three years alone, the state has doubled its number of primary schools and has witnessed a 50 per cent increase in primary health centres. The investment in the state has quadrupled during his tenure. He has left so far behind him, his most powerful competitors." The influence of Bajrang secretariat's on Prithvi seemed overwhelming.

"Bajrang Prasad is good at fudging figures," Pushkar butted in. "One cannot fall into the trap of statistics. Did you not read Professor Patnaik's article, Hidden Agenda of Development— in *New India Times* today?"

"And what does your Professor have to say on this," Hemendra was curt as he tore his eyes away from Money LIVE.

"The cold fact is that there is not a single new school that has opened in areas populated by minorities," Pushkar put it bluntly. "Those are also the areas which are lacking the basic health care facilities. The development is selective and lop-sided. The CM's hidden agenda is for all to see."

More pairs of eyes swooped down on Pushkar. Sudhanshu, Shahid, Binny, Yogesh and Amitabh appeared all set to enjoy Hemendra-Pushkar tug of war. Rajkishore gazed intently at Pushkar, suggesting that he perhaps was the only one with him, but without much ado drew away his stare and got back at tinkering on his mobile.

"Enough of your god-damned *gyaan*," Hemendra's stock were apparently on the slide and his body language more than betrayed his irritation.

"Does your Professor have any experience of administering a state? Has he ever contested an election?" Shahid never spared an opportunity to follow Hemendra word by word, sentiment by sentiment—like a four year old brazenly aping his father's mannerisms.

"I am a dumb-witted soul who cannot respond to such intelligent assumptions," Pushkar continued with his barbs.

"How can you trust the analysis of a controversial sociologist?" Ernesto joined the issue with Pushkar. "Moreover, Prithviji is right when he says that things have changed over the years. All his alleged communal acts have now been consigned to the past bin of history."

"May be your sense of history is better than mine," Pushkar rubbed in.

"I am just trying to be neutral," said Ernesto.

"Yeah... I know. As neutral as Stalin during World War II when he signed the Non-Aggression Pact with Nazi Germany," Pushkar smirked.

"This is enough, guys. If people don't like my conclusions, they are free to leave this room." Prithvi barked out his order.

Pushkar was sinking deeper into abysmal rage until his mobile beeped for a message alert: *'Mad felo. Dnt argu.'*

"I have been watching my circle of employees. They have the tendency to question the chair. This is a very dangerous trend and shall not be tolerated."

A stony silence engulfed the conference room.

"Don't get me wrong. I was not trying to question. I am sharing my thoughts about just and able governance," said Pushkar.

"Why don't you just stick to your *bhakti* shows? You shall be the last person I would turn to for editorial advice on politics," Prithvi was unrelenting.

"We are all aware of Bajrang Prasad's divisive politics that led to communal carnage in the state. Can anybody in this room deny this historical truth?" Pushkar may not have had a great start to the conversation but he is not quitting. "We cannot be seen holding on to the vestiges of the past. If somebody does some good work we have to acknowledge that," said Prithvi.

"Point taken, sir," that was Sabir's voice. He realised his silence was criminal. "But, the government discrimination continues without respite. With due respect to Haldi sir," Sabir continued after taking a while to process the information, "most of those bumped off in the fake encounters last year, belonged to the minority community. Certainly, there has to be some pattern to the way Bajrang Prasad administers his kingdom. Therefore, a word of caution always keeps us from oversimplifying things. That's all I have to say."

"I understand the pain of minorities, Sabir. But media cannot be seen as behaving like, an activist." Prithvi mellowed as if he had something to hide.

"His government has been accused of destroying evidences. Moreover, the recent undercover report on *Pangapost.com* has blown the lid off the roles of police and senior government officials in that carnage. Likewise, some of those fake encounters are now being scrutinised by different courts," Sabir displayed with equal grace and maturity a fine, well-balanced opinion.

"The state has come a long way since. There is no law and order problem now," said Prithvi.

Sabir had ignored a message alert beep on his mobile. He quickly pressed it open. It was Pushkar: *'Jst gv it bk 2 ths chutiya'.*

"That was a well-orchestrated drive to teach a particular minority community a lesson. Don't you think so?" Sabir dug in.

"If the state has buried its past and moved on, we should try and acknowledge the new fervour and enterprise," said Shahid clearly undercutting Sabir's viewpoint.

"The past always catches up with you Shahid bhai. His intentions were suspect then and even now." Sabir hinted Shahid to cut to the chase. "The new set of development initiatives is again discriminatory. The real motive seems hidden," Sabir added forcefully.

"He has not been pronounced guilty by any court. And, we have no reason to hang him either." Ernesto was on his legs, eager to make his point.

"Precisely... That's what my point is," Prithvi dittoed Ernesto.

"That's fine if you don't want to listen to others," said Sabir.

"Listen guys, I will do what I want to. I am running the channel here," saying that Prithvi turned to Hemendra and ordered, "Slot the interview for tonight's prime time. Please ensure that we put out a small promo ASAP."

"Sure. Will be done!" Hemendra obliged, and then turning to Ernesto barked out, "Sit with Shahid, work out a promo and show it to me ASAP."

"Shall we begin the meeting, please," Binny said as a sign of protest, addressing no one in particular.

"I don't think I can continue any more. There are capable men here to take a call on the editorial agenda." Prithvi got up from the chair and left the room. There was pin drop silence. Hemendra took a final glance at the BSE's update, collected his BlackBerry and started walking towards the door. The rest also filed out, leaving Sabir and Pushkar alone in the conference room.

They stood up, leaned across the table and did an impromptu *high-five,* acknowledging the rare sense of victory. As they walked back to the door, Sabir paused, cleared his throat and said in a formal tone, "I declare the meeting close." The conference room boomed with raucous laughter.

"Sabir *miyan,* this one from Dushyant is specially for you," said Pushkar as he broke into a couplet:

"Ye Sara Jism Jhukkar Bojh Se Dohra Hua Hoga
Main Sajde Mein Nahin Tha, Aapko Dhokha Hua Hoga."

Ernesto

"Look at Ernesto," Sabir nudged Pushkar as they walked towards Mamu's. Ernesto was frantically trying to light up Prithvi's cigarette with his Clipper, which seemed to have run out of gas. Failing in the first three attempts, he looked apologetic; it was not until the next successful attempt that his face lit up, sans ash.

Pushkar and Sabir went around the empty tables towards the other end of Mamu's and sat down.

"*Do* Secular *aur ek* Navy Cut," Sabir ordered.

"Will you have *band-makkhan?*" asked Pushkar.

"I would prefer a bread-omlette," said Sabir.

"Mamu, *ek* bread-omlette *aur ek band-makkhan bhi...*"

Pretending he was busy as much, Ernesto tried to steal a glance at the duo. He appeared to bask in the attention given to him by Prithvi.

"That's a funny way of holding a cigarette," Sabir said.

"Don't bother about it."

"I mean you can't hold your cigarette like you hold your hands together to draw on a chillum…"

"He clasps it like I used to hold my house flag in school, leading my squad in the march past."

"And he thinks he is some kind of a style bhai."

They broke into extended laughter in the midst of the most smoky surrounding. "By the way he defended Bajrang Prasad in the editorial meeting today, I seriously doubt his leftist credentials. What do you say?" Pushkar had a sparkle in his eye, while Sabir could manage through the haze of smoke an opportunity to strike forth.

"He is such a bloody fake," Sabir responded. "Let's call his bluff," he added as the twosome exchanged mischevious glances.

Meanwhile, Sabir saw Binny walking towards Mamu's with Raman in tow. She paused two tables short and dissolved into the crowd surrounding Prithvi.

"Can I guess how is your mood now…?" She threw a question at Prithvi and giggled. "You know you scare me when you leave the meetings!"

"DNN is not a ghost hunting site, madam. Where did you get this top?" Prithvi came down to brass-tacks.

"Oh, you didn't like it?"

"Can't I ask?"

"No tell me *na*, you didn't like it or what?"

"It's nice and upmarket," Prithvi stole a glance at nice little mounds of wheatish flesh that peeked from behind the top of her cups. Her clothes felt painfully tight, cutting deep into her young and bosomy skin. Prithvi's eyes travelled deep in imagination.

Binny giggled again.

Sabir glanced over Pushkar's shoulder to see Ernesto sagging in sudden ostracisation after Binny's arrival.

"Ernesto boss..." Sabir called out in a raised pitch.

He looked at Sabir and then at Pushkar.

"Please oblige us sir," Pushkar said waving his left hand to guide him to the table.

Ernesto appeared confused. Sabir and Pushkar could hear him mumble hesitantly to Prithvi, as if seeking permission to leave the table. "I can see Ernesto cosying up to Prithvi these days. He doesn't leave Prithvi for a second. What worries me is that he even coordinates his visits to the washroom with that of Prithvi's." Pushkar chuckled.

"Huzoor... Mohataram... Adaab... Please have a seat. What will you have?" Sabir's extra sugary tone was deliberate as Ernesto's figure loomed over the table.

"Nothing... I have to go. There are a couple of scripts I have to clear," Ernesto could read the duo's intention.

"Oh come on... Where's the hurry, have some tea."

"Just a little, then."

"Tell me Dheeraj, who gave you Ernesto?" Sabir initiated the interrogation on the unusually cool name.

"I got this in college. I was the General Secretary of the Students' Union."

"Why would people call you Ernesto?"

"I don't really know, but maybe because of my leadership style."

"You think it was patterned on Ernesto Che?"

"I never said that... But he has always been my idol."

"He is my idol too," Sabir quipped.

"Did you call me here to talk about Che?"

"Do you know Che worked for leprosy patients?" Sabir put it directly.

"Yes. He moved around on his motorcycle named *La Poderosa,* along with his friend Alberto and travelled across Latin America, cutting from corner to corner Chile, Uruguay, Brazil and Venezuela."

"You seem to remember the name of the motorcycle also. I wonder how the leprosy patients bid him farewell."

"They sang and danced and played music for the way, he treated them."

"Great! You know, Dheeraj, leprosy is a disease that preys on its victim's bodies." Sabir was gradually moving into top gear. He added: "It turns a human being into a scary lump of flesh, oozing puss."

"And in those times, it had little or no cure. Leprosy patients were left to die," Pushkar explained.

"I know, but why am I being told all this?" Dheeraj appeared a tad too curious and a bit exasperated.

"You know science has helped wipe out the scourge of leprosy from this planet, but we still have patients who suffer from mental leprosy. For which, I don't think there has been any antidote till date." The suppressed anger in Sabir took the better of him.

"*Hmmmm*... So?" Dheeraj was clueless.

"Che fought against dictators. He fought for people's rights. He suffered hardships, but fought on for people's rights. He tried to make people like you and I understand the meaning of democracy and freedom. Little did he know there would be renegades in the garb of followers. So, I am not surprised people like you find great virtues in Bajrang Prasad?" Sabir was blunt.

"See, I was talking from the point of view of the channel's well being." Dheeraj replied in a whimper.

"Which, of course is to be read as, Bajrang Prasad's well-being?" Sabir replied.

"My point is that the territory which Bajrang Prasad administers is our TRP area. The channel gains from Bajrang Prasad's, 'Muscle to the Last Man' ad campaign. We can never afford to ignore this aspect."

"I wish it were just that—Muscle to the Last Man—but this is no secret that Bajrang's count stops short of taking minority in its sweep." Sabir was caustic.

Pushkar was quick on the cue. "So you are scared of the three-legged monster called TRP, while Bajrang Prasad scares the minority by propping up a communal monster. You have a Chief Minister who considers well being of the minorities as a drain on his TRP."

"The recent state elections have proved beyond doubt that Bajrang Prasad remains the heartthrob of millions. The media has egg on its face trying to rake up issues that are no longer relevant. We have to draw the line somewhere and must not forget the state is a potential mine of business interests for our *seths*, the employers," Dheeraj explained with all the patience at his command.

"Goodness grief! How could I miss your concern for the channel's health. You should have been a marketing guy. You are wasting your talent rewriting scripts." Pushkar chuckled.

"You guys are getting it all wrong," Dheeraj insisted.

"No. We have you right. We understand you cannot be out of sync with Prithvi."

"Well...he is our boss. We will have to grant him a certain level of understanding."

"Yes, of course! An understanding for everything that is perverse, irrational and illogical." Sabir quipped.

"The TRP has been created by the same market that sustains you and me. If you don't respect that, it won't respect you back. The market forces shall work against you." Dheeraj sounded like been-there-seen-all-that.

"You are talking management, dude," said Pushkar visibly angry with himself, having invited Dheeraj over at the table.

"You guys seem to be totally off key!" Ernesto replied.

"...and our heads are already beyond saving! We are also clear now that it would take years to find an antidote for mental leprosy," Sabir concluded, throwing up a big smoke haze across Dheeraj's face.

"You guys are oozing pus. It's horrifying to see the stump your cranium has reduced to. Frankly, people of your breed need to be thwarted." Pushkar spoke each word with a pronounced stress, like a visual in slow motion.

"We are sorry to waste your precious time. You have to play a pivotal role, in shaping the destiny of the channel and of the entire TV news industry. Good luck to you!" Sabir extended his hand across the table for Dheeraj.

Dheeraj got up and groped for his wallet to foot the bill.

"Don't worry, consider this a donation for mental leprosy patients." Sabir said that with thc air of an athlete who has outraced his opponents.

As Dheeraj walked away, Pushkar ordered for another Secular before digging into Dushyant's treasure trove:

"Jo Aadmi Mar Chuke The, Maujood Hain Is Sabha Mein,
Har Ek Sach Kalpana Se Aage Nikalne Laga Hai."

Car-o-bar # 1 - Dear *Beewi*

Sabir and Ranvir sat silently in Ranvir's car, relishing every sip of Royal Stag whisky. Ranvir had gulped two pegs down his throat in one rapid swig, as if that would quench his parched throat. Now, he was in a mood to showcase his knowledge about dangers of alcohol. He could take you to a virtual tour of human anatomy as the whisky washed down his body, much like the nonchalant professional cab driver who knows his way like the back of his hand.

"About 25 per cent of the alcohol would be absorbed by the stomach. Absorbed alcohol is rapidly carried through blood. Once the absorption is complete, you have the same concentration of alcohol in blood at all points of the system.

"It will be some time before the alcohol in the blood travels to the cerebral cortex of the brain, making its consumer do extraordinarily outlandish things." Ranvir had explained once during a car-o-bar.

They had painstakingly identified, the safest location for their car-o-bar. Right across the corporate headquarters of Glorious Softwares, some 300 meters down the DNN. That would mean crossing over two lanes, or "one-cigarette-walk-away," as Ranvir would put it. The software company wore a deserted look after 7 pm, while the traffic remained off the road. An hour later, Ranvir's Corolla or Sabir's Honda City, or Baba's Zen would stalk the street. Sometimes Haldi would beat them to the game. His white Tata Safari was unmistakable under the small cluster of trees, adjoining the municipal park.

Ranvir was in a spirited mood tonight. He knew he could drink to his heart's content as he had exchanged his anchoring schedule with Saba.

"Where is Baba?" Ranvir suddenly changed the topic.

"There comes the devil," Sabir could see Baba in the side-view mirror. Lean and tall, he doubled up in long strides as if he had some news to break.

"*Aao thakur, aao...*" Sabir greeted him as he sat on the back seat of the car.

"Should I pour you a small one?" Ranvir asked.

"No, boss, I am off drinks."

"Since when?"

"Since last night."

"Come on! I know how long your self-denial lasts. Small one...?" Ranvir insisted.

"No, sir, absolutely not. I have promised my mother I will come home early. Amma and babuji are here these days." Baba sounded sincere.

"So, leave early, who is stopping you?" Sabir intervened. "Have a small one, at least."

"No, boss, I will rather avoid it tonight."

"Ok, as you wish. I can't insist any more," said Ranvir as he put the plastic glass in the glove compartment.

"*Hmmm*...OK sir, if you insist."

"*Whhhhhaaaaat?*" Ranvir turned around to stare at Baba.

"Just a small one, sir, if you don't mind." Baba was smiling like a child who has recovered from a severe bout of cold and cough; long enough to go blue, and begging his mother for an ice-cream scoop.

"Oh! What about amma and babuji now?" Ranvir teased him.

"I will handle them, no problem." Baba smiled.

"You are such a drama," Ranvir fished out the plastic glass and made Baba a 'Patiala', duly topped with ice-cubes.

"Do you know Hemendra misbehaved with Jamaal and threatened him," said Baba seeking everybody's attention.

"He threatened Jamaal that he shall not get a promotion in the appraisal due next month," said Baba.

"Tell us what happened?" asked Ranvir.

Baba recounted the story Jamaal told him. "Hemendra, that fucking crotch-scratcher, wanted to buy a penthouse worth 60 lakh at the Moonlight Towers. He cajoled Jamaal to use his real estate contacts and cut the deal for him for 40. Jamaal did manage to squeeze out an extra discount, but the builder refused to come down to 40. Ever since the deal broke off, Jamaal's has been a life on the edge in the newsroom."

"Poor Jamaal," said Ranvir.

"Finally, Hemendra struck a deal at The Seventh Heaven, which is being developed by Eternal Developers. My sources told me that he helped the DNN management broker a deal with Eternal Developers," Baba added.

"Oh my God! Now, I see the game plan. Eternal Developers is our official headlines' sponsor also. Isn't it?" Sabir said in amazement.

"Multitasking seems to be a necessary prerequisite of being competitive," said Ranvir, tongue firmly in cheek.

"This crotch-scratcher's lust for real estate is strong, man!" said Baba.

"He has residential flats in Delhi and Gurgaon. And he is a 'farmer' who owns an apple orchard and a villa in a prime hill town of Uttarakhand." Said Baba taking a quick swig from his glass.

"Sometimes I wonder are we members of the fourth estate or the real estate?" Ranvir announced.

Ranvir's assessment was greeted with an instant laughter across the bar members in the car.

"*Hush*! Just a minute, guys. Call from *beewi*..." Baba's tone suddenly turned serious.

"*Umm*...ya...no...I shall get late tonight. It has been a disconcertingly maddening day today," Baba was direct.

There was a long pause. In the silence of the car, Ranvir and Sabir could sense the danger that lay ahead of Baba once he got back home.

"No, Neelu, why would I lie to you? You know how Psycho is."

"Didn't you promise to share the dinner table with amma and babuji?" Neelima's voice penetrated through the thin air in the car cabin.

"Yes, I know, but can't help it sweetheart. Try to understand."

"Don't lie. You are not in office, I know where you are." Sabir and Ranvir muffled a laugh, attempting to draw malicious pleasure at Baba's pitiable state.

"Where is amma?" Baba tried to deflect the conversation.

"*Haan,* amma, why don't you and babuji have dinner? I shall be late. No, amma...can't avoid it. I have a meeting lined up with my boss. But tomorrow *pakka*... I will spend the whole day with you. That's a promise, my dear amma!"

Baba hung up and took a deep breath. "Yaar, how do these wives come to know about our binge sessions? Can they smell your breath from afar, like a snake on night prowl that locates its prey from the sound waves and goes for the precise kill?"

Ranvir and Sabir broke into a hearty laugh at Baba's hysteric outburst.

"You don't know how to lie. You are a bloody give away. I wonder if Ravina ever got to pry on my life, I would blast her like anything," said Ranvir.

"*Arrey* you *toh* have a feudal mindset," Sabir teased Ranvir.

"Wives are supposed to take care of their husbands. Right?" Ranvir shot back.

Sabir cut him short. "Supposed to do what? To allow you to lay her and serve you food on demand?"

"Absolutely. She will have to take care of all my needs, any time and every time." Ranvir held his ground.

"What are we discussing, gentlemen? It's my wife who called, you don't need to quarrel over women," Baba intervened and begged Ranvir for another small one.

"What about Neelima?" Ranvir teased him with a grin.

"A situation far less pleasant awaits me back home. I know I'll have to face the music."

Sabir suddenly opened the door from his side, stepped out and banged it shut with a loud thud.

"Oh shit!" Baba's drink spilled over the car floor.

"*Arrey* bhai, can't I go out to pee... Welcome to join me." Sabir said nonchalantly, as he strode towards a clump of huge Ashoka trees.

Car-o-bar # 2 - Roving Editor

"See, who is here!"

"Sir, just one," Uday seemed desperate as he opened the back seat door and tried to get in, next to Baba.

"Have a seat, handsome! You will get anything in this *jannat...*" Ranvir invited him into his car as if, he were ushering him into his living room.

"*Kya khabar,*" asked Ranvir. He then poured the whisky into a thermocol glass he fished out from under his seat.

"Sir, *ek bandar* newsroom *ke andar,*" Uday said excitedly.

"What does that mean?" Baba expressed surprise and shock.

"Sir, monkeys and ghosts are stalking the newsroom." Uday provoked a thunderous laughter inside the car, shutting out the chartbuster '*Kendi Po Po Po*' on Radio Mirchi.

"That sounds interesting," said Baba. "Give us some more dope on that."

"Two 'stories' have just landed at the assignment desk," said Uday. "A monkey is seen piggy-backing a goat. He is immediately dubbed as the goat's new lover," he added.

"Oh! You mean a metrosexual monkey." Ranvir quipped.

"This monkey is competing with a ghost. Because another related story has landed up on the assignment desk, the story about a woman who claims that a ghost shares her bed and makes love to her every night. So, it's a tie between *aashik bandar* and *the maha-aashik bhoot,*" saying that Uday gulped down a large swig from the glass.

"That's one hell of a smart ghost, I must say." Ranvir quipped. "He knows how to hog the headlines even after having been dead. What better platform than DNN." He added with a chuckle.

"You never know, he might just be the *bhoot* who can lift our sagging TRPs. Cheers to that!" Sabir raised his glass to the general cheer of those present in the car.

"I am going to suggest Prithvi to track this woman until she begins to enlarge," Ranvir quipped. "You never know, we might create history by being the only channel to cover LIVE a human being delivering a ghost's baby," he added as the car crew doubled up with laughter.

"I shall pray it's a boy, for his name's sake," Sabir butted in.

"What?" Everyone asked in unison.

"*Bhootni ka.*"

"Today, the reporter is dead. Let us toast to the death of a reporter," Ranvir said.

"TV channels don't need reporters, they need porters who can carry their wastes on their heads...their *paikhana*... Shit sells, man!" Sabir took a swig from his glass and gave it to Ranvir to refill it.

"The challenge before us all is to avoid spoiling our clothes. *Lekin hum kab tak bachenge, behenchod?*" Said Sabir.

Ranvir sank deep into his front seat, convulsing with laughter and slapping his hand down on the steering wheel. The car shook as if a minor quake had hit it.

"Sir, *aashik bandar* is already on air for 'Hila Ke Rakh Denge'. They have superimposed the visual clip with the song '*Bus Ek Sanam Chahiye-eh-eh-e Aashiqi Ke Liye*'," Uday crooned the song for effect.

"I am sure they will handle the *maha-aashiq bhoot* story with a creative flair," said Baba playfully.

"Cheers! Let's drink a toast to the *bandar-bhoot* duo."

"Cheers!" Baba said raising his glass to Uday's.

"By the way, did you guys read *Paagalvaani* on the media sponsored, self-immolation bid in Bihar?" asked Uday.

"He is bang on! Witty, cheeky, irreverent, provocative, call it what you will, there's something to be said about it. I'm a fan already!" Sabir was delirious with praise for the faceless *paagal*.

"He is too good yaar," Ranvir said excitedly. "Let me read out a brief snatch from his blog on the self-immolation story that every channel covered," he added as he pressed buttons on his smart phone and browsed the Internet. "There it goes and I quote, '*The day shall not be far when news channels will put out advertisements that will read somewhat like this, 'Book prime-time slots for LIVE coverage of suicide bids'. Hail to thee oh, Indian media, hail to thee oh, inspirational reporting! Shame on Indian media! But why am I not surprised?*'"

"That's very well said. Who is this *paagal* guy?" Baba asked.

"Well, he seems like someone from our fraternity. Whoever he is, let's pray the hits on the blog multiply by the day. More power to him!" said Sabir.

"Do you know they dropped the NCERT syllabus revision story in favour of Lovonita Berry's wardrobe malfunction for *Dus Ka Dhamaka*?" Uday brought the conversation back to the newsroom's agenda.

"Good that I'm not anchoring today," said Ranvir as he took another swig from his glass.

"Yes, we have finally procured Lovonita's sensational visuals," chuckled Uday.

"*Tch... Tch...* Poor girl will lose her honour yet again, on DNN." Ranvir chuckled too.

"Sir, let me share a little secret with you," Uday could not contain his excitement.

"Nothing will go out of this car." Ranvir assured Uday.

"I saw the silver glitter of Lovonita Berry, from the far end edit suite that is reserved for special programmes. Devendra, Sudhir and I, just the three of us; we went back and forth on the visuals and saw them on slow motion, repeatedly, almost analytically. Sir, *nasha chadh gaya*. It made me want to inhale the perfume she was wearing as deeply as I could, like a creep, totally immersed in her curvaceous body."

"You have spoken beyond your tender age, young lad." Ranvir turned around to pat Uday on his back.

"Devendra's impatience led him to transfer the visuals on to his pen drive," said Uday.

"You guys show that there is, in fact, no limit to anything, as long as you set your lust to it. *Ha ha!*" said Ranvir to the general applause of the car mates. "They sent Nidheesh to Lovonita's father, Brigadier Berry's farmhouse in Mehrauli for a sound byte. The angry Brigadier came out, apparently holding a gun in his hand, baying for the reporter's blood. He also fired two rounds in the air. Nidheesh ki *phat li* and Pawan forgot to roll the camera." Uday gave a blow by blow account.

"Come to think of it, what could they have asked the Brigadier?" asked Ranvir as he lobbed a bunch of hypothetical questions for his audience: *"Aapki beti ko nirvastra kar diya gaya... Bataiyye, apko kaisa lag raha hai? Bataiyye, kya iske peeche koi sazish hai? Bataiyye? Aakhri baar apne apni beti ko kab aisi halat me dekha tha... Bataiyye...?"*

Sabir took a long drag off the cigarette, and broke into a couplet from Dushyant:

"Main Inn Bepanah Andheron Ko Subah Kaise Kahun,
Main Inn Nazaron Ka Andha Tamashbeen Nahi."

"Isn't that Pushkar bhai's favourite?" Uday asked Sabir as they climbed out of the car into the moonlight that spread across the street.

"I am missing him tonight. He has gone to visit his ailing mother, let's pray for her speedy recovery," said Sabir as they leaned against the car.

All of a sudden, a pack of half a dozen stray dogs appeared on the scene and tried to snuggle around Uday and Sabir.

Perhaps, the pack could smell the chicken lollipops that Sabir had ordered from the local vendor, who was sitting at the far end of the other lane. Uday's loud cheers only egged them on.

"*Suno miyan,* this is not the right place for you guys," Sabir said patting two of the dogs as he knelt down to keep the conversation eyeball-to-eyeball. "They need you there in the newsroom. It is only through animals like you that the India's fourth estate is still alive and kicking. Go to the fourth floor, take the lift on the left as you enter the lounge, or should I escort you all 'sirs'. Please allow me this privilege. You are the new deities of TV news. I bow to thee with all humility." Saying that, Sabir kept his glass on the road and bent down, first in a double and then stretched his arms and legs to lie prostate on the ground. The dogs flinched. The mob moved back. One of them let out a small howl, trying to figure out the drama being staged, while the other that wasn't impressed with Sabir's antics, growled looking skywards; followed by two more growls in quick succession by his lieutenants.

"Hey Sabir. Come off it…enough of your *nautanki*." Ranvir tried to pull him back into the car. Baba stuck to his ground.

The dogs soon realised the height of nonsense human beings can create when they get drunk. So, they gradually hopped, stepped sideways and pranced back to where they had come from. The kiosk owner was about to close for the day and the mob looked forward to a sumptuous leftover to feast on.

One of the dogs came back from hunting though, and held his ground. He would not budge and kept wagging his tale, his hind legs spread wide, his head held high, his clean pink tongue hanging clear six inches out of his mouth, teasing Sabir regally. He kept staring Sabir into his eyes. Sabir, in turn, could see the disdain in his eyes and could hear him speak: "*First, you hunted us down for food. Though we loved the wild and tenaciously guarded our freedom, you terrorised us and domesticated us. You ill-treated all members of the entire animal kingdom. You started making money out of our corpses. However, from time immemorial we have given only loyalty in return. Not any longer! We are your masters now. We control your destiny. Don't give us 'air-time' and you are doomed."*

The dog's extended family howled hysterically from the other end, irritated at the fact that a fraternity member was in conversation with an insensitive human being. The cue was reasonably well understood; the dog turned around and let out a strong howl in solidarity, before sprinting into darkness.

He stopped midway, turned back to take one last look at Sabir. Sabir could read a question in his eyes: *"Hey, how did you find your new roving editor?"*

Maa

Sabir bhai, dropping me home tonight...?" *Baba* could barely speak a sentence straight. Sabir knew it was coming. It was already 11.30 pm. He collected himself, drew out a cigarette and said a cool "Yes".

"But it is no fun going back home. Neelima is not going to allow you to share the bed with her. Why don't you come to my home instead," he added.

"No, sir, amma and babuji..." Baba was slurring and Sabir could see the whisky flowing out in drips from the corner of his mouth. He was barely able to keep his eyes open.

"Ok, no problem. I will drop you home. Time to leave!"

"Here's for the road..." Sabir poured himself another peg and stepped out of the car, banging it shut with a loud thud.

"Long way for you, buddy. Just take care of him," said Ranvir as he slipped his car into gear and started driving.

"Where's your car by the way?" Sabir asked Baba.

Baba lifted his hand and pointed towards the office. Sabir realised Baba's car was safe in the office parking.

Sabir's Honda City was speeding towards Janakpuri. Sabir had switched off the AC and wound down the window glasses. A gust of cool breeze greeted the passengers.

"Sabir *bhai*..." *Baba* tried to speak something, but realised he has lost his power of speech to Royal Stag.

"Yes, tell me...you have had a peg too many. You should have avoided it today."

"Yes...rrright..."

"Then, why did you have it?"

"I lofe my mottthhher..." *Baba* blurted out.

"*Ube chootiya mat banao*... If you loved your mother, you would have been home long back."

"I love my mother..."

"I don't want to listen to you! Stop ditching people! They are your parents. They visit you once in a while and you're too busy wanking... That's unpardonable."

"Sabir *bhai*... I lovvfe my mottthher," *Baba* lapsed into silence again, staring blankly out of the windshield.

"I will..."

"What...?"

"I will...complete your sentence..." said Sabir as he switched on the FM radio.

"I love amma..."

'*Luka Chhuppi Bahut Hui... Saamne Aaja Na...*' Just when Sabir thought he had the situation under control, Lata's entry with her hit number from Rang De Basanti changed the direction and threats emerged.

"Sir, please change, sir..." *Baba* almost pleaded and even tried to reach out to the control buttons on the audio panel.

"I just love this song..." Sabir said, almost cutting his washed-out colleague midway.

"I will cry, Sabir bhai..." Baba came out clear for the first time. Sabir wasn't surprised.

'Aaja Saanjh Hui, Mujhe Teri Fikar...' The song with a tremendous ability to affect and manipulate emotions, played on.

"I love my amma..."

Suddenly, Sabir felt a water drop falling on his left arm. In no time, there was another hot drop. He looked outside the side window into the sky...The full moon was shimmering on the road ahead, almost overshadowing the bright luminescence of the sulphur street lights. Not a drop on the windshield either. How can it rain in a perfectly clear sky? Where did that water drop come from? He seemed thoroughly puzzled, but kept driving and singing along with the song that was playing, like his guilty pleasure. And suddenly, almost as an afterthought, he turned to Baba. He was staring out of the windshield, as if he was struck by the beauty of a painting beyond what its painter saw when he set it upright, and in the backdrop of the sulphur light, Sabir could make out a wet patch—two tear drops balanced precariously at the tip of the nose—on Karthik aka Baba's face, but he made no attempt to wipe them off.

'Mere Chanda Tu Hai Kahan...' Lata crooned on. Sabir pulled up the vehicle. He realised he was being a bit harsh on Baba. He put his left hand around Baba's shoulders and hugged him tight.

"Hey, come on man. I am sorry. You can always say sorry to your mother. Mothers are kind. We are so selfish that we forget our parents once we are away from home and settled in life..."

Sabir explained like a moral science teacher who teaches not only with mind, but also with heart.

"You are lucky, your parents visit you here," he added. "My mother is so unwell, she can't even move out of bed. And look at me here, I hardly get time to visit her. I go there as a guest. Now, I have decided to visit her at least once every month. You never know when you might lose them forever. We are extremely lucky to have them around. So come on, cheer up!"

Baba covered his face with his hands, his sobs buried deep in his chest.

Sabir switched on the engine and started the machine.

"Your mother loves you a lot. *Inshallah*, she will pardon you. If you love her, do try and keep the promise you made to her tonight." Sabir looked hypnotically to the road ahead as he crested the rising curve to the left.

The hot tear bubble slipped off Karthik's face, vanishing into the darkness of the car. Sabir slowed down his car before pulling up yet again. He fished out his mobile phone from his shirt pocket. Baba looked askance at him.

"Just putting a reminder..." Sabir gave him a reassuring look as he typed on his phone's keypad:

'To-do list 4 2day: Ttk bukng for Alld. Dad specs. MUST.'

Then putting the phone back into his breast pocket, he pressed the accelerator. He wanted Baba to reach to his parents even sooner.

Dysfunctional System

Sir, there is a bomb of a news we just broke," Binny rattled off as Prithvi took his seat in his plush swivel chair during the editorial meeting.

"What is it?"

"Sir, a young couple found dead in the car. Their bodies, clothed in their tattered undergarments, give it away as a case of a suicide pact," announced Binny.

"Who saw them first?"

"Sir, the bodies were discovered by a passerby on the Delhi-Noida Expressway."

"These days, boys and girls are seeking out innovative places for sex," Prithvi sounded like a sociologist, who was talking of a paradigm shift in customs and mores in India in his latest paper.

"The chick lit fictions are getting very creative with their suggestions of rather funny places for sex." Amitabh wanted Prithvi to indulge in a little fun. "Sir, forget cars, youngsters are now trying out in toilets of moving trains, in buses and in office washrooms as well."

"Do you mean to say even our office is a haven for the young and the enterprising?"

"The scope is larger in offices where they have unisex washrooms," Ernesto chipped in.

"Binny would throw some more light on this," Prithvi was steadily and surely getting into his element. Binny looked up and giggled without answering the question.

"Why, can't we plan a special on that?" Prithvi's adrenaline was pumping hard.

"Absolutely!" Hemendra was quick on the uptake. "This is a trend story. We must also educate our masses and help them understand the changes taking place in the sex trend among our youths," he was equally besotted with the idea. "Get top of the line guests from the world of fashion and entertainment. Tisca Fereira and Mahi are must," Prithvi thundered.

"Are we not digressing?" Pushkar's statement triggered an awkward silence in the conference room. There were a few coughs around the room and then overwhelming silence.

"I think we should stick to the investigation bit, rather than creating hype around the sex angle," Pushkar argued.

"I don't think I asked for your opinion on this," Prithvi cut him short. "I don't like people who speak out of turn."

"The floor is all yours, boss." Pushkar said in a resigned tone.

"How about calling it *Kaamtantra*?" said Amitabh, latching on to the subject close to Prithvi's heart.

"*Hmmm...*" Hemendra sounded tentative.

"*Kaamsutra...*" Ernesto was even innovative.

"Fine! Lock it for our prime-time show *Hila Ke Rakh Denge*." Prithvi ordered.

Three days later...

"What is the update on Ridhima-Nakul suicide pact?" Prithvi fired his first question as he sat on his swivel.

The police had not made much headway into the case, but Uday knew the repercussions of not providing an update on a daily basis. "The police have discovered a pack of condoms from Nakul's wallet." Uday announced reluctantly.

Uday knew his revelation would trigger a rush of testosterone among his seniors. He tried to filter information so that the whole process is still secretive with little details getting out.

"They were all unused. I know that this is a minor update on the murder case, but, of course, the police are stuck to their earlier version. Not ruling out murder yet!"

"So...what brand was it?" Prithvi posed the question directly to Uday.

"What, sir?"

"*Arrey*, the condoms! What brand?"

Uday stared blankly at the TV panel in front of him, the crudeness of the question sank into him. "It was Kkk... Kamasutra..." Uday stammered.

"Which flavour?"

This one stunned him. "Sir, I...I did not ask." Uday stammered again.

"Strawberry, I heard, is the flavour of the season." Ernesto said with a voyeuristic smile on his face.

"Why do girls love strawberry so much?" Prithvi sounded like he was going to reward the person who comes up with the right answer. He darted a look at Binny, who pretended to be busy playing with her mobile handset; an impish smile touching her lips. "Sir, you should tell us. You are the most experienced." Amitabh sought Prithvi's indulgence.

"*Arrey*, we never had options other than the much-trusted *sarkari* brand." Prithvi leaned back on his plush swivel, locked his hands behind his head and dashed a look at Binny. "Why is she silent?"

"Why do you look at me for answers?" she giggled, then raising her head up a little looked straight into Prithvi's eyes. "There are married people in the room, ask them," she broke into a giggle again.

"What has it got to do with marriage?" Haldi ran the comb over his head.

"Haldi bhai is right. In fact, these are time tested tools for unadulterated fun before marriage, safe and trouble free." Prithvi held forth in his typically histrionic manner. He couldn't resist the topic so he went on to add: "Girls have a lot many options today with all kinds of pills available."

Binny chose to ignore his remark and continued to fidget with her handset, while he grinned like that Hindi film villain who violated the modesty of a village belle.

"Let's plan a one-hour special on prime-time tonight on teenage sex." Prithvi turned to Shahid: "Can we have a power-point presentation on the plan by afternoon?"

"This is our kind of story and we must cash in on it," the crotch-scratcher latched on the idea with the fervour of a kite runner.

"Must get the sexologist Dr Ambrish Kothari this time," said Prithvi.

"How about slugging it—*Gupt Gyaan*?" Ernesto never failed to value-add on such occasions.

"Still better—*Andheri Raat Mein, Diya Tere Haath Mein…*" Shahid scored. Hemendra twisted his lips in a sort of a smile and acknowledged Shahid's contribution.

"Those are old fashioned. Make it more today types. How about *Kabhi Mere Saath Ek Raat Guzaar…?*"

"You are brilliant," said Ernesto.

'Bloody voyeurs...' Sabir sent it on group ID—*'The Gang'*.

A week later...

"Sir, the police are not ruling out foul play, they suspect the young couple was murdered in the car. It was not a suicide pact as the police suspected earlier." Baba put the story in perspective for the editorial seniors in the morning meeting.

"But, the Crime Branch has not ruled out sex before they were murdered," said Prithvi.

"Yes, that is alright, but I think the viewers shall be interested to know the suspects and the motive behind the murder," said Uday. "The post-mortem report clearly indicates bruises on their necks."

"We must give our viewers a wholesome platter. Let's put two teams on the story. The first team, led by Uday, should clearly focus on the investigation bit; I want every goddamned information, every minute update, even if hearsay, on the case. The second team shall focus on the lifestyle, the craze for pre-marital sex among youth today and the increasing acceptance of live-in relationships; get Anushka in the loop. Nobody can do this stuff better than her," said Prithvi.

"Let's hear daily updates on Ridhima-Nakul scandal. Haldi *bhai* make sure the two teams do not work at cross purposes," said Hemendra.

"*Arrey,* don't worry. The Additional Director General of Police is an old friend. God willing, DNN shall have an exclusive by evening." Haldi fished out his knife-comb and launched into his drill with aplomb.

'This comb mst b a gft 4m sm goddamned IG or DIG... Ha ha ha ha...' Sabir opened the inbox on his mobile to see Pushkar's message.

A week later...

"What is the update, Uday? Visphot beat us squarely. They had the report on the vaginal swab." Prithvi launched without preliminaries. It seemed like the DNN torture chamber had come to life again. "Sir, I tried to confirm but..."

"...you were caught unawares? You must pull up your socks, errant lad this shall not be tolerated." Prithvi was spitting fire.

"Sir, we had only unconfirmed info," said Baba.

"You had the info, but you chose not to share it with your seniors?"

"Sir, Uday did tell me about it in the afternoon, but I asked him to cross check. After all, it was a sensitive piece of information on molestation and death of a young girl. Uday could not get an official confirmation until late last night. Even Visphot did not have the confirmation; they ran it on hearsay."

"The fact is we missed it and it is inexcusable." Prithvi was rabid.

Baba could feel the lava pools starting to pop up all over the place. "How can you expect me to put out half-baked information on air? Facts are sacrosanct, we cannot afford to play with them." Baba kept his cool.

Prithvi turned to Uday: "You are a crime reporter, but you don't think like one. You don't have that killer instinct."

"Sir, no official was willing to bet his service on that. So, we decided not to run it," Uday was bolstered by the support shown by his immediate boss in the meeting room.

"That's lazy thinking! I see slackness in the team. Let me warn you, Uday that you are going to pay for this," Prithvi barked like a psycho.

"Sorry to interrupt you, sir, but we broke this story. Uday has been ahead in the race right from the start. We were the first to say that there was foul play in the whole case. We need to recognise and appreciate his efforts. We don't deserve such harsh words from you," Baba spoke out with firmness and resolve of a team leader.

"But, how can you sit on info like this?" Bubbles of spit leaked out from Psycho's mouth, as he turned rabid.

"It was an unconfirmed report, how could I have allowed it to go on air? It would have been a huge compromise with the channel's credibility. And you know how Yashwant sir always talks of credibility." Baba now drew out his ace.

"It was Yashwant boss who called up to inquire about the miss. Later, the marketing head also called me up and complained that we shall be ruined if we lag behind in this business of breaking news. What do I tell them? That I have a bunch of dumbwits working for me." Prithvi was livid.

"Then you set the credibility criteria," said Baba.

"Do not act smart with me." Prithvi shot back. And then he turned around to address those sitting around the oval table. "I would not save your jobs if the company loses its market. This should be very clear to one and all," he announced.

"It seems I have lost your trust. I had better resign. You can get the marketing chaps to run the newsroom for all I care." Baba got up from the chair and in two quick strides was at the exit door.

"Hang on, you cannot talk to me like that," Prithvi shouted from his chair.

"You will have my resignation in the next 100 seconds." Baba appeared business-like and talked like a thorough professional when he looked straight into Prithvi's eyes.

Everyone around that oval table was now looking at Baba. Rajkishore was scratching his beard as if he had developed a rash. Everything in his looks betrayed if he had any take on this incident. He made a 180 degree head movement, trying to take in the drama unfolding, but gradually sank his head into his chest and resumed Solitaire on his BlackBerry.

Another resignation was the last thing Prithvi could afford at a time when professionals across editorial departments had quit in the past two months. Moreover, Baba was not just somebody. He had a solid reputation as an ace reporter and was popular among his team-mates and colleagues and was a favourite with the Super Boss.

"Yaar, you guys get unnecessarily emotional. Come on, be a sport," said Prithvi trying to calm Baba.

"But this is sheer humiliation. I cannot compromise my self-respect." Baba pulled at the doorknob once again ready to dart out.

"Come on Baba, don't be silly; come on here and take your seat." Prithvi was fast on his feet. "Don't behave like a juvenile," he added.

"Sir, I am behaving in a professional manner, but there are people who lapse into fits of excitement every now and then." It was clear the remark was meant for Prithvi and Hemendra. "Some people don't know how to talk to a senior colleague." Baba was never so direct and firm.

"*Arrey*, come on, nobody is humiliating you," said Prithvi. "Now, please take your seat."

Baba quietly returned to his seat. The moment he sat down, he saw a message on his mobile:

'Puraane Pad Gaye Darr, Phenk Do Tum Bhi,
Ye Kachra Aaj Bahar Phenk Do Tum Bhi.'

"So, what is it we need to do today?" Prithvi sounded normal.

"This is beyond my jurisdiction. It's up to you to decide that," said Baba.

"Do we have a confirmation on the swab today?"

"It's confirmed! Uday has already given a phone-in in the morning and he has a LIVE lined up in the next hour," said Baba.

"I suspect the vaginal swab is going to be a clincher," asked Prithvi.

"We should avoid going ballistic over the swab info right now," said Uday. "I mean...I am just sharing a viewpoint," and completed himself by playing safe.

"But the public mood is not ruling out the involvement of sex," Prithvi insisted. "Once the swab report is confirmed, we must tell the viewers that we were spot-on when we claimed on the second day that the couple had sex before their bodies were discovered in the car," said Prithvi sounding like Sherlock Holmes explaining a point to Dr Watson.

'Ye madarchod nahi sudhrega.' Pushkar sent the message to *'The Gang'*.

Three days later...

"Uday is likely to get the vaginal swab report." Baba announced in the meeting, expecting the piece of news to ease rising professional tensions.

"That should be wonderful," Prithvi smiled at the prospect of another sensational exclusive. As the scant group of well meaning journalists sat around the oval table, worrying about their viewer's fears on receiving unfiltered updates on the latest murder, Psycho was basking in the reflected glory of investigating the crisis and unearthing a scandal of astounding proportions.

"According to our sources, the hired *goondas* could have well turned into rapists. They may have killed Nakul first and then gone on to rape Ridhima before doing her in too," said Baba.

"Why would they kill her?" Prithvi was surprised.

"Because they feared Ridhima would spill the beans," Uday supplemented Baba's point.

"You mean to say Nakul never had sex with Ridhima that day?" Prithvi asked like it was the most complicated riddle he wanted solved.

"It is too premature to suspect Nakul for that," said Uday.

"Now, we must do a story on the goof-ups of the police. They are still groping in the dark," said Baba.

"Tell me...are Ridhima's parents above suspicion yet?"

"My sources tell me that the parents had sent hired goons to teach Nakul a lesson. There was no brief to kill their daughter. Even if there was, it has not been established yet," said Uday.

"But, the parents turned out to be murderers." Prithvi concluded.

"Well...you can't really say at this point of investigation," Baba looked askance at Prithvi.

"Sir, I have an appointment. I shall leave!" Uday was desperate to leave the room.

"Sure, best of luck! Anushka did a brilliant interview with Dr Kothari yesterday. Exclusive one on one. You must try to get the Police Commissioner's interview."

"*Madarchod, laundiyabaaj, tharki saala,*" Uday mumbled a volley of curses at Psycho for praising Anushka as he opened the door to leave. He turned around and looked at Prithvi straight-faced: "I shall try my best, sir."

"Let's play it big, folks," Prithvi announced.

"We should invite a forensic expert and a gynaecologist in the studio," said Shahid.

"We must ask the gynaecologist if she could simulate those anatomical nuances for the benefit and understanding of our beloved viewers." Ernesto chipped in.

"That's a brilliant idea! What do you say, Haldi bhai?"

"It's fantastic! It's the best way to explain to viewers the complex human anatomy." Haldi fished out his comb once again.

'*Human anatomy...? Thz ppl r sick.*' Sabir shared the message with '*The Gang*'.

"Get down to business. Get Sudhanshu in the loop. I want this on air at 8 pm." Hemendra ordered Shahid.

"Slug the show—*Ye Andar Ki Baat Hai.*" Prithvi puffed up his chest as if he had dictated a letter of thanks to the Nobel committee, for having nominated his work.

Web Chat

Paagalvaani.blogspot.com

Suddenly, the dead bodies of two teenagers, a boy and a girl have become the subject of many a thesis on voyeurism in the electronic media. Today, I shall present to my readers brief excerpts from the live web chat, organised by Association of News Channels. The questions were answered by a panel of Managing Editor/Editors-Owners of top three channels—Rizwan Abbas of Angaar TV, Umang Tyagi of Visphot News and Yashwant Thakur of DNN. Eighty per cent of the viewers grilled the panellists on the news channel's coverage of the Nakul-Ridhima case, which has brought the media under public scrutiny like never before.

I would refrain from commenting on the webcam chat. I know the readers are intelligent enough to draw their own conclusions.

Amit Negi: Don't you think our media has behaved irresponsibly in Ridhima-Nakul case?

Rizwan Abbas: It is unfair to blame TV channels. If anyone was carried away, it was the State CID. The police came up with multiple theories; we only reported what we were told.

Ashish Mathur: The media ran a parallel investigation into the case. How far do you agree?

Umang Tyagi: We realised the police failed to do a neat investigation. We only did what was expected of us. We wanted to help the police crack the case ASAP.

Nibha Sinha: So you came up with new theories every day?

Rizwan Abbas: We don't believe in concocting stories, that is the most sloppy piece of investigation. The unpopular decision made by the police is bound to draw a lot of dissension from the media.

Rakesh Raman: I suspect the media speculated in order to push their TRPs.

Umang Tyagi: TRP is like a monster which needs to be constantly fed.

Yashwant Thakur: Our primary responsibility as a journalist is to reach the truth. Incidentally, the way to truth is through a heap of conjectures.

Arshad Fakhri: The news channels did not even care that the honour of so many families were at stake when they speculated about the Nakul-Ridhima relationship.

Rizwan Abbas: The Indian media is not from Mars. We are part of the same society which, some say, is highly voyeuristic. Sometimes, we do feel helpless.

Rishadat Kabir: Far from it, sir, you in the media seem to be titillating viewers with such stories.

Umang Tyagi: We have no intentions to titillate our viewers. But, at the same time I would like to share the findings of a survey the Association of News Channels has got done recently. Shows that scream sex, crime and cinema always get us the maximum TRPs. We call it the three Cs and one S formula! Cricket also gets us high viewership.

Vijay Kapur: So you are soon going to set up a sex-shop on your channel and sell vibrators, tampons, sex toys, condoms and pills?

Rizwan Abbas: I don't feel the need to reply to that question.

Tabassum: How else would you describe your coverage of Ridhima-Nakul death mystery?

Umang Tyagi: Look at you there, even you are terming it as a mystery. The police are still groping in the dark, trying to make a spectacle of the investigation. We are just acting tools to help crack the puzzle. The TRPs are just an indicator that the viewers are equally concerned about the way investigation is allowed to be dragged.

Ruma: At around the same time when Nakul-Ridhima were found dead in the car, 22 people died in hooch tragedy in Andhra Pradesh. That got a passable mention on most channels. Why?

Yashwant Thakur: It is unfortunate that many poor, faceless people, die of consuming hooch in our country every year. As far as news coverage of such incidents is concerned, there is a general sense of fatigue about such newsbreaks. We, in media, always look for a novel angle. In Nakul-Ridhima case, we had a face to the story. Imagine the teenage couple taking each other's lives in a suicide pact near the national capital. And then, investigations point out that it could be honour killing.

Shivendra Bahadur: Do you think journalism has not remained untainted by consumerism?

Rizwan Abbas: Your guess is as good as mine. We all have to accept there has been a general decline in the ethical standards in our society.

Yashwant Thakur: We have not invented the market. Like everything else, the market has invented the media.

Sanjay Bannerjee: Do you see a crisis of credibility in news channels?

Umang Tyagi: I am very optimistic about the role of the fourth estate in shaping the destiny of the country.

Saira Khan: How! By dishing out trivia 24×7?

Rizwan Abbas: It is easy to hang the media. Please try to appreciate the good we do.

Manish Ojha: So you will continue to work with no accountability.

Yashwant Thakur: A journalist knows that he is accountable to not only his viewers but also, his conscience.

Part II

Tathaastu

Tathaastu Steel Project

"Sir, Ullasganj is up in arms," Satyendra sounded excited over the phone. "The farmers and forest-dwellers, including the Bhambhuki tribals have decided to take on the government."

"What is the ground situation there?" asked Haldi.

"The villagers, especially tribals, are brimming with anger. The tribals fear Nilamata Parvat, which they revere as their deity will be poached upon and taken away from them," said Satyendra. "The district collector has started the land verification exercise already."

"The government's standpoint?"

"The state government has found out ways to cut corners. They will go all out to grab the land for the Tathaastu steel project. This could mean disaster for those 16 villages. More than 2000 people will be displaced, leave aside the impact on the flora and fauna. The project is bound to threaten human rights outrightly."

"What does the 'Friends of the Forest' act says?"

"Right now the laws are heavily skewed against the tribals and the forest dwellers. How can the government take away their land without their permission?"

"And the farmers, what about them?"

"The farmers are worried on two counts: first, that their irrigational lands are going to be taken away at throw away prices. Second, the resettlement and rehabilitation that follows."

"The government has already laid out the resettlement plan. Hasn't it?"

"They don't feel reassured on that front any way."

"So, Tathaastu will have a smooth sail?"

"They are in the process of setting up the refinery. A part of that project is on forest land. They need to mine iron-ore and other minerals and as you know, Nilamata Parvat stores precious minerals under its belly. Tathaastu is not leaving anything up to chance this time."

"What do you mean?"

"There is talk of Aryan International—the parent company of Tathaastu—having replenished the ruling party coffers, they are ready to bribe anyone to get their project through."

"Stop talking in riddles," Haldi's patience ran out.

"I am likely to get some revealing dope on the story soon. You will get exclusive investigative story very soon. But, sir, I have a question."

"Tell me."

"*Ummm*...will the channel run this kind of a story?"

"Cut to the chase."

"*Hmmm*...because it is going to impact the state, its development and its people," said Satyendra. "This is far from *Chamatkar Ko Namaskar* stuff," Satyendra put it bluntly.

"You don't know, *Chamatkar Ko Namaskar* has great TRP potential. People will love it. In fact, we ran your UFO story for two hours on prime time the other day. You are doing great stuff! Keep at it!"

"You only instructed me to borrow its footage from our rivals. It was no UFO-Shu-ef-aw, but a pilotless plane. Truth be told, the Airforce Command Office was experimenting with their new design. I told you everything before you ran the story."

"But, people got scared. They watched it in horror and awe. The story gave us maximum eyeballs on that day. You shoud know this." Jagat snapped at Satyendra.

"I only wish to know whether I should pursue my investigation against Tathaastu? Is the channel interested in such stories?" Satyendra probed.

Jagat Singh knew it was difficult to dissuade Satyendra from a story. He knew Satyendra was not talking out of his hat. He also knew well Satyendra had done his research. "Tathaastu is the Indian arm of Aryan, and Aryan International has access to power corridors in the countries it has set up its business. It should be a watertight investigation." Jagat finally gave in to Satyendra's persuasion.

"Does that mean, I have a go ahead?" Satyendra could not contain his excitement.

"We cannot be seen as activists. Show me the explosion and I promise your story will be on prime time," said Jagat.

"Sure, sir!"

"Coming down to Delhi for Super Boss's meeting?" asked Jagat.

"Yes, sir. Got my tickets booked already."

"See you soon then!"

"Bye."

That night before he went off to sleep, Satyendra hurriedly wrote this down in his blue diary:

Whatever you do will be insignificant, but it is very important that you do it.

– Mahatma Gandhi

Chamatkar Ko Namaskar

Paagalvaani.blogspot.com

Physicist and cosmologist Sir Stephen Hawking should visit India and see the contribution of Hindi news channels in propagating his theory, 'the presence of extraterrestrial in other parts of the universe based on mathematical calculations,' to ludicrous proportions. For a lay TV news follower, any flying object in the sky is a potential alien. Sir Hawking may still be grappling with numbers to work out exactly how do aliens look like, but little would he know that the self-sufficient Hindi news channels have unravelled the mystery already. They have worked out the looks and dress code of the aliens, down to the last cut. An average TV viewer would know everything about the lifestyle and behavioural tendencies of aliens, except the way they procreate. Perhaps, this could be a new area of interest for Sir Stephen Hawking to apply his genius mind.

Even otherwise, TV news channels have gone where no man (not even Sir Stephen Hawking's mathematical mind) has gone before. So, when a news channel takes you around on a stroll to the gardens of heaven, in a series titled *Swarg Ka Darwaza* and another one gets you an exclusive interview with the man who voluntarily set up a rendezvous with our very own

Yamraj (the death messenger in Hindu mythology), you can be sure that the pundits of superstition now graced the exalted newsrooms. With a heady mix of astrology, news channels are pulling you deep down into the *paataal* of superstitions, desperately feeding on your fears.

They scare you with all kinds of ludicrous Big Bang Theories where the universe shall end—stopping just short of telling you that only roaches and TV journalists will survive the Big Bang—resurrecting and writing together, a new world order.

What does the future hold?

If an alien were to meet a News Manager, it might ask a modest for royalty for using its clan's footage without permission. It might even slap a defamation suit against news channels and film producer Rakesh Roshan for showing its clan as little green men, walking about after UFO touchdown and as senile dwarfs.

Lessons drawn:

Don't fall into the traps of news channels, if you haven't already. They have a specialised group of con artists, masquerading as TV journalists. Scare the media by skipping their channels every day during prime time.

Synergy

"*Ama miyan, khul gayi dukan aapki?*" Sabir took a dig at Shahid, who was glued to his work station monitoring the stock market."The Super Boss shall be here any moment," he added.

"*Bleh*...there is still time," Shahid said nonchalantly without even caring to look at Sabir. And then, sounded chirpy the very next moment. "I had an excellent start, have already gained 20 grand since the market opened today. Hope the trend continues for few more weeks." Shahid appeared happy with the rising sensex.

Those in the newsroom who invested in stocks swore by Shahid's analysis. "Can you please check the fate of Teekay?" asked Sabir.

"It has improved slightly," Shahid replied without looking at the terminal.

"Oh...that's great! I am safe. I am a *chhota-mota* investor Shahid bhai. You are the king of stock market."

"The king has become a pauper," Shahid was rueful.

"Can we have everyone in studio number two? The Super Boss is expected any moment." Binny made the announcement and in no time, her colleagues herded towards the meeting venue.

"Come, let's go and hear out boss's ATN" (ATN meant 'Address to the Nation'—a newsroom lingo used whenever the Super Boss wanted to address the newsroom in person.)

"Let's see if our jobs are safe," said Sabir as the two walked down the stairs towards studio two, on the third floor.

Haldi often boasted about his closeness with Yashwant in a rather peculiar way. *"See, short people rule the world. Look at me. Look at Yashwant!"* Yashwant and Haldi shared many similar physical attributes, but for Haldi's fair complexion and a receding hairline. For a man of an average height, he had a sharp and pointed nose upon which his rimless glasses fitted snugly, defining his broad chin more deeply.

"Hi friends, it's been one hell of a journey for all of us. In a short while from now, we shall be celebrating the fifth anniversary of our network. Time to introspect and chart out our growth plan. We are living in different times and we have to change with the times. We cannot sell a product that has gone past its expiry date. We have to innovate ourselves constantly.

"There's more competition knocking at the door and we have to pull up our socks to meet it midway. There is an old anonymous quote: 'If you don't create change, change will create you'.

"But, we must understand that there is no compromise with the credibility. Sometimes, we tend to get carried away, but let me remind you all, our USP is our credibility. We have to secure it."

"Already under question, boss..." Muskan mumbled under her breath. Sabir trifled a laugh.

"Always remember, the viewer is the king. We cannot afford to upset the king." Yashwant's voice boomed across the newsroom.

"So now I'll open the floor for questions," said Binny. There was a long, pregnant silence.

"Go ahead, guys, this is an open forum." Yashwant's reassuring words eased the palpable tension and offensive malaise, that enveloped occupants of the studio.

"Sir, it is now established that the man who died after dousing himself with kerosene, was egged on by a bunch of local stringers who wanted to make some quick buck. His life could have been saved. Doesn't our credibility take a hit when we decide to give air time to such news items?" After waiting a long time, Satyendra finally tossed a question at Yashwant.

"I do think the visuals were tempting and I mean no disrespect to the dead. Whoever took the call to put those visuals on air, actually followed good TV. I would still say that we were the first to take it off air, after the report of his supposed chance of survival was confirmed. And, I congratulate the news managers, here for having taken such a wise decision in time."

"What rubbish! Prithvi knew it all along," Bhoomi whispered into Binny's ears. "You remember that?" Binny pressed Bhoomi's hand so hard she almost screamed in pain.

A reluctant hand went up. It was Muskan.

"Sir, we are a news channel, but why do we show so many entertainment related shows?"

It was an innocent question, but Prithvi and Hemendra did not bargain for such a question from Muskan.

"We are a news channel and shall ever remain so." Yashwant was abrupt. "But, there is a market out there for such shows. We are doomed if our product fails to capture the minds of the consumers."

Binny stepped forward and announced, "One last question before we wind up."

"Sir..." a hand went up. It was Iqbal's, DNN's bureau chief in Hyderabad.

"Yes, Iqbal. Go ahead." Yashwant replied.

"Sir, what can we do to be different so that we don't have to follow any one?"

Yashwant looked supremely embarrassed, and that was the reason he kept toying with his wrist watch. When he raised his head to launch his reply, his eyes looked blood shot.

"We don't follow others, in fact, it's exactly the opposite. I am told, an assistant engineer and two inspectors of the civic agency were suspended after we ran the famous undercover operation on manhole deaths. Other channels followed up on our exclusive story. That's what I call news with an impact. We are credible, we are different, the credibility quotient is our differentiator and that's what everyone should remember."

Ranveer, Sabir and Baba's mobiles buzzed simultaneously. They had a message waiting in their inbox from Pushkar:

'Tumhare Paon Ke Neeche Koi Zameen Nahi,
Kamaal Yeh Hai Ki Phir Bhi Tumhein Yakin Nahi.'

"By the way, we are working on rebranding and I strongly believe that the marketing-editorial synergy will work wonders for us." Saying that, Yashwant turned around to shake hands with Prithvi, who was standing next to him. That was a cue for Binny.

"That's all, guys! The boss has to leave." Binny announced. "He will host a new talk show from today on State Television. It's on youth icons. Sidhartha Sawhney is his first guest," she added. The mention of his name was greeted with a lusty round of *'Ooohs'* from a large section of girls present in the newsroom.

"Can I be a part of the show audience? I want to meet Sidhartha, he is so cute…" Bhoomi could not contain her excitement. "Me too," Shalini joined the chorus, along with Tavleen and Nigar.

Yashwant looked at Bhoomi and smiled. "Yes, come along if your boss permits."

Bhoomi turned to Binny. "Sorry dear, you can't. Let's go and hit the canteen. Chicken biryani and rogan josh are waiting for us."

"Take care, guys. Happy weekend!" Yashwant bid adieu to colleagues as Prithvi, Hemendra and Jagat escorted him to the lift.

"What could you make out of Yashwant's ATN? Was he trying to justify everything the channel was up to?" Ranvir tossed the question in his fascinating 'though-I-know-the-answer-but-I-want-your-answer-first' style. The gang members took the table at Mamu's after hogging the chicken biryani and rogan josh. The emergency meeting was called to analyse Yashwant's ATN. Sabir had already ordered for tea.

"He couldn't have been clearer," said Sabir.

"Is it curtains for news then? The final nail hammered?" asked Ranvir credulously.

"*Ram Naam Satya Hai*!" Pushkar clapped and burst out laughing.

"He spoke of market and editorial-marketing synergy. Let's not forget he's never before, in all his earlier speeches, raised such issues in public," said Baba.

"We must not forget that Yashwant is an entrepreneur and in the throes of an ever-increasing media empire. His one-point agenda is, mopping up *moolah*. I heard he is soon going to launch an IPO," Ranvir announced.

"You are right! He is too ambitious and secretly strives to wield the political clout, more than anything," said Sabir.

"Maybe, he's just waiting for that one big ticket to come his way," contemplated Baba.

"He has the knack to strike friendship across parties; in the ruling alliance and outside it." Sabir appeared in a mood to tell a story. "The UPDGA is facing the biggest political crisis, following withdrawal of support by the Gate Crasher Party. My information is that Yashwant has been tasked to get smaller parties on board with the UPDGA," added Sabir.

"And at whose behest is he doing that?" asked Ranvir.

"Sidhartha, of course," replied Sabir. "*Aah*...That's what I call synergy," said Ranvir, tongue firmly in cheek.

"Can we say our future is safe in Yashwant's hands?" Pushkar asked innocently.

"Who cares? As long as they keep paying my salary, it's fine by me." Ranvir argued.

His reply was greeted with silence. Sabir tipped Nandu generously, before the foursome left the table and walked back to DNN Tower.

Satyendra had no check-in luggage. Just a handbag from which he fished out the blue diary, before he secured it in the luggage cabin. He wasted no time, either, in fastening his seat belt. He opened a fresh page in his diary and wrote in bold capitals:

SUPER BOSS ATN

Below the slug-line, he reproduced a quote of one of his favourite authors, Milan Kundera:

Nothing requires a greater effort of thought, than arguments to justify the rule of non-thought.

India Gate

"Hi, what's up?"

Muskan never answered unidentified callers on her mobile but she answered this by sheer chance.

"Rits... Is that you?" Her voice choked with emotion, "Where the hell did you disappear?"

"Just like that. Hope you are fine."

"I am fine. But what happened to you? You have stopped answering my calls, stopped responding to my messages. And then one fine day your mobile goes dead. I don't know what has taken over you and your life. Why did you do that to me? Relationships die when the two people in it stop talking."

"I have got a job."

"*Hmmm*...OK...great. Where?"

"With Channel 91. It's a local channel, not as big as yours."

"Oh...come on, Rits. I am so happy for you." She appeared distracted by her phone as she walked out of the newsroom.

"Can we meet today?" asked Ritwik.

"Sure, Rits. Why not."

"Right, then, let's meet at Café Cofi Korner at 5.30 pm."

"See you there!"

Muskan flung herself on Ritwik from behind, throwing her arms around him and kissing him like they will never meet up again, at the corridors of Connaught Place. The façade of the century old structure, built as the shopping complex for the *phirangs* when they ruled India, was under massive face-lift as part of a 'Clean Delhi, Green Delhi' drive. The entire area had been dug up and one had to negotiate an intricate web of iron and bamboo stilts to reach, any destination along the corridor.

"You know, I vowed not to speak to you ever again. I mean, how can a person just disappear? Do you ever realise somebody could be worrying herself to death?" said Muskan as they walked down a flight of stairs, to take the corner sofa in the basement of one of the popular cafés in the capital city.

"You broke the vow for me?" Ritwik teased her.

"Shut the fuck up! *Bencho*...! I went looking for you at your house, met your landlord, he said you don't live there anymore; that worried me even more. You didn't even leave any message for me with your landlord?"

"What? Why would you go and speak with the property owner? Am I a bloody escapist that I would just disappear and stray into the woods? Why do you try to play my mom and come after me?" Ritwik snapped at her.

"You don't have to be rude to me. I don't expect such a sullen behaviour from you in our first meeting after so long."

"OK... I am sorry." Ritwik calmed down after having realised his mistake. "What shall I order for you?"

"You don't even remember that, Rits? You have changed!" Muskan needed some pampering. "I'll have Korner Khallas?"

"Oh, yes, how could I forget your favourite ice cream, your sinful dollop of hot chocolate poured over it, you fatso?"

"I am not fat and I am not talking to you."

"Not again," said Ritwik as he got up to place the order.

"What is that?" Ritwik asked settling in his chair. While he stood in a long queue placing the order, he could see Muskan scribbling something on the paper napkin on the table.

"Can't recognise yourself? That's how you look when you are rude." Muskan drew an emoticon that looked serious and stern.

Among the most striking features of the attractive emoticon were the markedly deep-wide eyes, the prominent big nose and its full lips suggesting anger. The two horns seemed to mirror the devilish look.

"That devil cannot be me. That could be your boss Psycho, not me. I have such a pleasant personality," Ritwik concluded in light banter.

"That's definitely you. You creep. *Achcha,* tell me about your new job profile." Muskan stretched her hands out along the seat.

"I shall be heading the channel. They are paying me well. You know they are the biggest producers of dairy products in the national capital region. They sell it under the brand name of 91. That's the name of the channel too."

"When are you guys launching?"

"Most certainly the next month."

"So, is the licence through, and the satellite in place?"

"Oh yes, of course. Ahujas are making their mark in the real estate sector. They were confident they will get the licence," said Ritwik.

"So you are a boss now... You will call the shots at the new channel." Muskan said that in a matter-of-fact tone.

"Well, the MD has reposed faith in me. The responsibility is huge."

"But how did you land up a job here? How did you get in touch with the Ahujas?"

"I met the junior Ahuja at a friend's party. I realised we share our passion for bowling. He was looking for someone to introduce him to power corridors. I helped him with that," said Ritwik.

Muskan couldn't digest that Ritwik had agreed to work with the Ahuja's. She did not like his expression, either—*I helped him with that*. That was not the Ritwik she knew. It was difficult to understand how he could have helped the industrialists? She just knew something was not right. Ahujas have been mired in controversies. Will he now speak from the standpoint of an employer? Was he the same Ritwik who helped Mahesh draft a rejoinder to the DNN HR, when questions were raised on Mahesh's long medical leave? Was he the same Ritwik who defended Amulya from Prithvi's wrath for running a breaking story, on a fire in a *jhuggi* cluster that left 8 dead, in place of a sponsored show? Was he the same Ritwik? "Are you with me, young lady?" She could hear Ritwik's voice. "*Helloooo*..."

"Oh... I am sorry. I am really sorry. Rits..."

"Come on, finish the coffee. We are going to India Gate."

They walked out of Korner Café, hands locked against each other's backs. They took the subway towards Palika Bazaar and came out at the parking lot.

"Where's your bike?" asked Muskan. "I am not going to walk all the way to India Gate."

Ritwik did not reply. He stopped in front of a brand new car at the parking lot. He took out the remote key and pressed a button; a squeaky noise followed by the sound of the car doors coming unlocked. It was a golden Honda City. "Come on young lady, our new *ram pyaari*."

"Oh...when did this happen? How so lovely!"

"I am heading the bureau of a *chhota-mota* channel. It does not mean I can't buy myself a car?"

"But this must be huge money. Isn't it? You shouldn't have taken such a mammoth of a loan for the car," Muskan reacted like the ubiquitous housewife who would invariably complain about how the price rise has played havoc with her budget, and taken away the happiness of her family.

"Relax! This is part of the package," Ritwik declared while steering the car on to Janpath Road.

"So you don't have to pay EMIs for this?"

"The company has put in the initial amount. The rest can be paid via EMIs. And the car shall stay with me if I quit work after 36 months."

"So a brand new Honda City at half the price?"

"Precisely. Now, tell me."

"Tell you what."

"Are you happy?"

"There is no reason why I shouldn't be."

They got down from the car. Ritwik bought two huge balloons. A blue and a red. He put the red one inside the car and gave the other one to Muskan as they crossed the chained demarcation and stepped into the lawns; the imposing India Gate looming in front of them, resplendent in its nightly armour of shining lights, washed with thousands of megawatts of sulphur bulbs.

"That's your favourite colour, isn't it?" he said expecting an assuring nod from her. Meenu didn't answer.

"Mind some *chana jor?*" Ritwik called out the seller carrying the mobile kiosk around his neck at a distance. Meenu didn't say a word.

They took a stroll along the lawns, walking towards the Raisina Hills. "Why don't you say something, Meenu?" Ritwik casually put his right hand across Muskan's shoulder, holding the paper cone in his left hand.

Muskan would fall in love with herself every time Ritwik called her Meenu. Her parents used to call her Meena. So did all of her friends. In USA, she was just Musi for friends and colleagues on campus. Nobody had called her Meenu until one day Ritwik whispered the word softly in her ear, while they were making love at her one room barsaati in Lajpat Nagar.

Muskan slipped her arms around his waist and rested her head on his shoulder. She did not say a word. She wanted to put all her doubts to rest and enjoy the moment with her beloved.

"Bhagwan jodi salamat rakhe... Haye haye... Munni, tujhe chand sa beta hoye..." Muskan and Ritwik were strutting along the lawns when lanky 18-year-old-somethings, dressed in tight top and jeans tried to solicit Ritwik.

Muskan was terrified when she heard the characteristic *hijra* clap. "I don't like them. Just shoo them away, Rits, please."

"Just get lost!" Ritwik waved a disapproving hand at them as he held her tight and paced up towards his car.

"Let's go to my place. I need to talk to you," said Muskan.

"Do you have vodka at home?"

"Will pick it up on our way," she replied. Ritwik was too excited at the thought of spending an evening with Muskan, whose face had suddenly turned grave.

Mafia

Never tried this one before. Hope it suits our pallete," said Ritwik pouring Fuel into two shot glasses.

"They say it's a nice vodka. Make me a stiff one." Muskan ordered Ritwik. "I was quite impressed with the beaker shaped bottle. Nice straight lines."

"To our good health and my new job," Ritwik toasted as Muskan raised her glass.

"And to our new *ram pyaari*...cheers..." He raised his glass for a toast again. Ritwik sensed that Muskan was not quite impressed with his first car.

"Can we have some music? Do you have the audio of *Jodhaa Akbar*?"

"No, but I can play it for you on my computer. I have a custom list of music tracks that is made up from songs on my drive. Here, plug in the pen drive."

"*In Lambo Ke Daman Mein*..." She started crooning. "I just love this movie. Hrithik looked so suave and debonair, his portrayal of Akbar is a magnificent one."

"How can you discuss Hrithik in front of me?" Ritwik said.

"Why, he is my favourite on-screen hero."

"Who is your off-screen hero?"

"Well, there used to be one. Now I can't say that with the same conviction."

"Why do you say that?" Ritwik was nonplussed to discover this.

"Just like that," she replied.

"Well, maybe, I am not as good looking as him. It's up to you lady. Take it or leave it."

"You seem to be narrowing your options rather too soon," said Muskan.

"Now this is double-edged. Come out clear, will you, young lady?" Ritwik could sense a hint of sarcasm in Muskan's voice.

"I am a nobody to question your decision. But why would a journalist of your caliber want to associate with a city channel whose existence is as much in dark as the credibility of the people who are behind it?" Muskan persisted. She added: "I wanted to discuss these things with you the day you broke the news to me, but I did not wish to ruin your happiness."

"What do you know about the Ahujas?" Ritwik looked annoyed.

"I know that 21 innocent people perished in the '*Mera Ghar*' residential complex built by the Ahujas, when the roofs caved in year before the last. Their graveyards were dug in their dream houses. Your Ahujas' used such inferior quality material. Don't tell me you don't know about that tragic incident." Muskan was scathing.

"I know all about it. I covered that accident as a reporter for your kind knowledge." Ritwik explained. "There were reports of sabotage as well. These are corporate wars you would never understand. Anyway, there is a CBI inquiry into it. In fact, the matter is now sub-judice at Patiala House courts." Ritwik explained.

"Yes, precisely. The Ahujas' are under the scanner."

"Well, the court shall take stock of that and punish the guilty. Who are we to judge things?"

"They are murderers. And their guilt shall be proved in the court one day. The death toll would have been much higher, had it not been peak of summer. Many families were out on vacations. Do you understand the magnitude of the tragedy?" Muskan rubbed it in.

"Clap Clap…young lady… You would certainly make a good prosecution lawyer." Ritwik said sarcastically.

"You can't build a tower on edifice of greed, Mr Ritwik," Muskan would not stop.

"The Ahujas have never shied away from investigation. They are cooperating with the government agency," he explained.

But Muskan was unstoppable. "I never thought a person who swore by ethics and integrity would have such major change of heart overnight. You have absolutely no sense of moral unease," she said looking straight into Ritwik's eyes.

Ritwik's patience was running out. He got up to fix himself another drink, and didn't bother trying to stop her.

"A small one for me too!" Muskan ordered.

"If you consider this as the high point of your career you will be best served to join them as their Public Relations Manager. You know you shall be a mere tool in their hands." Muskan continued with her tirade.

"You are harsh in your assessment of entrepreneurs, and about me," said Ritwik as he handed over the vodka glass to her.

"'I come from a business family. I understand entrepreneurship, I appreciate enterprise, but an enterprise which is not built on the foundation of ethics, is bound to crumble'. These were your words, remember? I am just repeating those words for you, just in case you forgot." Muskan's anger swelled.

"I remember having said that, but you don't know how the world operates, Meenu." Ritwik argued.

"I dreamt of seeing the world through your eyes. I saw promise in your eyes."

"And now you don't. Is that what you are trying to say?" Ritwik was beginning to lose his cool.

"I envisioned us together. But you chose a different path." She slurred. "I lost you somewhere."

"Meenu, I discovered my life's purpose in those six months. When unrelenting misery, disappointment, setback, and deceit came knocking at the door, everyone turned their back on me. Do you even know how difficult it was to seek a job after I resigned from DNN? I thought I had paid Hemendra in the same coin by challenging him. But I realised it was a mistake. Sooner, I got his message loud and clear. The mafia was at work. And I couldn't take it all single-handedly." Ritwik paused, picked up his glass and upped the bottom in one large swig.

He got up to make himself another one. He was feeling groggy and miserable. "Shall I make you another one, sweetheart? Or are you drunk on the potion of hatred against me?" Ritwik's anger was palpable.

He came back after the refill and sat down on the floor with Muskan. "I learnt it the hard way. The mafia has a wide sweep. It has its members and associates across channels. Across *EVERY* newsroom. The mafia ensured I don't get offered a job. Strange, isn't it? You can only challenge the mafia at your own risk. No blood gets spilled and the person gets executed in broad daylight. Everybody shut their doors on me."

"So, you, in turn, decided to shut *your* door on me. You decided to disappear because the market would not offer you a job?" Muskan snapped back to life.

"They drove me to the edge. There was a point when I decided to give up my life. But, what's the use of telling all this to you."

"Since you're alive now and are picked up by the Ahujas, you are on top of the world, isn't it?" Muskan's sarcasm was not to be missed.

"You don't even know how I lived off my life from railway platforms. My landlord had turned me out. My brother had lodged himself in the hostel. I had packed off my father to my sister's place. I went through hell. Do you realise that?

"No, I don't. I don't want to." Muskan snapped.

"You know, Meenu, I was thinking of you when I decided to give up my life by throwing myself before a running train. When suddenly somebody pulled me away, I thought it was you. I thought I would live to see another day, I thought I would return to you one day when I would be back on my feet again."

"Clap...Clap... Of course you deserve a Bharat Ratna for what you have achieved. No...?" Muskan's sarcasm was scaling hysteric heights.

"Let me tell you one thing, sweetheart. I realise I have a better hang of how this *dhandha* operates." Ritwik was not ready to give in easily. "This *dhandha* is not for the meritorious. There is no place for talent. The only talent is to be a sucker. I would rather play a sucker to somebody with loads of money than those mother fuckers sitting in glass cabins."

Ritwik was never so coherent four pegs down. He looked for the glass for another refill and found it had taken a tumble down a couple of feet away, and the vodka was spilled.

"Remember, you are going to be sitting in one such cabin yourself." Muskan's voice wafted up to him as he fixed himself a large one.

"What has come over you, Meenu? Why are you behaving in this strange way?" Ritwik persisted. "Ok, let me change the music for you. Care to listen to the latest romantic number, written by our favourite Gulzar sa'ab?"

Ritwik kneeled over and reached out for the mouse on that small computer table. He clicked on one song and put it on repeat mode...

Catharsis

He came back and snuggled up close to Muskan. "Tell me, sweetheart. Why to spoil our evening fighting over small things? You will have to give me some time. I have to get back my name, my honour. I don't want to be called a loser."

He held Muskan across her shoulder and pulled her head to rest against his chest. His fingers ran slowly across her back. On the floor, bed-cum-sofa amply cushioned for comfort, the twosome struck a perfect couple pose in their moment of solitude.

'Dhaage Tod Laao Chandni Se Noor Ke... Ghoonghat Hee Bana Lo Roshni Se Noor Ke...' Raahat's searing and a quiet romantic number wafted into the room...

"Bol Na Halke Halke... Honth Se Halke Halke..." Ritwik hummed the song on cue from *antara* back to *mukhda.*

Ritwik could feel his bare arms getting wet. He ignored it for a while, but the trickle would not stop. He looked down at Muskan. Here face looked swollen with tears.

"If you think the sobs will move me, you are absolutely... bang on...my dear." He took a deliberate pause to dramatise the effect.

Muskan kept sobbing, her head still buried in Ritwik's chest. Seized by a fit of riding passion, she suddenly flung her arms around Ritwik and kissed him on his lips.

Her sudden manoeuvre caught Ritwik by surprise. He reciprocated with equal passion. He pulled her to himself as he lay with his back to the floor.

In one swift movement, Muskan pulled off her T-shirt and threw it away. She struggled to yank off Ritwik's shirt. It was the same with his vest, which was tucked deep into his trouser and secured by the leather belt. After putting much effort, she was able to pull off the vest. Soon after the couple was off to a flying start.

Muskan moved down, her tongue mapping Ritwik's hairless chest. Her mouth worked seductively on the small tuft of hair around Ritwik's nipples. She found it funny, as even she had tufts of hair around her nipples. One big curly strand would surface every fortnight around both her nipples, which she would uproot mercilessly first with the scissor and then with the hair removing cream to stamp out its tiniest trace. She thought she was the only girl in the universe to work a hair remover across her breast. Muskan felt proud holding the most secret record. Ritwik moaned with pleasure as he allowed Muskan to take complete control of him.

The dim light from the kitchen crept close by making it easier for the lovers to catch the expression on each other's face. Suddenly shadows moved on the wall. But the formation did not. It took some time for Muskan to realise she was now reeling under somebody's body weight and someone's breaths stoking her neck, like a hot blast from a furnace.

Ritwik's breaths were coming in short spurts. "Just take it easy... *Bencho*...!" Muskan's voice dropped and rose in keeping with her movements.

But Ritwik was in for another surprise. By deft manoeuvring, Muskan was on top once again. "Now, you will plead for your death...but I shall show no mercy... *Bahut sataya hai tumne...*" Muskan growled like an angry cat as she found herself riding another wave of passion.

"I am ready to die in your arms." Ritwik spoke the language of surrender.

"Stop making those funny faces, will you...?"

"I thought it was a huge turn-on for you...baby."

"Stop it...will you, sto....p...I say...*Bencho* . ." She realised words were hard to come by as she closed her eyes and dived deep into pools of ecstasy.

She went through the motions as if this was the last time they would be together. Ritwik went through a wave of catharsis himself. This was his moment to catch up on the lost moments with Muskan.

It was all over before long. Their bodies lay intertwined, laced in love-sweat. Over their conjoined short and quick breaths, Raahat tip-toed quietly and crooned softly into their ears... *'Kaisa Lage Jo Chupchaap Dono... Ho-oo, Pal Pal Mein Poori Sadiyan Bita Dein...'*

It's Quits

It was past 9 am when Ritwik stirred in the bed at the Lajpat Nagar *barsaati*. His head was a little heavy. "Goddamned it," he cursed himself as he ran fingers across his head. "I've had a peg too many last night. All because of Muskan," he thought aloud. "I don't know what came over her last night, man." He looked around for Muskan. He called for her. No one responded. He got up and headed for the terrace. The morning sun greeted him straight in the face. He could hear the din of traffic across a few houses away.

He came back into the room and picked up his mobile. A couple of messages awaited him. He opened his inbox to find a message from Muskan:

'door keys and locks are on the fridge. No milk! Green T is red melmoware jar and sugar in the yellow jar on the shelf right above the gas stove.'

The message from Muskan brought a smile on his face and last night's memories came rushing into his head, parking themselves bumper to bumper. He moved towards the kitchen to make himself a cup of green tea.

As he sat down with his cup of tea and morning newspaper, it crossed his mind he had to reach his new office by 11 am for an important meeting with the Managing Director. He managed to do a rush job and succeeded. He checked for his car keys in the jeans pocket. There was a piece of paper that came out with the keys. He opened it. He could recognise Muskan's handwriting.

Dear Ritwik,

I did not take up my family business because I wanted to carve my own niche in the field dear to me. I always yearned for fame than money. When I took up the profession, I promised myself I shall have all that but I will never resort to means my conscience would not allow.

Business parties only invest in what they feel shall be a profitable venture. I also invested in one such stock. And that was you, Ritwik. You were the voice of my conscience. And I used to feel proud of my instinct, as someone who could invest in a stock whose value shall ever go up and up.

I realised I was wrong. The developments over the last few days have crashed all my hopes. I can see the value of my stock nose-diving. When I look back, I find the long separation between us did not cause as much pain as the new avatar of Ritwik Sinha I got to see of late. You really are a changed man. I wanted to find MY Rits, but it seems I have lost him forever. His goals are different now. The means of reaching those goals strikes at the very foundation of our relationship. Because I sincerely believe that a person will have to be intrinsically good to be able to be a good journalist.

You pronounced your final decision last night. I realised I did not figure anywhere in your decision. There cannot be a greater affront to the love and integrity of a person who used to be dreamy-eyed about a young man who will one day take her as his bride.

Let's call it quits, Ritwik. Please do not try to get in touch with me ever again. Return the keys to Chawla aunty downstairs before you leave. Let me assure you, she won't be surprised to see you in my house.

Muskan

As he sat on his car seat, Ritwik drew out the paper from his jeans pocket and read it all over again. He could not believe Muskan could do this to him after such a passionate encounter last night. Muskan's behaviour puzzled him to no end. He put the first gear and said to himself: "Don't get emotional, Ritwik. You have to conquer the world, so that no motherfucker in this world can dare threaten you without taking stock of the consequences that might befall him."

Aandolan

"Tathaastu Go Back...Aryan Go Back!
Door Hato Aye Duniyawaalon...Yeh Zameen Hamari Hai...
Sarkar Haye Haye...Tathaastu Group Haye Haye!"

They came in trickles. They came on bullock carts. They came on bicycles. And then there were some who trekked barefoot into the city, from villages as far as 60 kms. They all gathered to partake symbolic sit-in outside the District Collector's office. Some of them carried bows and arrows over their shoulders. Everybody followed the traffic rules and filed in disciplined manner, before congregating at the destination.

The police deployment outnumbered the protestors by a long shot. And they had come prepared, if the deployment of riot-gear policemen and water cannons atop two vehicles were any indication of the administration's might.

They were a motley crowd of villagers, artisans, cattle herders, small-time farmers and forest dwellers, and the dwindling Bhambhuki tribes people, other Bhambhu tribal groups of adjoining villages that were supposed to be swallowed by the Tathaastu project. The cries of injustice rent the sky:

"Tathaastu Go Back...!

Door Hato Aye Duniyawaalon...Yeh Zameen Hamari Hai..."

Satyendra and his cameraman colleague, Altamash jumped into the melee, trying to get close ups of the agitating forest dwellers and tribals in their primitive gear.

For a few months, now, they have been hearing talks of acquisition of their lands by the government for setting up steel plants. The government wanted private sector to participate and had already opened doors to foreign multinationals. Signing an MOU with Aryan International (AI) in 2005. The AI's Indian arm—the Tathaastu—was to execute the project that is mine iron-ore and other ores and to establish an integrated steel plant.

The district collector had visited some of the villages twice in the last three months, trying to gather land details of each family in those villages. This had only set the villages into a grip of panic and fear. That's when they decided to set up the Jan Kalyan Sangharsh Samiti, to fight 'evil forces' that were out to usurp their land.

"We should have been covering it LIVE," said Altamash as he went about filming the protestors.

"It was only after I raised the spectre of violence to Haldi that he allowed me to cover this. Of course, without the OB van for LIVE coverage." said Satyendra.

"Are we expected to manufacture violence for them? Strange fellows, yaar." Altamash sounded irritated.

"Delhi foxes me no end. Don't ask! The crude fact is that we can't go LIVE with the visuals."

"But, aren't we supposed to cover the dog show LIVE tomorrow, in which the deputy CM's pet bitch, Rani is also participating?" Altamash paused on his camera. "I saw Binny's mail. And then subsequent mails by Haldi, Sudhanshu, Shahid and Hemendra. Prithvi boss wrote a one liner in bold capitals like that telegraphic message: 'REPORTER PTC FEEDING THE BISCUIT TO THE WINNER MUST.'"

"Yes, I saw that. Binny ma'am told me I must send her a 'walkthrough' with the dog," said Satyendra as both broke into a laughter.

"The deputy CM has reluctantly agreed to take out Rani for a walk. He insisted that we must have breakfast with Rani only," Satyendra explained.

"We will have to do some dog-biscuits shopping tonight," observed Altamash.

"Otherwise, our place for the guillotine is assured," said Satyendra.

"Lucky bitch!" Said Altamash as they broke into a hearty laugh. They both laughed at Psycho's expense.

The farmers had laid siege to the collectorate. The local media was present in strength but only Angaar, other than DNN, represented Delhi media. A local stringer represented Angaar, though. No OB Vans in sight.

"You can only take away our land over our dead bodies. This is our message to the world," said a young bearded man.

"Door Hato Aye Duniyawaalon, Yeh Zameen Hamari Hai..."

"But the government shall be launching development projects on that land. It says you will be adequately compensated." Satyendra tried to argue with a young protestor for a sound bite.

"Why do we leave our fertile lands? This government is anti-farmer. This government is anti-poor. This government is anti-tribals."

Another torrent of slogan went up the air.

"No one can dare touch our land and do whatever they want, without the permission of the Gram Sabha. The government is bypassing Gram Sabha," said Naveen.

Altamash could see a thin veneer of smoke rise up on his lens. Behind him, he could hear strange noises that were clearly distinct from the noises of surging slogans of the shouting crowd. It was as if someone had opened fire. He could hear the commotion around him. Suddenly, someone pushed him from behind: "*Betichod, chalao goli...*" A village lad was screaming his lungs out.

Before Altamash could realise, he doubled up coughing. The police had lobbed teargas shells to disperse the agitated villagers.

The protestors dispersed like bees from the hive smoked for honey.

"Run... Let's go. I can't tolerate the smoke," said Satyendra as he disappeared in the haze.

Satyendra was asthmatic and therefore always carried an inhaler. Altamash carried another one for Satyendra. His camera kit was incomplete without a stand-by inhaler, just in case.

"You stay clear. Go ahead, I will join you sooner. Let me get some quick shots."

Satyendra ran across the street and into one of the lanes that opened to the other trunk road. He quickly fished out his inhaler and pumped in 4-5 quick spurts. He sat down on a bench at an abandoned tea shop, inside that narrow lane and dialled up office.

Binny came on line. "Binny, police lobbed teargas to disperse agitating farmers. You can take my phone-in."

"Just hold on," the voice on the mobile said. "Sudhanshu... it's Satyendra on line...some urgent news...farmers have been tear-gassed..." Satyendra could hear Binny shout.

"Why...you should take it, *yaar*. He says he has got some great visuals too... It was a massive gathering of farmers..."

"Did the police lob teargas shells or it fired? Has anybody got injured?" Binny asked Satyendra.

"The situation is getting out of hand. It's chaotic here. I can hear the sound of gun fire now."

"Sudhanshu, you must take his 30 second phone-in, at least," Satyendra could hear Binny plead Sudhanshu.

"I can't break the recorded show," Satyendra could hear Sudhanshu sir's voice wafting over the phone.

"*Yaar*, the boss's show is on air. I will again pitch for your phone-in after ten minutes. So be on stand-by."

"I will wait, Binny."

Satyendra came rushing out of the lane and crossed the street to join Altamash. But he could not spot him in the milee. He could only see farmers scramble to safer locations and policemen chasing them with *lathis*. He put his mobile phone on video mode.

In that three-inch screen, he could spot a policeman aiming a rifle at a protestor. The mobile camera zoomed in. "They have opened fire at us. Do you have the courage to say that, *bhadwe saale?*" Satyendra heard a man shouting at the top of his voice as he ran past, hurling abuses at him.

Satyendra again dialled Binny on her mobile. "The police have resorted to unprovoked firing. We are here at severe risk to our lives. Anything can happen now," Satyendra's voice raised to the level of panic.

"Hold on." Binny again shouted for Sudhanshu. And after a pause, her voice came back. "I am putting you through to the production control room."

"It was simply unwarranted. The police are trying to suppress this peaceful agitation by force. I saw two farmers falling down in the hail of bullets."

"Do you have eyewitnesses around?"

"Oh yes, of course," said Satyendra as he caught hold of a farmer seeking refuge in the lane and plugged the Nokia handset onto his ear. The farmer got the cue. "My father has gone down in the hail of rubber bullets. Are we criminals? We were on a peaceful *dharna*. We didn't provoke anybody."

Two other teenage lads stopped by and started shouting slogans. They insisted on speaking on the mobile by holding it in their hands.

"We will fight the battle till our last breath. Fuck the police, fuck the government," the youngest of all declared, his eyes dancing with the confidence of a brat straining to launch his most innovative mischief.

"*Chala goli, betichod.*" He said one last time into the phone mouth for effect.

DNN went LIVE.

Development

I would like to know who allowed him a LIVE phone-in." Prithvi was livid. "You tell me, Binny."

"Sir, it was Sudhanshu's decision."

"Get him on phone." The morning meeting started off on a grim note yet again.

Binny took Sudhanshu on a conference call. "Hello…"

"Sudhanshu, this is Prithvi. Tell me honestly, who took the call to put Satyendra on LIVE phone-in yesterday?"

"Sir, it was a collective decision."

"Whose decision was it?" Prithvi shouted to a stunned silence.

"Sir, Binny passed on the call and I put it on air."

"Did you ask for it or was it forced on you?" Prithvi's pitch went a notch higher.

"Sir, it was kind of forced on me. I had refused once," the voice on the phone said.

"What do you mean, Sudhanshu? You are lying. I never forced it on you. Don't lie in front of bosses, OK?"

"Why should I lie to anyone, yaar? Is this not true I told you I can't cut LIVE?"

"True, but that was when the recorded show was on air, and you said you can't drop it."

"Yes, I thought you had nothing new to offer at the time. Since you insisted, I gave in. And I did no wrong." Sudhanshu defended himself.

"Well, the situation was hot there. Why would Satyendra lie to me?" said Binny. She was irritated that Sudhanshu would put the blame on her in front of the bosses. Wasn't Sudhanshu the one she shared the most notorious office gossip unabashedly with, she thought.

"Stop fighting, both of you," Prithvi barked. "Who will take responsibility of whatever went on air?"

"Sir, it was a LIVE situation. I could not have helped it. Satyendra should have been more careful at his end."

"You can utter expletives LIVE and get away with that. Anything can happen on this channel. You guys have fucked it all up." Prithvi's voice boomed.

"I told Satyendra we don't need any LIVE phone-in. I mean, for *some* goddamned protest over *some* issue of land and that too in *some* tribal area, does not make good TV." Hemendra dusted off last vestiges of guilt.

"Get Satyendra on line," Hemendra ordered.

"He must be with the Deputy CM right now. He has gone there for a 'walkthrough'. Let me check."

"Hello, Satyendra, you are on conference...in the morning meeting. Are you through with the CM?" asked Binny over the phone.

"Yes, I am back in office. Was about to send the feed."

"Hello... Hello... Hello...! Satyendra, can you hear me?"

"Yes Binny, tell me."

"Who gave you the permission to go LIVE with your phone-in?" Hemendra lifted the phone instrument, brought it close to his mouth and barked into it.

"Sir, I...I...I spoke to Binny. And sir...yesterday you only gave me the permission."

"When did I ever give you such a permission? Don't lie. You are a blood liar!" Hemendra raised his voice.

"Sir, you only said the headquarter will cut LIVE if there was violence."

"Was there violence?"

"Sir, police broke into indiscriminate firing after the initial round of tear gas."

"You call that violence?"

"Sir, six farmers died and four are battling their lives in city hospitals. More than 40 got injured. Opposition parties have condemned this act of the police."

"Do you work for this channel or for those goddamned tribals or those fucking opposition parties?" Hemendra was screaming as if somebody had pulled his chair from behind.

"Sir, I thought that it is good developing story."

"You think only *you* understand news and we all are fucking *chootiyas, haahn...?*" Satyendra could make out Prithvi's voice in the background.

Altamash could hear everything on the speaker phone. "*Haan, bhonsadi ke tum chootiya hee ho,*" Altamast muttered under his breath as Satyendra pursed his smile.

"Why would police fire at them without being provoked?" This was Hemendra now.

"Sir, there was no provocation from the protestors. It was a peaceful sit-in," said Satyendra.

"The protestors had come all armed with bows and arrows and you say there was no provocation from them," said Hemendra.

"Sir, bow and arrow is a part of Bhambhukis' traditional gear. They don't move out without that anywhere. But, they didn't use it at that time. And not all protestors were tribals, sir." Satyendra explained calmly.

"An arrow could kill a person," Hemendra insisted.

"Not if it is not used, sir." Satyendra tried his best to pacify Hemendra a little.

"They could have used them on the policemen yesterday." Prithvi endorsed.

"But, sir, that's their traditional gear. And what about those group of volunteers belonging to Chief Minister Bajrang Prasad's party's many outfits, who stage marches on city streets brandishing naked swords?" Satyendra dug in his heels.

"That's a cultural outfit. They serve the community." Psycho poured out his *gyaan*.

Hemendra extended his hand and snatched the phone from under Psycho's nose and held it up in air before barking into the speaker: "Satyendra, don't try to derail the conversation. The police did claim the tribals with bows and arrows had put on a semblance of collective threat."

"Police forces are the same everywhere. Who can dare challenge their might? At least not those poor farmers, innocent tribals and forest dwellers who sat on *dharna* yesterday," Satyendra argued.

"Can you vouchsafe for their intention?" Hemendra roared.

"Sir…I mean…it's not…"

"Don't argue, Satyendra." Hemendra butted in. "The police were perfectly within reason to get provoked. Someone must have mocked an aim at the police just to tease them. In fact, the police did claim later that arrows were shot at them, too," 0said Hemendra.

"Hemendra is right. By the way, do you know what went on air yesterday?" Satyendra could clearly distinguish Prithvi's bark.

"Yes sir, I ticked off that boy LIVE on air and then wound up my phone-in." Satyendra replied.

"You did not wind up, you were taken off air. Do you realise that?" Hemendra turned his chair around from the share market LIVE news to speak into the phone.

"We shall talk to you later," Binny spoke into the phone as Prithvi gestured her to switch off Satyendra.

It was time for Prithvi's 'thought of the day.'

"We must understand news is not where the protest is. This is a strange country. Nobody is happy here. People sulk. They have grievances. But, we must look at the big picture. India is on the threshold of a giant leap towards becoming a super power. Development is the key. Development is pivotal to the government's economic policies. We must try and become a cog in the wheel of country's development."

'What about you, madarchod? You always run on flat tyres.' Sabir keyed that furiously on his smart phone before sending it out to *'The Gang'.*

"So, folks," Prithvi continued, "we have to be very careful at the stage of selection of stories."

"Yes, you are right, Prithvi. Perhaps, it was my fault. I should have stopped him right in his tracks yesterday itself," said Hemendra almost apologetically.

"I should not have sent him there in the first place," said Haldi as an afterthought.

"We can't afford to repeat such mistakes," Prithvi announced. "It's telling on our TRP. We have to take immediate measures to arrest the downslide or we are doomed." Turning to Hemendra, he instructed: "Please set up a meeting with show producers and team leaders. Time for some introspection."

"Sure. But we have string of meetings lined up for today, one with the marketing team as well. Can we put this meeting for tomorrow, if it suits you?"

"Fine by me, but no further delays," Prithvi replied.

"Time for special tea. Why don't you arrange for Mamu's Secular today?" Said Hemendra turning to Shahid.

"Given the heat generated in the past half hour, I think we would be better off with some cold drinks." Shahid's repartee evoked a ripple of laughter across the conference room.

"You shouted at me," Binny finger-pointed at Prithvi. "Now, you owe me a treat." It was time for her to sulk and be pampered by Psycho.

"Oh, come on. I wasn't wrong, was I?" Prithvi grinned like a toddler, having just been plied with his favourite toy.

"The boss is never wrong." Hemendra said as he pursed his smile and turned his swivel chair to catch up with the latest on the stock market updates.

Atom Bomb

Paagalvaani.blogspot.com

Sex sirens from Bollywood are becoming brand ambassadors of news channels. Today, I am going to present a brief case study of one such channel, which showed a half hour interview with a sex siren—Mahi 'Mindless' whose music album, *Ek Chumma Udhaar* has been a recent chartbuster—on its prime time yesterday. The country was caught in the grip of Mahi Mania. She was more popular as Mahi 'Mindless'. The channel in question is DNN. No prizes for guessing the interviewer. The celebrated Anchor-cum-Managing Editor of Diamond News Network, Prithvi.

But first, the show promo that ran an ad-nauseam on DNN. The show promo scaled a new high—a whole new phraseology that puts to shame, lacy dialogues of a C-grade Bollywood film.

I am reproducing the promo lines as they ran on DNN:

Woh Leti Hai
Woh Deti Hai
Bus Ek Chumma Udhaar
Dekhiye Aisa Husn

Jo Josh Jagaakar
Hosh Uda De
Aisi Adaayein Jo
Dil Machlakar
Deewana Bana De
TV Par Pehli Baar, Dekhiye
Dilfenk Haseena Ke
Dehakte Jism
Aur Bindaas Jawaani
Ke Raaz...
Dekhiye...
Atom Bomb!
Sirf DNN Par...

P. S: This sure seems to have been written with the excitement of a teenager, climaxing his first masturbation.

And now, excerpts from the interview itself. You decide who of the two is more 'Mindless':

"I have a charge sheet against you. I represent your innumerable fans. And I will read out that charge sheet little by little." Prithvi, the Managing Editor was all over the screen, grinning, even as he readied to lob questions at her.

"Charge sheet? Oh my God! Am I a criminal that you will prosecute me?" Mahi readied for what she was best at—nautanki. (In one of her recent interviews to a filmy monthly, she claimed she could easily head a news channel because she knows how to deliver TRPs.)

"You are in the public's court."

"Right now, I am your prisoner. Do whatever you want to. Shoot."

"So, why do you call yourself an Atom Bomb...?"

"Am I not? Am I not? Take a good look at me…from head to toe…" Mahi started swaying her hands like a woman working up lather under the shower, in a shampoo advertisement. Mahi had a strip of near-translucent cloth in hues of red and green holding her honour. (The show's first TRP moment.)

"Have a good look at me, baby." She said flailing her arms about herself.

"Oh…yes… I can see that…" Prithvi started grinning.

"What did you see?" said Mahi indulgently.

"I can see countless bombs ticking inside you…"

"Oh…thank you very much." She smiled coyly.

"How do you keep yourself so fit… errr… shall I say hatti-katti?"

"That's a secret."

"Oh, come on. Please share the secret with our viewers today. I believe you went in for plastic surgery."

"I am natural…can't you see?"

"Yes, I can see that. But is this not true you went in for some silicon makeover?"

"Take a good look at me… Do I look like plastic…anywhere…? Take a good look…" (TRP moment number 2.)

She winked at Prithvi with an oomphish twist to her lips as she rested her elbow on the round table, offering a veritable feast to Prithvi's eyes.(TRP moment number 3.)

The screen split into half. Mahi winking at Prithvi and the camera caressing her cleavage. The right side of the screen showed Prithvi grinning from ear to ear, a hint of voyeurism dancing in his eyes.

The ticker band was pulled out. After all, democracy cannot survive without transparency.

Lessons drawn:

Next time you are feeling a little horny, just switch on any Hindi news channel on your LCD TV—for a wider and sharper perspective to your secret desires.

Perform or Perish

"Guys, let me come straight to the point." Prithvi started without preliminaries. This was a monthly meet on channel's TRP. The show producers and department heads sat across the oval table.

"We cannot afford to be losers. I hate the number two tag." Psycho fired his salvo as soon as he took his swivel chair.

"Some people here have attitude problems. They need to be ready to face the music," he thundered.

There was a lull. But another storm was building up.

"We want results." Hemendra was waiting for the right cue to take over from Prithvi.

'They failed 2 delivr. Thy shd leave. Hahaha!' Pushkar pursed his smile as he opened the inbox to find Sabir's message in his inbox.

"Sir, how do we take the TRPs further up from here," Brajesh mustered up the courage to break the silence.

"You want everything to be spoon-fed, isn't it?" Prithvi shot back.

"It's a regular peaks and troughs for my show *Akkad Bakkad Bambe Bo*. It is mind-boggling to see a show on superstition registering such dramatic ups and downs," said Brajesh, expecting seniors to offer a solution to his problem.

"We are all facing similar problems. I don't know if my best performance would translate into higher TRPs. I wonder, who are the people who watch our shows," Meghna asked innocently.

"I do not want excuses," Hemendra shot back. "Look at Akhil. He has something new for the viewers every day." Akhil had recently scaled the biggest peak of his career. He was the new 'jewel' in Hemendra's court, after, of course, Sudhanshu and Karuna.

"You guys should start using your brains. Look at Amitabh. When he handles a show, I feel reassured," said Prithvi. "Amitabh has done us proud."

"I agree with you." Hemendra endorsed Prithvi. "Amitabh has energy. He takes up challenges. He is pro-active. The way he handled the wardrobe malfunction story with Akhil's assistance was extraordinary."

Shahid darted a furtive look at Hemendra. He read visible traces of deceit on his face. Sometimes, Hemendra's moves puzzled him—as though he was going to trip his oldest friend. Would he ever cross him? "But didn't he last year, when he gave a double promotion to Amitabh, bringing him at par with me? And if Prithvi had his way, he would promote Amitabh again. I never questioned Hemendra. And he always trampled over my ambitions." Thoughts such as these were common in newsroom. This time these were Shahid's; pondering upon his future and his colleague's mean intentions.

"Look, Prithvi, we try to innovate every day. Those in my team put in extra hours daily. This is the level of dedication," Pushkar butted in.

"What has been your achievement, Pushkar? You keep repeating the old format," Prithvi latched on to him.

"When I turn to you for suggestions, you tick me off saying I should know how to handle my show. When I innovate and experiment, you charge me of bypassing you. You want to trust me when it suits you." Pushkar was not in a mood to give up easily.

"Well, as a senior, I expect you to be pro-active," said Prithvi.

"Didn't I suggest we must not give space to Dharmadhiraj Maharaj on our channel?" Pushkar retored. "After the sting *Sambhog Se Samadhi Tak*, shown by Vishphot, it was better if we discontinued with Dharmadhiraj's two sponsored shows. It is proved beyond doubt that he is a trickster and a fraud."

"Dharmadhiraj Maharaj pays two crore annually to the company for using our platform. The company can hire a dozen people like you for that amount," said Hemendra.

"But we should not cheat on the integrity of our viewers by giving platform to criminals like him. We cannot fiddle with our credibility for a few crores."

"Enough of your moral lecture," Hemendra said folding his hands in utter exasperation. "He has large swathe of overseas followers. We have a market there too. It is not that easy," explained Hemendra almost reluctantly.

"I only know we need to have clarity on our editorial policy," said Pushkar.

Heads turned. Rajkishore looked up to Pushkar in disbelief. His eyes met Pushkar's. Pushkar could read endorsement in his eyes. "Will he speak up or remain silent as always," Pushkar thought. Rajkishore proved him right once again as he retreated his gaze on the mobile he held in his hand. He made it all appear as if he was not present in the conference room.

"Now, that's a very good lecture." Prithvi butted in. "Strangely, it comes from a person whose show's TRPs are dipping by the week. The channel has to bear the burden of his failures and we become victims of his fucking lectures too."

"But I agree with Pushkar." Ranvir was getting fidgety on his seat. "How can we have tainted Babas going around as our channel's brand ambassadors?"

"The question about the channel's goal and agenda was clearly settled by Yashwant boss in his mail the other day. Are you challenging the Super Boss?" said Prithvi pointing his finger at Pushkar.

"We don't challenge that," Ranvir stepped in again. "Let me talk about my show, *Nexus*. It used to be a show that exposed corruption in the system. But it seems the show has fallen from grace. My team has been severely truncated."

"Well, the show's TRPs have been on the downhill from the past couple of months," Hemendra rubbed it in.

"Not yet, but I can't guarantee that in future," said Ranvir.

"Will talk about *Nexus* separately, Ranvir." Hemendra waived his hands dismissively.

"I do not want problems. I want solutions," said Prithvi.

"I think the message from Prithvi boss is very clear. You got to perform or perish." Hemendra declared as he got up to leave.

As everyone dispersed, Pushkar, Sabir and Ranvir sat glued to their seats. The tension was palpable. Pushkar suddenly got up from his seat and walked up to the white board, to the other end of the conference room. He threw a playful smile at his friends and comrades and wrote this on the white board:

Yahan Darakhton Ke Saaye Mein Dhoop Lagti Hai,
Chalo Yahan Se Chalein Umr Bhar Ke Liye.

Pushkar's sudden act relaxed every one present in the room. And he was not done yet. He immediately launched into mimicking Prithvi: "But let me tell you guyj," he announced, I sall not give up eajily. I swear on my pug, the Ghunghroo." The threesome burst into laughter as they got up to leave the conference room.

Nexus

Look Ranvir, we called you to discuss something important." Hemendra broached on the subject he had been avoiding, after moments of impregnable silence.

"What is it?" Ranvir's deep baritone cut through the air of the cabin like a knife through butter.

"We have a problem at hand. Prithvi and I concluded that only you can help us solve it." The air smelt faintly of deceit.

"Why are you people talking in riddles? Let's hear the problem."

"Well, we have to launch a women's show," said Hemendra breaking the suspense.

"Go ahead," Ranvir cut him short. "Is it going to be the *Agony Aunt* thing?" his voice was laced with sarcasm.

"Well, no," Hemendra said, his facial expression now resembling a forced smile. "It's going to be a beauty show. The idea is ready and we have titled it—*Main Sundar Hoon*."

"Oh, wow! Good. So?" Ranvir could feel his legs shaking with nervous excitement. He still could not figure out the reason he was called to the glass cabin.

"So, we wanted *you* to produce this show for us." Hemendra said that and leaned back on his chair.

"You must be joking! I mean, you can't be serious." His hands stopped at coming to blows.

"We are serious. Why should we crack a joke with a senior guy on such a serious matter," Hemendra reasoned.

"You mean, a senior anchor like me will produce a show on beauty tips for women?" Ranvir's huge frame of six-feet-one convulsed with palpable anger.

"*Hmmm*...look, we thought we will give this show to a young woman. But then we wanted to experiment." Psycho spoke for the first time during the conversation. His eyes stayed fixed on the palm-sized TV panel on his large table.

"We are getting the pretty young things on the show with you." Hemendra returned bearing slime with a glint in his eye.

"I won't do that. Not my cup of tea. You can keep your harem with you," Ranvir retorted as he got up from the chair.

"Hey, hey... Ranvir just hang on. This is going to be the most watched show in afternoon prime time. We can turn things around with this show with a repeat on late prime time." Prithvi tried to cajole Ranvir.

"For someone who is producing *Nexus* and is also the face of the channel, I consider this proposal demeaning."

"Well, we intend to discontinue that show," Hemendra butted in.

"You mean you are discontinuing *Nexus*?" Ranvir's eyes popped out in disbelief.

"We would not be able to continue with a perception-based show any more." That was Prithvi, still fiddling with the TV remote.

"That's the only show which accords an image of sanity to the whole channel and you guys plan to stop it?" Ranvir's argument was greeted by silence.

"But not the best of TRPs, I am sorry to say," pat came Prithvi's response.

"*Nexus* has had its life. It needs drastic overhauling." Prithvi declared as he continued to play with the TV remote.

"Now I know why you guys gradually pulled out people from my team. You had already decided to drop this show, right? I should have seen this coming." Ranvir felt he had been deceived.

"You are reading too much into our decision. We admire your work and your talent, Ranvir," said Hemendra.

"We don't want to lose you. You are an asset to the company. You will continue to anchor prime time news shows. But for all the practical reasons, your area of focus will be your new show—*Main Sundar Hoon*. Hemendra will put out a mail as early as possible."

Ranvir kept quiet. He realised he was shaking with nervous rage.

"And allow me to share good news with you. We are redesignating you. You will no longer be only the senior anchor. Your visiting card will now read—Associate Editor. And we are only giving you what's yours." Psycho held out his hand for a handshake with Ranvir.

"Congratulations, Mr Associate Editor!" Hemendra stretched out his hand, too.

Ranvir looked at him and then at Prithvi. He got up from his chair and left the cabin, shutting the glass door violently behind him.

"They are dropping *Nexus*," Ranvir broke his silence after gulping down the first sip of Royal Stag in his car.

"I knew it. I knew it." Baba popped up. "Psycho cannot stand someone's scoring on popular ratings better than the show he anchors," he added.

"*Nexus* had built its niche viewership over the years and you were the face of the show. Prithvi had to clip your wings." Pushkar analysed the situation to the general approval of all who were enjoying the blissful car-o-bar. Pushkar was special invitee to the car-o-bar at Sabir's request.

"But the reasons could be elsewhere. The marketing guys told me that Yashwant is under tremendous pressure from the cable mafia to compromise on the agenda. And he, after giving it much thought I reckon, is game for that," said Baba.

"What do you mean? The cable mafia is dictating DNN's news agenda!" Ranvir asked accusingly.

"Yes, precisely. See, your show *Nexus* took on local politicians and petty bureaucracy in small towns, where most homes are still on cable," said Baba. "And in most states, cable business is owned and run by state-level politicians and their families. Your show hurt their interests, that is it."

"Yes, Baba is right!" Pushkar butted in. "Yashwant had no choice but to strike a compromise with the cable mafia. *Nexus* was destined to go off air, if DNN were to survive," he added.

"Quite right! Yashwant knows how to play his cards. He does not want to die just another media baron. He thinks he is destined to fly higher," said Baba as he poured himself a stiff one.

"So, now, our hot-shot anchor will sell botox and anti-ageing skin care...to middle-aged post menopausal women, eh?" Sabir teased Ranvir.

"The dramatic proposal caught me by surprise," said Ranvir. "Frankly, I hadn't bargained for that. Not in lieu of *Nexus*."

"But, why didn't you say 'En Ow' to producing the fucking girly stuff, whatever the name."

"I did, but...forget it! All the pent up anger will bust out like a volcano."

"But then why walk out like a person who has lost the battle?" Sabir almost challenged him.

"Assumption is the mother of all the problems. What do you think? I sat there like a lamb bleating?" Ranvir was visibly provoked. "I protested in the strongest possible terms."

"You should have thrown the resignation letter at his..." paused Sabir.

"That's easier said than done," Ranvir took a large swig from his glass, threw the cigarette butt out of the car window and sank into the chair as if exhausted.

"At least you could have threatened...to resign," said Pushkar endorsing Sabir's view.

"Why should I? Why should you, I and all the good guys quit?" said Ranvir.

"That's a valid point," said Pushkar.

"I phoned my father and asked for his opinion. He also advised against resignation," said Ranvir.

"Yaar, then why do you go against these *chootiyas* when you don't even mean it?" Sabir showed his dispproval. "And your lofty ideals of good journalism, whatever happens to them." He reasoned and challenged Ranvir.

"*Journalism gaya maa chudane,*" Ranvir just flew off the handle. "I don't aspire to be the next Larry King. If I am pushed into a situation I don't feel comfortable being in, the job is in focus, not journalism. I am very clear about that."

"About...? I think this could have been the right excuse for you to bid adieu to this mad house." Sabir insisted.

"He has redesignated me as an Associate Editor," said Ranvir with a sense of pride.

"Oh...your talent has been finally recognised?" Sabir was caustic.

"I don't want to lose your company *re*," said Ranvir lightening the mood and alleviating the tension that surrounded their conversation, as he deliberately blew a smoke ring at Sabir and then added with a stern face: "Let me be very practical, Sabir. Why should I forego salary just because these motherfuckers do not have a job profile of my liking? All said and done, I, like everybody in the car, love what money does to my nerves."

"He is right! We all have to run our families. We have to pay off mammoth debts as EMIs. We cannot commit this *hara-kiri*," Baba's face turned grim.

"We all saw what happened to Ritwik," said Ranvir. "He was without a job for over eight months," he added.

"He was a victim of the newsroom mafia, if any one of you doesn't know," said Sabir. "The same mafia who is suffocating us in their death grip here."

"Quitting is not a solution," Ranvir persisted.

"*Hmmm*...but we should put a stop to newsroom humiliation and then be prepared to face the consequences." Sabir argued vehemently.

"When we already know the consequences, where is the need to hasten that up," said Baba.

"So you will continue to put up with abuses and humiliation, because you have the EMI's sword hanging over your head?"

"Is that a question, Sabir or a statement? If it's a statement, I endorse that. If that's a question, I would ask you to ask yourself. Don't preach." Ranvir's voice added savage gravity to the conversation; a voice so sharp, it could be considered a weapon hanging over Sabir's head until he gratified the listeners' need for a balanced answer.

"Well...what have I done to preach you like a saint? I lack guts myself. Perhaps, I am also scared of the consequences. Sorry Ranvir bhai, I take back my words." Sabir abruptly opened the car door and stepped out into the darkness of the night.

"Hey, where are you going? Listen, stop. Sabir...wait..." Ranvir kept calling for him, but Sabir did not look back. Without warning, with his hands in his pockets, Sabir strode away into the murky night, only his silhouette now visible in the side-view mirror.

A mysterious silence enveloped those still in the car. Strains of a couplet broke through the chilling silence:

> *"Sabse Khatarnaak Hota Hai Murda Shanti Se Bhar Jaana*
> *Na Hona Tadap Ka, Sub Kuchh Sahan Kar Jaana*
> *Ghar Se Nikalna Kaam Par Aur Kaam Se Laut Kar Ghar Aana*
> *Sabse Khatarnaak Hota Hai, Hamare Sapno Ka Mar Jaana."*

"By the way, that's Paash's poetry," said Pushkar as he stepped out of the car, closing the door behind him.

For the first time, Ranvir and Baba hated the poet in Pushkar.

Those Six Pecks A Day

The phone rang… Oh no, must be amma. She does not like you. But I love you. I love you Tiya. I will handle amma, don't worry. I will be back soon." India's 20-something super model, Tiya was a frequent visitor into Uday's dreams. Every time she visited his dreams, they ended up in a passionate lock. Uday would convulse in ecstasy, only to find tell-tale signs of the night's orgy in his underpants the next morning.

Sometimes dreams with Tiya around ended up in nightmares. When Tiya would be chased and driven out by his mother. Uday could never figure out why amma hated Tiya so much. What does she have against her?

The phone rang continuously. Uday gradually opened his eyes and groped for his mobile handset. A hint of luminescent white rushed to fill his field of morning vision.

He soon realised it was his mobile handset throwing off that luminescent light. He soon also realised he was no longer dreaming and somebody wanted to connect with him, on his mobile. He picked up the handset reluctantly. The screen announced 'amma'.

"Karmanye…wadhikaraste… Maa phaleshu…kadachan…"

For a few seconds, Uday could hear only shlokas from the Holy Gita on his earpiece.

"Hello, Guddu, *kaisan ba...*" His mother's voice bommed into his ear.

"*Theek bani...*" he said reluctantly. "You spoiled such a beauty of a dream!"

"You must be dreaming about that mini-skirt *chudail...!*" Uday's mother hit the bull's eye.

"You kept intruding my mind..." Uday spoke with a deliberate hint of mock disapproval. "Why did you chase her away. Why do you do that to me."

"What did I do to get subjected to such early-morning rudeness," Uday's mother snapped at him.

"You were chasing that girl," Uday said as he broke into a laugh. "What is this noise I am hearing in the background? Are you watching some serial?" said Uday.

"I was watching *Om,* one of the few good shows on your channel."

"How come you watching news channel? Have you given up on Baba Prasannmukh?"

"His is the first show I watch every morning. He is my guru..."

"TV guru...you have never met him, *na...?*"

"So what, a guru is always a guru..."

"Why does your guru keep making those non-sensical political statements? Why can't he stick to teaching yoga?" Uday teased his mother.

"Don't be silly... He does not need the trappings of a politician. He already has millions and millions of followers," she retorted.

"I have information that he is going to launch a political party." Uday persisted much to his mother's annoyance.

"That's all bunkum! Maybe politics need such good souls like him. By the way, I have not called you to talk about Baba Prasannmukh."

Uday realised it was time to change the subject. "Ok...so you have been watching *Om*? Isn't it?"

"God bless the person who produces that show..." Amma was a rather fast learner. She would understand the TV lingo, much like she did her son and his antics.

"*Arrey*, that's Pushkarji...remember, that decent guy you met in Delhi?"

"Oh...of course, I do remember... He has mastery over *Vedas* and *Puranas*. He is a *pavitra atma*."

"Yes, he is the one who produces this show...!"

"The *Krishna janm* episodes are very well made. The narration is superb! I fell in love with my *kanhaiyya* all over again after watching these episodes. God bless this guy! Give my love to him."

"And amma, what about mine...?"

"You don't deserve it... You don't listen to me."

"How can I not listen to my amma..." Uday sounded like an obedient child.

"Promise me, you are going to heed to my advice," Uday's mother persisted.

"What do you want?"

"You really need to settle down in life now. Your papa and I have decided it's high time for you to be married."

"Oh...come on, amma, not again!"

"Yes, now is a perfect time to act. You feel lonely and you need a companion; look at the way you keep your house, it's all a mess."

"It's clean! The maid takes care of it."

"I want someone to take good care of you and your house."

"*Oh ho,* amma… I have hired a maid."

"I want someone to take care of you all the time."

"There is no such maid, even they demand weekly offs," he chuckled at his mother's forthrightness.

"Don't you dare talk like that… I have had enough!" Amma was clearly agitated.

"Ok, will talk about it later."

"That's not done, Guddu. Tell us if you have a girlfriend. Your papa and I don't mind that, but for God's sake, make up your mind."

"This is ridiculous. I don't want to get married now. And yes, please stop playing a *palan karta* in my dreams. Period."

"What…???"

"Nothing," Uday dismissed the question. "Will talk later, buh-bye… Give my love to Daadu. I will call him up tonight."

"No, listen…"

He hung up.

Uday kept holding his mobile handset for long. Nostalgia took over him. How, as a kid, he longed to be by his mother's side. He had missed his amma around the house, missed her kisses and missed that as an everyday feature. He missed his quota of six hugs and six pairs of kisses he used to get in a day, fixed liked his fixed six meals.

The first, when she would wake him up for school, soon followed by the second when he would leave for school on a cycle rickshaw. The third, when he would come back and the fourth when he would wake up lazily from the afternoon siesta. The fifth came with double and sometimes infinite bonanza, when he would recite a poem to her heart's delight. She would shower him with kisses on his cheeks and his forehead. And the last set was reserved for bed time, after she had lulled him to sleep. While he was half-awake half-asleep, his threshold consciousness would not help him remember those bed-time pecks and so often he would complain to her the next morning. His mother would plant an extra peck on his cheek and tell him, "*Buddhu...*"

Those sets of hugs and kisses continued even after he became a sixth grader, until one day when amma planted a peck in front of the waiting school bus. He became incredibly uncomfortable with his mother's way of showing her affection and love towards him in public.

As he stepped into college, there was a role reversal. It was Uday's turn to give. So every time he would feel low or depressed, he would walk up to his mother and give her a warm hug. During other times, when he would be in a jovial mood, he would throw his arms around her and not leave her, until she shook off his embrace to attend on a chore more important than tending to her son's mercurial moods.

Sitting far away in Delhi, he was denied those warm hugs, but he could always reach out to her on phone, as he did now, to the warmth of her voice. That was enough to sooth his frayed nerves.

He got up from the bed, put on his pyjamas and went out to check the morning newspapers.

It was a story spread across eight columns on the front-page bottom of *The NCR Mail* that caught his attention. It talked about a recent survey on work-related stress. The survey was done extensively, across 20 corporates, covering a sample size of about 2000 employees. It revealed a rise of 57 per cent in work-related stress, and almost 50 per cent jump in the number of suicides as an escape from it.

The survey report categorised work-related stress under three broad categories. The first concluded that the high demand of performance lends unrealistic, unhealthy and unreasonable pressure on an employee. The second category talked about technology as an all important cause, since it heightened expectation for productivity. Workplace culture was termed as the third villain.

At 26, Uday was all too familiar with work-related stress.

Don't You Love Me, Papa!

Uday was setting out for a shoot but Prithvi's fresh outburst, which seemed like this longest goddamned *gyaan-updesh* ever, had turned him off. He wanted to unburden himself so he sent a short message to Pushkar, requesting him to join in at Mamu's.

"That *madarchod* is always after my life. What's his problem, man, doesn't he get enough of sex or what?" Uday launched into an agitated monologue as soon as Pushkar joined him.

"You must understand you are talking to a mentally unstable person." Pushkar explained. "He dropped my investigative piece against Ranjit Diwakar. I showed you the story, wasn't that a top class story, Pushkar bhai?"

"Dushyant has an answer to that," said Pushkar as he broke into one of his favourite couplets:

"Gidgidaane Ka Yahan Koi Asar Nahi Hota,
Pet Bharkar Gaaliyaan Do, Aah Bharkar Bad-Dua."

Pushkar broke into a hearty laugh after reciting the couplet but Uday seemed caught in his web of thoughts that revolved around Prithvi aka Psycho.

"Is there an end to evil in this world? Neither is there any end to his wickedness," Uday reasoned.

"Lord Sri Krishna said in the holy Gita: '*Yada Yada Hee Dharmasya...Glanir Bhavti Bharata...Abhiyuthanam...*' Uday, my dear young lad, like the cycle of birth and death, there is a cycle of good and evil. No two seasons are the same; the monsoon clouds come as a welcome sign only after summer has scorched your energy and strength."

Uday listened to Pushkar intently, his face held by his two hands which were balanced on his thighs.

"Yes, I agree the bad patch sometimes lasts a bit longer, but you keep your calm, hold your ground and have confidence in yourself, the evil forces will never harm you."

"I have never seen you losing your cool," said Uday. "It is like an impossible feat, considering games these *chootiyas* are always up to against you..."

"There are times when I go into depression. You know, there are days when I am not able to meet my children. I get to see them only when they are sleeping. I don't get time for my two daughters, my family. I didn't realise Sia has turned five and Siddhi has become a little toddler, learning to lift her legs and walk a confident walk. You'll be shocked to hear what Sia told me on phone the other day. She said, 'Papa, why don't you see me often? Don't you love me?' I went to bed that day and cried like a child. Even Mandakini, who I consider stronger between us two, broke down. You sacrifice your family and this is what you get in return. *Zillat!*"

"Sir, why don't you speak to Yashwant sir?"

"I tried speaking to him once. The only thing he told me was that he had great expectations from me. Who is bothered about our expectations," Pushkar seemed hurt and aggrieved.

"That's unfair of him," Uday could not avoid his annoyance.

"Forget it! Why don't you come home some day? Mandakini will be happy to see you and you will fall in love with my *jaans*, Sia and Siddhi. Siddhi is picking up vocabulary fast and Sia makes friends easily." Pushkar's face illuminated with uncanny warmth as he spoke about his family and children.

Pushkar called for Nandu as he got up to leave. "I will pay, sir. Sorry, I didn't realise the time, have held you up for long," said Uday.

"*Arrey*, no problem. Always remember, you must never give up. Be positive, that's the mantra of success and happiness. I leave you with this inspirational couplet of Dushyant:

> *"Kaun Kehta Hai Aakaash Me Surakh Nahi Ho Sakta,*
> *Ek Patthar To Tabiyat Se Uchhalo Yaaron."*

"It is always a relief talking to you, sir," said Uday as he shook hands with Pushkar and waved him bye.

Sia

"...but you said you had an off," Mandakini was preparing breakfast for Sia, but her dart was directed at Pushkar's back. He didn't try to stand clear of his wife's annoyed tone and similar expressions and found her anger perfectly justified.

"I shall be away for a little while and back, sweetheart. It's an emergency!"

"How can you do this to Sia?" said Mandakini whose demeanour did not change much since the last question. "Come on, sweetheart! I shall be back sooner. Swear on you."

"Think of our children, Pushkar. You are never there for them."

"Now, please Manda, don't start it all over again. I have an important meeting. I promise I shall compensate for this some other day," pleaded Pushkar.

"That day will never come," Mandakini refused to be pacified.

"Will take an off next week and we will all go to Batkal lake," said Pushkar flinging his hands across his daughter's shoulders, who sat on the dining table with her mug of milk and corn flakes.

"Ok, papa."

"My little Sia is the only one who stands by her papa," Pushkar said darting a look at Mandakini, who now got busy in the kitchen.

Pushkar got up and tip-toed into the kitchen. He took Mandakini by surprise when he flung his arms around her. "I love you more when you are angry, sweetheart… Hope the *koftas* are shaping up well, *huh?* Prepare for a grand feast, Sia is five today."

"When will you be home?" Mandakini showed signs of cooling down.

"Before five."

"OK! Fetch some more milk from Mother Dairy on your return. I forgot to get enough for *kheer*."

"Will do, sweetheart! And yes, Uday might swing in by in my absence. He is very fond of *koftas* and *dahi vadas*…"

"Have enough to feed your entire office, but don't get them here in the evening. I have only invited Sia's friends," Mandakini warned Pushkar knowing him all too well.

'The Lights Are Hurting Me'

Pushkar did not respond to Sia's cheerful "hello papa" when he entered the house. He thrust the milk pouches in his daughter's hands. She had already got into her brand new birthday dress and looked disappointed at her father's ordinary nod. Walking slower than his usual brisk gait, he seemed to be a father whose very persona and appearance were such as to have no impression on his child's friends. Sia embarrassedly saw him walking straight into the bedroom, without even caring to look at the festoons and the balloons hanging from the ceiling. Mandakini could hear the door bell from the kitchen, but could not hear the excited tone of her daughter welcoming her dad over the din of Cartoon Network cacophony.

"Who is it, beta...?"

Sia came rushing to her in the kitchen, dumped the polythene bag into her hands and ran back into the living room. "Hey listen, send your papa in here..."

But Mandakini knew it was impossible to get Sia off her favourite Tom and Jerry. She came out of the kitchen and looked for Pushkar in the living room. "Where is papa?" Mandakini then came looking for him in the bedroom, only to find him gasping for breath, his feet twitching, breathing laborious. As soon as Mandakini switched on the room's lights, Pushkar covered his eyes quickly with both his hands.

"Just put those lights off. Put 'em off," he ordered.

"What happened...? Are you alright?" she asked as she switched off the lights and moved towards the bed side where Pushkar lay.

"I have a constant throbbing pain in the back of my head."

"You don't seem alright. What happened? A bad day at office, is it?"

Pushkar rested his arm across his eyes. Mandakini held his hand and tried to take it away from his face.

She tried to jolt him out of his comatose state, to get him to speak to her. She persistently failed in her efforts owing to Pushkar's strange behaviour. "Has something been troubling him and he could never share with me; he never before complained of a similar symptom, though, so what could this possibly be? A minor stroke? Hypertension?" Too many questions criss-crossed her mind as she shook him once again. Pushkar lay on the bed like a log.

"I have put off the lights, Pushkar now open your eyes, speak to me." Mandakini was getting hysteric.

"I can't feel any sensation," he announced.

"What do you mean?" Mandakini fears were now coming true.

"I could see that you lifted my hand away, but I didn't feel anything." Pushkar spoke in the sound of a man's heavy breathing.

It was time for Mandakini to panic. "Pushkar, what's happening to you?" A dead silence greeted her.

"Speak to me, Pushkar." Mandakini's voice almost rose to a level of shriek.

Pushkar mumbled something, but his voice refused to come out of the throat. Mandakini put her ears to his mouth, but failed to make out what he said.

"Let me call the doctor. O...o... no...it will be better to take you to Yashodhara hospital." He did not respond, Mandakini called for the taxi.

"Will you be able to walk up to the taxi?" she asked expecting an answer.

Pushkar made an attempt at speaking but his strength gave way. "What is it, darling? Tell me...what's troubling you?" He would not open his eyes.

"Say something. Just speak up! Please." Mandakini broke down. His pupils appeared dilated. It scared Mandakini no end.

She dialled Sabir. She was incoherent and Sabir could only hear staccato muffled sobs.

"Hello...hello...yes, Mandakini. Tell me, what's happened?"

"He is not talking. What happened to him in office? First, he did not allow me to switch on the lights and then he said he could not feel the sensation in his hands. Now, he refuses to speak. What is this bhaiyya...?" she was sobbing uncontrollably.

"Is there anyone around? Somebody who can take him to the hospital? He needs immediate medical attention. Don't lose time, just rush him to the hospital."

"Yes...taxi should be here anytime."

"Rush him fast! I am on my way, don't worry."

"Please come, please come fast..."

Mandakini tried to lift her husband, but could not muster the strength for the ordeal. She left Pushkar on the bed and ran towards the door. "Taxi *walleh* bhai sa'ab, will you please help me? Will you please carry my husband from the room? He is not able to walk on his own."

The sardarji was an old man, old enough to understand a distressing emotion aroused by impending danger.

"*Oye, koi gal naii...*" he gave her a reassuring reply.

She led him into her house and ushered him into the bedroom. "No lights here, so you will have to be a bit careful."

The taxi *wallah* realised the body weight appeared too heavy for a lean frame like Pushkar's. Pushkar lay like a log on the taxi *wallah*, making no attempt to move. He was lapsing into unconsciousness.

"What happened to papa? Why is the uncle carrying papa like that? Has he taken ill? Are we going to the hospital?" Sia's questions were never ending. Mandakini chose to ignore them.

"Come fast," she instructed Sia as she lifted Siddhi in her arms and darted towards the car.

Those were the most nightmarish fifteen minutes to the Yashodhara Hospital. The cab driver rushed in to get the ward boys, who'd wheel the patient inside the emergency unit.

Mandakini came out to pay the fare to the taxi driver, but could not find the taxi on the spot it disembarked her. She stood there for a moment before rushing back inside the reception area and found, to her utter surprise, the taxi driver standing beside Pushkar's stretcher, near the emergency unit.

Pushkar was wheeled into the minor O.T. A young doctor came out of the O.T after a few minutes, asking for the patient's relative for a chat regarding his condition.

"What has happened to him?" Mandakini asked.

"This seems to be a veritable case of brain haemorrhage."

Mandakini was devastated. "Haemorrhage...he is not even thirty-five!"

"Ma'am, this has nothing to do with age. These are lifestyle problems. We have been getting even younger patients."

"You will have to save him. What is to be done?" Mandakini fired questions as if she were under a spell of delirium. Her world seemed to collapse. A ward boy rushed in to help her, and the bounteous sardarji comforted the little Sia, who was crying herself hoarse.

"Is there nobody else with her? Tell her that the patient will have to be operated upon immediately, so someone should complete the formalities," the lady at the reception barked.

It was the taxi *wallah*'s turn to make use of his big-heartedness. He helped Mandakini sit on the bench. "*Rab rakha*, everything will be all right!"

Sabir asked Uday to park his vehicle and made a dash towards the hospital reception.

"The doctors are saying weird things...haemorrhage rrhage...how could he have a haemorrhage?... Sabir bhaiyya, please do something..." Mandakini lapsed into hysteric sobs.

"Control yourself...nothing will happen to him... Don't worry..." Sabir thought these words would comfort her, but he was mistaken.

"Where is the doctor?"

He rushed into the doctor's chamber in the corridor, right of the reception. Dr Avinash was a bespectacled man in his early forties.

"Was he a chain smoker?" Dr Avinash asked.

"No, he does not smoke and is a teetotaler."

"Was he over-stressed? You know...family problems, work pressure etc...?"

"Well, he did seem under stress at work," said Sabir out of concern to reach at a correct diagnosis, so that the doctors get down to brass-tacks and bring back Pushkar to his normal self.

"See, Mr Hussain, it has now been established that haemorrhage is also the result of stress. The blood vessels in his brain have ruptured and blood has spilled over his vital tissues and brain cells."

"What is the prognosis?" Sabir choked.

"He has to be operated upon immediately, but there is no guarantee the operation would be successful. Look...this is a sensitive operation. We may be able to locate the clot and remove it. But you never know...if the clot has caused enough damage to restrict his body functions. The patient might have to give up functionality of a body organ, or organs, as an after-effect of the stroke."

"You think it could happen to him?"

"From the symptoms it does look like the haemorrhage might have taken its toll. We have sent him for the CT scan, let's wait for the report."

"Will he be his usual self after this operation?"

"*Hmm*...that is what I was about to tell you. We have seen patients who have suffered memory loss or paralysis."

"Paralysis...?"

"It could result in partial paralysis...for instance, he might lose power of speech. We keep such patients under strict care of doctors and physiotherapists. Patients do recover, but over stretched periods of time. Let me also warn you that there are far more acute consequences that are painful for the entire family in the long run."

Sabir could hear a faint sob from behind. Mandakini had walked into the doctor's chamber and was listening to their conversation, standing afar at the door.

"Mandakini, these are just scenarios the doctor is discussing. Nothing is going to happen to our Pushkar." He got up from the chair and escorted her out of the doctor's chamber.

"I told him he should quit this place. The office was getting on his nerves. It has upset our lives. Sabir bhaiyya, why did it happen to us? Why, on a day like this? It is Sia's birthday." Mandakini was getting hysteric.

"Calm down, Mandakini. Pushkar will be fine and will be in company of you all sooner than later." Throughout the conversation, he was also trying to convince himself of the same.

"Why was your Prithvi after my husband's life? Who gave him the right to harass and bully my husband? Pushkar had asked for a day's leave but your Prithvi chap refused. I curse him, he shall never be a happy man himself. I curse him, he will meet a fate worse than this. Just tell him Sabir bhaiyya for all I care."

Was he also responsible for Pushkar's condition? Why couldn't he help to save him and his family from a crisis that has almost devastated them? Sabir's shirt was washed in Mandakini's tears, her head with Sabir's.

Muskan and Farhat joined in and comforted Mandakini. They sat on the bench in the corridor as Sabir walked away towards the hospital lobby, where Ranvir and Baba waited for him along with Uday.

"Sir, Pushkar bhai had invited me over to his place in the evening for *koftas* and *dahi vadas*. But I didn't know we will end up visiting him in the hospital," Uday's eyes filled with tears as he narrated his conversation with Pushkar to Sabir at the hospital.

"Pushkar sir seemed a trifle upset with the way these situations were being engineered to push him against the wall," said Uday.

"He definitely looked upset when he came out of Prithvi's cabin at around 3.30 pm," said Ranvir. "I could see him locked in some animated discussion with Prithvi and Hemendra. I wanted to take him out at Mamu's then, but before long he had disappeared," he added.

"He told me that Prithvi was out to paint him a loser, so that he could replace him with Akhil as the show's producer," said

Sabir. "This is what they do to a person who gave them a show that topped the TRP charts for sixteen consecutive weeks?"

"I heard they were preparing a case for his retrenchment," said Ranvir and took a long drag on his cigarette, the top of the filter pinched between his thumb and forefinger, slowly expelling the smoke.

"They have succeeded in that, even though it is just partial. Pushkar will not be able to attend office for months together, may be never at all," Baba's eyes were wet with tears.

"Let's not lose hope. Pushkar is going to be back on his feet very soon," said Sabir with a tone of confidence. The meeting dispersed suddenly as everyone ran towards the emergency ward. Mandakini's cries were unmistakable.

"The CT scan report has confirmed the haemorrhage. Pushkar will have to undergo surgery, immediately," the doctor announced.

Mandakini's Steel

Five-year-old Sia was tall for her age and showed great composure; she ushered Uday into a small room that had a clean, slippery floor.

"Hello Pushkar bhai. How are you?" said Uday as he sat next to him on the bed. On the other side of the bed, Mandakini held a small bowl, full of curd and mashed banana in her hand. She was feeding Pushkar little by little with a soup spoon, taking care of him like a baby while baby Sia kept a napkin ready, wiping the corners of her father's mouth every now and then. There wasn't a day since Pushkar was operated upon that Uday and Sabir had not been by his side in the last three months. The thought that Pushkar would recover fully one day and recite Dushyant and Paash, never left them.

Pushkar's operation was a success, but the after-effect of the stroke had left him paralysed on the left side of the body. It had severely restricted his body movements and had also taken away his speech. Uday would come and sit next to him, touching and pressing his hand. The large black pupils would dilate, travelling from one end of his big, bulging eyes to another and freeze, not necessarily aimed at Uday but there was a clear hint that pleasantries have been exchanged mid-way. He did attempt to speak but his speech died in the cave of his mouth.

"He makes that attempt only when you or Sabir bhai are here. You can read his irritation behind that failed attempt. But for me, it's more than a hint of his presence. He is most alive, most connected, and most content when he sees Sia and Siddhi around." Uday could see Mandakini's eyes turning wet.

At times, Pushkar would simply ignore Uday, not caring to look him in the eye at all. "It seems he has seen my story today and didn't like it. Isn't it, bhabhi? That is the reason he is not talking to me." Both knew they were only faking assurances. Mandakini knew her husband will never be able to ask her to make *koftas* for Uday. Uday knew Pushkar will never be able to share the table at Mamu's, lifting his sagging spirits with his inspiring words and his *sher-o-shayari*, always tailor-made for the occasion.

"Mr Jain is in the final stages of the draft. We will file the case in the court early next month," Mandakini announced with an air of finality, as two year old Siddhi played with Uday's mobile.

"So, what is the compensation amount you have decided?" Uday asked.

"Compensation is just a component of the petition." Mandakini spoke slowly, yet firmly. "I want justice! I know my husband was an honest, hard working and a diligent professional who never compromised his integrity and honesty. He did not deserve this vegetative state. The way he was treated by his seniors, gnawed on his self-confidence and that manifested in our marital relationship too. I don't care whether there are any precedents in such legal battles. I will make these bosses pay for all their misdeeds, will ensure their defense fails to pass muster in the eyes of public who make icons out of TV journalists." Mandakini oozed determination and grit, ready to pounce back like a hurt tigress.

Uday's eyes caught something in motion across his right side. Something in Pushkar had moved. Perhaps, his eyeballs. Perhaps, for hundredth of a millisecond. Perhaps. Was he dreaming or was it wishful thinking. Whatever it may have been, deep inside Uday knew that Pushkar had heard his wife and acknowledged her steely resolve.

Bhai Sa'ab

Ritwik was returning home late that night when his crime reporter, Harsh Ranjan called up to inform about an accident. "Sir, an SUV has rammed into roadside hutments here and mowed down a few people. It was apparently driven by business tycoon Vikramjit Singh's son, Veer."

Ritwik had negotiated the road which leads him home to his house, past the DDA market, in Saket when he received the call. He asked his driver to take a U-turn.

Veer, all of twenty-three, stood by the roadside. Ritwik went up close. A thin stream of blood travelled down Veer's head, mixing with tears on his face. A strong gust of alcohol hit Ritwik as he approached Veer. Two young girls, who seemingly accompanied Veer in his SUV, stood next to him. They were crying themselves hoarse. Probably they, too, sustained injuries. But Ritwik soon discovered they were not crying out of any apparent pain, but by the unexpected and unfortunate position they had suddenly found themselves in. An old man wearing a white shirt and a pair of white trouser sat by the roadside, crying in pain as he positioned his head in his hands. Veer told Ritwik that the old man was his driver.

Ritwik could immediately recognise Veer. He was a page 3 regular and was much talked about as the most sought after bachelor in the Delhi's elite circuit. He remembered how he had once sent a reporter across to him to get his comments on multiple partners. "*The society is changing; the more the merrier.*" Ritwik had played it up on prime time.

There was a commotion up there. The hutment dwellers threatened to descend down on the spot. "I don't know how I did it. Please don't write about it, please, I beg of you," Veer said spotting Ritwik's car with the sticker labelled 'Press'. Ritwik came close, shook hands with him. "Were you driving the car?" he asked. There was a sheepish "yes". Another police gypsy hooted up to the spot.

Ritwik stepped ahead and whispered something into Veer's ears.

"How can I do that?" Veer was puzzled.

"You can take care of the driver's family; he will be more than willing to take the blame on himself," said Ritwik in a cold tone.

"He will be ruined." Veer sounded concerned for the driver.

"It's a bailable offence. You can fight the legal battle for him. But you stay away from it if you can. Make up your mind. You don't have much time." Ritwik surprised himself by giving advice to a complete stranger on how to escape punishment, for a crime as severe as murder.

Veer nodded and walked up to the driver. He grabbed his arm and took him away from the vehicle. Ritwik could see the driver folding his hands. And almost on cue, Veer took his hands into his, begging him the similar way.

There were no eyewitnesses as such. Ritwik knew he was playing on high stakes.

"I was passing by when I saw the SUV climb on to the side walkways. The driver looked drunk and sleepy." Ritwik told the police.

"I did not know he used to drink on the sly. He is sorry for what he did. He is an old man, please be lenient to him, sir." Veer blurted out Ritwik's script.

The police PCR did not wait for the ambulance. Two police personnel lugged two injured persons on to the vehicle and sped off. The ambulance turned up soon and lifted the other two injured. Ritwik had calculated the damage. "Two of them are serious. Impossible that they will survive," he mumbled.

One of the young assistant sub-inspectors went up to Ram Subhag and slapped him tight across the face. The driver fell on the ground... "Sa'ab, *galti ho gayi,*" said the driver, blood oozing from his nose and mouth.

"Betichod, kitni pi hai taine?" He lifted the driver by his collar. *"Madarchod,"* another slap landed on the driver. He shook uncontrollably before falling down unconscious.

"Oh! Hi, Ritwik! Long time!"

In the darkness of that lone strip lined with hutments, Ritwik could make out Anushka's voice.

"You are a big man now... Channel Head, *huh?!*"

"Just a city channel, you know. But I am more than happy."

"Oh yes, I know! What is the Channel Head doing on the spot?" It was not difficult to miss the sarcasm in her voice. "Oh, nothing, I was just passing by when my reporter informed me about this accident. I was the first to arrive."

"Atul, please get some more lights on. It is too dark for the shoot. I do not want the shoot to get spoiled." She barked her order at the cameraman.

"Tell me *na,* what happened here? Where is Veer? He is amazingly handsome yaar. I am dying to see him, like, this close for the first time." Anushka said animatedly.

"Veer has left for the hospital, he'd sustained injuries. By the way, the drunk driver has admitted to his guilt before the police." Ritwik gave a low-down to Anushka as if he was Veer Tulsania's press information advisor.

"Let me talk to the families of the victims and the police; will join you soon, Ritwik."

"You keep at it! I'll take your leave. My reporter is right here."

"You remember your promise, *na*? You have to take me to a bar for the terrific story on night shelters turning den for prostitution."

"Ya, ya, I remember! Sometime next week."

"Sure, chow..."

"Chow..."

The next morning Ritwik called up Veer. He did not answer. Ritwik then called up Veer's father, Vikramjit Tulsania.

"Can't imagine a perfectly normal day turning out to be so scary, but I shall ever remain indebted to you. Tell me, what can I do for you?" Vikramjit Tulsania was full of gratitude towards his son's savior.

"Nothing, bhai sa'ab..." Ritwik could not believe he would address a business tycoon as 'bhai sa'ab'.

"Oh come on, give us an opportunity to do something for a *farishta* like you," Vikramjit Tulsania was not willing to take a 'NO' for an answer. "I just need your blessings, bhai sa'ab. How is Veer now?"

"He was first taken to the hospital. He's got seven stitches on his chin." Vikramjit sounded like a concerned father. "The police let him go after recording his version. He came early morning, now sleeping in his room. Poor soul. Everyone in the family is shaken after the incident. Should I wake him up?"

"Oh, no, not at all bhai sa'ab. I will speak to him later."

"What is the toll, if I may ask?"

"Two dead."

"Oh my god!"

"Hope you have spoken to the Police Commissioner?"

"Yes I have! He was my classmate in Dehradun. He sat for the civils."

"Hope he's handling things at his end," asked Ritwik.

"He assured me of all possible help."

"The driver should keep his mouth shut or our plan goes for a toss." Ritwik spoke with concern.

"You are right."

"You will have to act fast. You must meet the driver's family. And before it's late, call the press and announce a decent cash compensation for the deceased. Take care of their children's education expenses. See if you can give employment to their wife or children." Ritwik laid out the blueprint for Vikramjit Tulsania.

"Sure, right over. Thanks, beta for whatever you have done for us. Come home sometime!"

"*Hmmm*... I will," said Ritwik as he hung up.

The numbness hadn't worn off before he received another phone call. It was Anushka's.

"I did a sting on the driver. Initially, the hospital authorities did not allow me to talk to the driver. That was when it struck me that I should go inside with a spy-cam," she rattled off. "As they say pen is mightier than sword...sure it is. The pen did the job for me," said Anushka.

Ritwik's pulse raced uncontrollably. He had not factored this at all in his operation 'cover-up'. "What did he tell you?" he asked.

"He was very repentant. He confessed he was driving the vehicle, feeling sorry that his sa'ab had to go through a troublesome phase, because of his mistake. How do you find my *exclusive?*"

"Oh… That's brilliant, simply brilliant. You deserve a treat."

"I am near Parliament. Let us meet at 1 pm at…*hmmm*… at the Press Club. Fine by you?"

"That's fine!"

"Meanwhile, I will feed my story from the Parliament OB. Chow…" Anushka hung up.

"I am so happy! This was the first scoop of my career and I am celebrating its success with you. You know, Ritwik, I want to confess something today."

"What?"

"I used to secretly admire you and your work. My admiration for you went up when you took on Hemendra sir and resigned. You have some guts, man and I love you for that."

"*Hmmm….*" Ritwik listed to her intently.

"And ya, thanks much for this latest story." Anushka pressed Ritwik's hand in an affectionate gesture.

"Anything for you, baby! Care for a 'Bloody Mary'?"

"I would love to have one today! Let's toast to our good old friendship."

"You know what? Right now Veer and his father must be on their way to visit the driver's family. This is our exclusive, but I don't mind sharing that with you." Ritwik was working on Anushka's mind.

"*Aww,* great! Hope there is still time…where does the family live?"

"They are in Jehangirpuri. They have a nice double-storeyed house; all because of Veer's father, who has been a nice employer to Ram Subhag."

"Thanks, Ritz. You are such a help... Love you!"

"You go and enjoy the shoot... I am not leaving this place before having yummy *biryani*. Should I get some packed for you?"

"Ya, sure. Get one packed for Sukhwinder. He is at the Vijay Chowk lawns...will just call him over."

"Sure, baby. Now let's drink to our memories."

"There is nothing that I like, more than drinking a fabulous Bloody Mary. *AAAhhhhh*!"

Do Bigha Zameen

"The entire area, as far as your eyes can see, will be taken away from us," Naveen Kumar led Satyendra and Altamash to show them the spread of paddy field that lay before them in acres, meeting the sky at the far end.

Ever since Tathaastu spread its tentacles into the state, Naveen Kumar, a strapping youth of twenty-four and the only graduate in the village, has been spearheading a movement to 'throw out the devils'. He had formed a youth brigade under the banner of Ullasganj, *Yuva Jan Jagran Sangharsh Samiti,* mobilising people affected by the Tathaastu Steel project.

A slogan went up the air:

"Tathaastu Haye Haye!
State Government Down Down!"

"We had a peaceful sit-in outside the collectorate today. You missed it, but there was a considerable turnout."

"Can you provide me some visuals of that *dharna?*" asked Altamash.

"That's not a problem. You will have a CD before you leave."

"Have they not promised to pay you well enough for your lands?" asked Satyendra.

"We are not going to accede even an inch of our land if we don't get the price we demand," Naveen Kumar described in a manner, which would be peculiar to the weak hearted.

"But, the government says the steel project will help the villagers. The company shall be giving each of the displaced family members a job in the new project." Satyendra persisted.

"And what about our children?" a senior voice tore through the crowd of youths. "Let them give stakes in the company, so that the generations to come also live off it."

"Maa Ka Sauda, Nahi Karenge, Nahi Karenge...
Door Hato Aye Duniyawaalon... Yeh Zameen Hamari Hai...
Sarkar Haye Haye... Tathaastu Haye Haye!"

"The government claims it has necessary power to take away the land 'in the interest of the public.'" Satyendra threw a direct one at Madhavi.

"Whose interests are they trying to protect is amply clear now. The amendments to the *Gift the Land Act* have been stalled by design, by big corporate houses, over the last decade. The parties in power, in New Delhi, lack the political will to introduce the necessary amendments in Parliament." Standing amidst the throng of protestors in blue-checkered cotton saree that had a strikingly red striped border, Madhavi Abhyankar burst out in anger, a streak of white on her head only enhancing the gravity of her statement.

"So, it's an advantage to the big corporate houses?"

"The government goes all out to woo the corporate, getting land for them by hook or by crook. And, at rates much below the market price. There was a feeble attempt at drafting the new bill without caring to remove the loopholes of that archaic

Gift the Land Act. My first opposition was to the very title of the Act, which was framed by the Britishers when they ruled us. The government will have to give a more humane name to the new bill. The land grab cannot be considered a gift to the government from a poor farmer," said Madhavi, her ubiquitous *jhola* swinging animatedly to her mood as it went back and forth like a disciplined soldier, waiting on cue for the next command of its officer.

"*Maa Ka Sauda, Nahi Karenge, Nahi Karenge...*" Naveen and his co-workers again raised the slogan, denouncing the government and the Tathaastu project.

Madhavi's passion for social work went back to her college days, when she participated in the Chipko Movement (or the 'forest satyagraha'). She travelled all the way from North Karnataka to Chamoli, in Uttarakhand (then part of Uttar Pradesh), in the late seventies to contribute her bit for the Chipko Movement. Her paper on 'The Politics of Development—the Case of Dams in India', won her praise from noted economist, Dr Murli Prakash Rao. She later became the sole voice of tribals and villagers in their fight against what was touted as development projects.

Altamash had now de-plugged the gun-mic wire and loitered around the area, exploring a vantage point to capture the serene landscape of the village.

"Who is going to listen to these hapless people? The local media has either been bought over or browbeaten to toe the government line. This is the first time since the last three years that I find the presence of national media here."

"You can't generalise about the media and its antics, ma'am." Satyendra was on the defensive.

"You are right! But, how do you explain your conduct? The other day I was LIVE on Channel 365 on the same issue. Suddenly, they decided to put me on hold for some breaking news. Apparently, a reporter had got visuals of the elder Damani brother's twenty-five-storeyed-mansion. Somebody told me the reporter had discovered a lift that opens into Magan bhai Damani's restroom. He surveyed the restroom, sat and used the pot to give a ring of authenticity to his reportage, giving pieces to camera from every angle before climbing down the same lift. You guys have time to report about corporates' shitpots and their 400 crore mansions, where not more than six people would stay, but you turn a blind eye to the lives of 2000 people who will get affected by the project."

Satyendra realised that it hurt when somebody told the truth about the media industry, but he put up a cheeky defence: "Well, we are not all that bad as some make us out to be. I have been here once before and have been in regular touch with Naveen."

"Where were you when the poor Bhambhukis fell to government bullets? The so-called 'national media' ignored the entire coverage. The local media turned out, no doubt, but their reportage was blatantly slanted."

Naveen Kumar had got a Marshall jeep and called out for Madhavi didi. They were leaving for Nilamata Parvat. Madhavi invited Satyendra to hop in for a drive to the village of Bhambhuki tribals.

Satyendra was waiting for this moment with a bated breath. The prospect of seeing Bhambhuki tribals—on their own land, for the first time—overwhelmed him. Before that fateful day. when police firing killed seven, which included two Bhambhukis, he had only seen Bhambhuki tribals on picture postcards, they sell to foreign tourists on Janpath and on government tourism literature. The last time he saw Bhambhukis was on DNN, in an advertisement put out by the state government to attract tourists to the state. The Bhambhukis were seen in their traditional attire, with the proverbial bow and arrow; the womenfolk sporting even colourful headgear and bangle-sized earrings.

Nilamata Parvat area was perhaps one of the few places Satyendra had not traversed during the course of his reporting assignment. The tribals revered the Nilamata Parvat as their lord and deity, little realising that the government was going to barter their deity to some alien traders for money.

"Of the 2,500 acres of land given for Tathaastu's steel plant, 800 acres was classified as forest land. Many people of the area are eligible for rights over this land, especially the lands they are cultivating, as they have been living in the area for more than 75 years. Also, under the *Friends of the Forest Act,* you cannot go ahead with the project without the village Gram Sabha's approval," said Naveen Kumar, who stood as an interlocutor for the tribals.

"The government has clearly overlooked the impact of mining iron-ore on the environment. The stage one 'environment clearance' has been granted to the project. Already, the Bhambhuki community is on the verge of decline; they are a close-knit community of people who do not marry outside their tribe. And now, you decide to make them extinct in one stroke," said Madhavi.

A war cry rent the air:

"Door Hato Aye Duniyawaalon... Yeh Zameen Hamari Hai..."

As Satyendra returned from the Nilamata Parvat area, he asked his last question to Naveen Kumar: "Why would he reject the government proposal to rehabilitate and resettle the affected families?"

"The case of Bokaro Steel Plant is a stark reminder of how rehabilitation and resettlement plan of a similar kind can go awry. And, in the last 40 years, we do not have any law for rehabilitation and resettlement," said Naveen.

"At best, there is a government policy," Madhavi butted in. "The state governments are free to ignore it," she added.

"The government is likely to read this as opposition to development." Satyendra lobbed a direct one.

"Development has to be just and equitable and should travel beyond one generation. Human sensitivity has to be cared for, respected and valued. The moot question still is: whose development are we talking about? For the needy or for the moneyed? At the moment, development is perversely tilted towards the latter," said Madhavi.

"What is the future of this agitation?" Satyendra asked.

"If voices of the farmers and forest dwellers are crushed for long, they might resort to whatever means to get even with the government. If Tathaastu goes ahead with its project, the government should be prepared for a showdown," warned Madhavi Abhyankar.

"Are you sure we are camping here tonight?" asked Altamash.

"Absolutely! Tomorrow, it's going to be crucial. It will be your day, Altamash. Maybe, we are very close to making history," said Satyendra.

It was getting on to seven in the evening when they checked into a non-descript motel, built in the bylanes of the busiest market of the town. Looking at its façade it was clear that the plot of land was meant for residential purposes and not for a motel.

Both were bone tired and wanted to have a quick shower before they settled down for a peg of Old Monk rum they had picked up on the way.

Satyendra's phone rang incessantly. "Who's is that?" Satyendra shouted from inside the toilet.

"There's no number on the screen."

"Pick it up, please."

"It was Naveen's. I told him he should expect a call in ten minutes," Altamash announced to Satyendra as the latter got out of the shower and stepped into the room.

The phone rang again. The conversation was short and crisp. Satyendra screamed in excitement: "It's going to be a big day for us tomorrow. Time for operation 'Deep Woods.'"

As Altamash poured rum into the water stained glasses, Satyendra wrote a quote by one of his all time favourite authors, Milan Kundera in his blue diary:

People are going deaf because music is played louder and louder, but because they are going deaf, it has to be played louder still.

Operation Deep Woods

Dhanpat Deenbandhu's mansion stood in Ullasganj's green belt, where construction activities were banned under law. It was two kilometers off the highway leading to the Capital, Himmatganj. Naveen found the whole tract—leading from the highway right up to DD mansion—metalled. It was clear that DD's writ ran in the entire area and the environmental laws were given a grand go by. Naveen was greeted with crisp, tight royal salutes by two mean-looking mustached *durbans*, as he pulled up his Marshall in the portico.

Naveen appeared fidgety and nervous as he toyed with the pen that was clipped to his shirt pocket. It was an ordinary pen, but had extraordinary qualities. Hidden inside the pen was a camera that would get activated as soon as the pen was 'clicked' to a functional mode, like any other ordinary pen. Beads of sweat broke out around his nose and forehead, and it seemed as if he was going to enter the college examination hall.

'*This is going to be a test of my grit and determination all right, but am I getting unnecessarily nervous? Am I scared? Have I not taken too much of a risk at the instruction of a reporter? If I am caught, would DD bury me alive in his backyard?*' A rush of thoughts crowded his mind. '*I will have to be brave. If I succeed, Tathaastu will be in big trouble. The press will hound it so much that they will have to give up their project.*' Naveen tried to explain himself as he climbed the stairs leading to the hallway.

A resounding laughter greeted Naveen as he stepped into a big hall. Dhanpat Deenbandhu was sitting on a large sofa, surrounded by his *chamchas*. The bartenders floated around in the room, serving liquor and roasted kebabs.

"*Aaiyye* Naveen *babu*..." Dhanpat got up from the sofa, walked halfway across the hall and shook hands with Naveen, before escorting him to the sofa next to his.

Dhanpat Deenbandhu was the elected member of the Legislative Assembly from Ullasganj. That was the shortest and the only legal introduction to Deenbandhu. For those who never voted for him or for that matter for any other candidate, DD was the Mafia. His writ ran large in the mineral rich belt of Ullasganj and Mitrapura. Last year, when he laid the foundation of a 50 bed hospital, he took upon himself the title of 'Deenbandhu', or, 'a friend of the poor'. From Dhanpat Deshraj, he had now become Dhanpat Deenbandhu.

But, it was his craze for self-publicity that always outshone his entrepreneurial acumen. In the run-up to his second election, his public relation managers went around hunting for the best copywriter to come up with slogans that suited their client's image. Many promising young writers excused themselves, saying they were too small a fry to be writing slogans in honour of a 'great soul' like Mr DD. Finally, a lyricist, whose recent album, '*Aaja Raja Le Le Maja*' had become a super-duper hit, agreed to do the honours. The deal was inked on a condition that the name of the lyricist shall remain anonymous. The lyrics were set to the tune of the title song of a Bollywood blockbuster, *Omkara*, with small fillers thrown in for effect.

Maa, Beta, Dada-Dadi, Ho Ya Apni Didi,
Vote Padega Usi Ko Jiska Naam Hai DD, DD, DD...!
Reh Jaenge Sub Phisaddi,
Jab Daudega DD...!

The city's who's who were in attendance at the Deshbandhu mansion. Naveen could recognise a couple of Municipal Corporators, the opposition MLA Ram Charan Misra, the Revenue Collector, Kranti Kundan and Anil Wilson, Tathaastu Group's PR Manager and the most visible face there.

Prakrit Kumar, who headed DD-owned 'Deshbandhu TV' was one amongst the team of usherers. Subhashish, the local representative of an English language daily sat wedged between Kranti Kundan and Anil Wilson. Naveen also recognised Sumant and Sohail who worked for the TV Red. He had often interacted with them ever since the Tathaastu controversy sprang up.

"What will you have, young man?" Deshbandhu asked putting his arms around Naveen.

"Nothing, bhaiyyaji… I'm alright."

"Care for a little scotch? This is imported. Can't offer you *ganna* juice here…" The *durban* broke into laughter.

"I will rather eat something," said Naveen as he tentatively stretched out his hand to grab chicken tikka from the triangular-shaped platter offered to him.

'It seems I have made a late entry into the guest list,' Naveen pondered for a long time. He got a call at 6.30 pm from DD, 'requesting' him to attend a small get-together. Seeing the preparations at this small get-together, it was clear the party had been planned much earlier and inviting him over was just an afterthought. *'Why would DD call me at such a short notice? Why would he shower me with so much of attention? Am I reading too much into all this?'* Naveen pondered even more.

Suddenly, DD got up from the sofa and started walking towards another room, to the far end of the hall. Others quickly followed suit. Anil Wilson came up to Naveen and whispered something into his ears. Naveen swiftly sprang up on his legs and followed others on the double.

It was a much smaller room with a set of sofa thrown in and a few chairs. Altamash's instruction came swimming in, *'Smaller the room, better the audio-visual clarity.'* Naveen thought this was just the right room-size for the camera to give its best results. The bartenders also followed, but soon enough they were ticked off by DD with a wave of the hand.

"The idea is to get all the like-minded people together. Such 'chaupaals' only help us grow. Welcome to the inaugural meet, 'DD *ki chaupal*'." DD spoke like he was throwing open the biggest sports meet as the Head of the Host Nation.

Naveen's fingers slid up his shirt pocket and reached the tip of his pen. He was cautious about it, lest it gave away the game. Altamash's instructions came floating back into his mind: '*You have to time it, otherwise the battery will betray you at the most crucial moment.*' He made a rough, mental calculation. He had switched the camera on just as he entered the DD mansion. He had precisely 80 minutes of battery life left.

Dhanpat Deshbandhu aka DD was sitting too close for comfort. '*Will he be able to read the nervousness in my eyes?*' Naveen decided not to pay extraordinary attention to his pen.

"A team of experts is coming to visit the steel plant site next week. What do you think about the new development project in the area?" DD expected to hear euphonious answers. Naveen, on the other hand, had waited for this very moment for ever.

"I think this is the best that could happen to Ullasganj in its entire history, right from the times of Mahabharata," a corporator said.

Another seconded him. "We should welcome Tathaastu with open arms."

"Sir, believe me, the real estate prices are going to shoot up the roof once the project comes up," another corporator chipped in.

"But, the farmers and forest-dwellers are the biggest stumbling block, sir," Kranti Kundan butted in, throwing a disapproving look at Naveen. "People like you should really mobilise people for the project. This is only going to benefit Ullasganj and its people in the long run," he added.

'*Try to participate. Keep them engaged in the discussion.*' Satyendra's words rang in Naveen's ears. "The farmers are not averse to development. They are willing to give barren lands but not the ones which give them source of livelihood. The farmer's very existence is at stake." Naveen contributed to the discussion with his two-penny bit.

"At stake is the development of Ullasganj. We can achieve so much if farmers cooperate with us. Bhai sa'ab has already laid the foundation for a hospital. Moreover, we are working towards opening an intermediate college. If you insist, we will have it opened in your village," Kranti Kundan added.

"The price offered is not acceptable at all. We are worried about our future. There is no rehabilitation and resettlement plan from the government." Naveen persisted.

"That shall come about in due course. Have faith in our government. As for prices, we are ready to give you the market price." DD assured as if he were running the government.

"That does not suffice. Our demand is 50 per cent more than the market price, a job for every displaced family and their next two generations in the new project and, of course, shareholding."

"Don't you think that is unreasonably greedy?" said Kranti Kundan.

"What about the Bhambhuki tribals and other forest-dwellers? They shall be the worst sufferers if Nilamata Parvat, which they rever as their deity, is dug up for minerals." Naveen said inching closer on the sofa edge in excitement.

"Of course...a portion of the Nilamata Parvat shall be ours for a price." Anil butted in.

"You can't do that! You can't put a price to that! Taking permission from the Gram Sabha is mandatory under the new law and the Gram Sabha is not willing to part with even an inch of Nilamata Parvat." Naveen shot back.

"We conducted the public hearing. A set of protestors came up with false claims. Their lands do not come under the forest area, as defined under the law. So, as far as the government is concerned, we have a clean slate. There are no claims for forest rights." Kranti Kundan was visibly provoked as he gulped down a big swig from his glass.

"That is what you have claimed, but it is far from truth Kundan sa'ab." Naveen was direct.

"We have received more than 200 applications from villagers and forest-dwellers who say they have no objection to the project," Kundan shot back.

"People must realise the project is for their own good. Those who know Tathaastu and the Aryan Group are well aware of its expansionist nature." DD barged in.

"Yes, I can see that," Naveen quipped.

"And, sir, Tathaastu is one of our own. Tathaastu is a dream project of Mr Oswal ever since he migrated to the English shores in the early sixties. But, he is much in love with his motherland and wants to give back what he got from it," said Kranti Kundan.

"The law is the same for everyone," said Naveen.

"The government has already drawn the blueprint for rehabilitation and resettlement packages." Kranti Kundan was quick to defend.

"It's not public yet. Where is the hitch? Why can't the government announce its rehabilitation and resettlement programmes to the general satisfaction of all shareholders?" Naveen dug in. "The problem is with the government. Its intention is suspect," Naveen rubbed it in. "The government cannot play the role of a usurper. It is the servant of the public."

"*Arrey*, servant my foot! Do you think I am your bloody servant?" DD flew into a sudden rage.

'Don't get provoked. It tends to end the discussion. Your job is to get the conversation going.' Satyendra's words echoed in Naveen's ears.

"Bhaiyyaji, I was just trying to tell you that the government will have to convince the people about the price and the resettlement and rehabilitation programmes," said Naveen in a rather mellowed voice. "But, unfortunately, the government has already launched the drive to grab the land."

"What do you mean?" Kranti Kundan sounded angry.

"The district collectors' office has fabricated sale deeds in the name of farmers. This is cheating," Naveen said.

"Those are perfectly valid documents. You do not know these people. They have got their due and now they are going to the town, saying they have been cheated," said Kranti Kundan.

"*Dekho* Naveen bhai, you should also think about yourself. You have a great future. Our party shall be proud to induct you as its member. In fact, I will make you an unopposed district president."

"Who shall I serve, if I lose the confidence of my own brethren?" said Naveen.

"Naveen bhai, many youngsters like you have migrated to big cities after selling off their lands. In Chiragganj, villagers have sold off part of their lands and now each house has a couple of SUVs and crores of rupees as bank deposits." DD was direct.

"I know that. But, the land they sold was not meant for irrigation. Perhaps, they did the right thing by selling that off. Whereas the soil in Ullasganj is fertile; it has been a source of livelihood of farmers for generations. Their lies the difference."

"I only know that if you decide, you could make a difference to your life. You shall have two crores credited into your bank account. This would be over and above the price you fetch for selling off your land to the government." DD had sharpened his predatory claws by now.

"Two crores from my party too," Misra jumped in. "But, one wrong decision now and you will regret for life," he remarked in a threatening gesture.

"We can get an account opened in any country across Europe." Wilson sprang to life.

"You quote the price, Naveen bhai. After all, you are like my younger brother." DD threw his trump card.

"That is so nice of you, DD bhai. But, I shall rather keep doing what I am best at," said Naveen with a straight face.

"Tathaastu's parent company—Aryan International—has a big heart. It always recognises the good deeds of friends and well-wishers. You shall get a plot of your choice for each of your family member in the land government earmarks for rehabilitation." Anil Wilson laid out the road map.

"Thank you very much, Aniljji. I shall not be able to digest all that," Naveen said without batting an eyelid. "I shall be happy if you make all those farmers and forest-dwellers stakeholders in your company," he added.

His nervousness had given way to oodles of unprecedented strength. '*They have all come prepared. This is a meeting to buy me over,*' he thought.

"*Behenchod...!*" A booming voice hung through the hall. DD got up from his seat and lunged at Naveen. In one swift movement, he held Naveen by his shirt collar. As Naveen struggled to pull himself free, he could find DD's grip tightening on his neck. DD lifted him from the sofa, dragged him and pushed him to the floor. Naveen tumbled over in two quick loops before falling down. His pen could not handle the sudden violence and fell out of his shirt pocket on the carpeted floor, without making much noise.

Naveen collected his wits, immediately gathered his pen and put it back in his shirt pocket.

"Throw him out!" DD lashed out at Naveen, almost using a whip on him and kicking him in the face brutally.

"You will kill him, bhai sa'ab. Control yourself!" Writhing in pain on the floor, he could see Ram Charan Misra pulling away DD. The two mustached *durbans* came running inside and took Naveen by his arms. As he came out of the living room, he eased his grip free of those muscled men and paced down the stairs. He could see his Marshall parked under a clump of trees, to the left of the portico. As he made it to the vehicle, he adjusted his spy pen one last time before hopping on to the driver's seat.

As he drove out and took the highway, Naveen saw DD's mansion fading in the rear view mirror. He sank further into the seat and smiled at his victory.

Nobody Can Touch You!

Muskan saw Thethar put down his executive leather bag on his table. He was alone this time and the twenty-something babes were not in tow. This was an odd sight for Muskan. Ostracised by colleagues, Thethar had been keeping to himself since the Gayatri episode.

"Gayatri was a fresher, an intern. She claimed that Kumar Amrendra (alias Thethar) misbehaved with her in a hotel room, where he had taken her to meet a political bigwig. While they waited for their host in his room, Kumar Amrendra 'pawed at me. When I resisted, he threatened me of dire consequences'. Those were her exact words in the written complaint submitted to the channel," Anika had told Muskan.

The incident shocked Muskan, but Anika, Assistant Manager (HR—DNN) wasn't surprised. "A couple of interns had come to me earlier with complaints of misconduct against Kumar sir. I discussed those complaints with my seniors, but they would tell me to ignore the complaints as interns were 'not going to stay beyond a month.'"

"If he was indecent with interns, he can misbehave with us too," Muskan sounded angry.

"An intern once complained that Kumar groped her in the office lift. I was furious! I took the matter up with my seniors. 'How do you know she was not doing it for some cheap publicity' was the answer I got!"

"Cheap publicity? I sincerely pray it happened with their daughters. Bencho...! I cannot believe that he is my friend," Muskan thundered.

"Kumar is close to Yashwant sir. Nobody touches him. Sometimes I feel so helpless. The HR is supposed to act as the bridge between the employees and the management, and we end up being pimps of the management." Anika exploded like a volcano at the Mamu's.

"That's not funny, yaar... We have Rati's case staring at us. You guys did not have the guts to take action against Hemendra then," said Muskan.

"And nothing is going to happen to Kumar now," said Anika. "Please don't quote me anywhere. I will be doomed."

"Oh...come on, Anika. Don't be silly. You can trust me on that," Muskan reassured Anika.

Gayatri had stopped coming to office. There was buzz in the newsroom that she had resigned. The management had succeeded in playing down the incident until one day, when *medianautanki.com,* a portal dedicated to news from the world of news channels, splashed Gayatri's interview. She talked in detail about those 'embarrassing five minutes when I resisted with all my might Kumar Amrendra's moves' to take her for a 'loose woman'. He said, 'I should know how to dress up, if I were to make my name in the industry.' The creep then followed it up with an even vulgar comment.

He said, 'You should display what you have. Don't hide it from the world.'

The hits on *Medianautanki.com* multiplied by the hour, so did DNN's embarrassment. The portal was taken off the inventory of sites accessible to the DNN employees. The damage, however, had been done. There was pressure on the channel to conduct an internal inquiry. Gayatri had threatened in the interview that she would approach the Women's Rights Commission (WRC) if the channel management did not punish the employee adequately.

The management's HR Managers swung into damage control operation. Female employees across the two floors were roped in to give out brief interview to *medianautanki.com*. They were effectively tutored to talk about the 'healthy working atmosphere in DNN', which was 'like our home away from home'.

The management put out statements like, 'Gayatri wanted a job with DNN, but failed the internal test. It's a ranting of a failed and frustrated intern.'

The matter died down gradually and the channel threatened to take legal action against the news portal if it tried to stretch the issue any further.

'If people could forget Rati, they could conveniently forget an intern named Gayatri,' Muskan thought. She looked up her computer screen and darted a look at Kumar's table; she could only find the executive leather bag.

Thethar took the lift down to the ground floor. He was furiously looking for a number on his mobile. "Here I come, Nilofar Goradia. Here I come, India Heights..." He was mumbling to himself.

"How are you, ma'am?"

"I am fine, Kumar… Tell me. What's up?"

"I have a breaking news for you."

"Don't tell me if it is a bad one…"

"I would not call you in that event."

"Tell me…it's been long since we have had some good news."

"You are through."

"What…? Kumar, please come to the point straight away."

"Buddha has laughed…boom…!"

"Are you serious?"

"It is two hundred and one per cent confirmed, ma'am. It is going to be Raju at Climate Tower."

"That's really good news, Kumar."

"You will get the official confirmation in a day or two."

"You've made my day. I have always had faith in Yash. He always delivers."

"He is the modern Chanakya. You know he is from Patliputra, I mean, Patna," said Thethar.

"Now, if your words were prophetic, my client would be only too happy to deliver what is expected of him," said Nilofar. "I think it's time for you to live your dream at India Heights," said Nilofar.

"Thank you very much." Thethar was grinning from ear to ear. "When can I see you, ma'am?"

"Very soon, Kumar."

"Sure…will call up and fix the plan."

"Thanks Kumar, you have been a lucky mascot for me."

"Let me also warn you here. Your client is being followed, so keep everything *hush-hush*."

"Don't worry, we will take care of that. Do convey my regards to Yash. Hope to catch up with him, soon," said Nilofar.

"You are always welcome, ma'am!" said Kumar as he pressed the red button on his mobile.

"I am the king-maker. Nobody touches me." Soaked in the luxury of self-admiration, Thethar took long, steady steps towards Mamu's for his puff.

Newsroom Lech

Paagalvaani.blogspot.com

They abound in every newsroom. They are mostly people in position or Team Leaders. They usually target innocent, young girls who are keen to make a mark for themselves, or those who refuse to give in to their threats and harassment. When they are on the prowl, their psyche works along the thought: *The 'net asset' of a girl remains the common denominator for identifying the potential victim.*

They look out for reasons to befriend female colleagues and never lose an opportunity to touch them. With sadomasochistic zeal, such people will go all out to harass and hurt their victims and paint them as 'women of easy virtue' when their overtures are spurned.

Such lech are usually adept at devising new ways to come around a female colleague who has spurned them. This gets reflected in ad hoc allotment of late night shifts, picking faults with their dress code (if they happen to be anchors, or even if they are not, the outfit often becomes the butt of their sexist remarks), allotting them tasks beyond duty hours and passing double meaning remarks.

Such people are usually protected by their seniors and are above, any kind of disciplinary action.

Conclusion:

For a secure workplace environ, such dogs should be taken head on, exposed and made to pay for their misdemeanours. Better still, they should be sent packing to an asylum and given shock treatments, depending on varying degrees of sickness.

Amen...!

Climate Tower, New Delhi: 4.30 pm

"Come on in, Yash," Sriram Raju got up from his chair and greeted Yashwant Thakur halfway through the carpeted floor of his office. "You don't need permission to visit me," he added as he stretched out his hand and led him to his seat across his desk.

"Oh, come on. You are a minister now, Sriram." Yashwant said indulgently.

"Not for friends like you," Raju reached out for his intercom. "Two coffees," he ordered into the mouthpiece.

Beautiful landscapes of varied Himalayan ranges hung in massive photo frames on two side walls of the room. Country's tribal community—spread across the length and breadth of India's terrain—grinned in a 10 megapixel collage in a massive portrait right behind Raju's chair. The Bhambhukis smiled at him from the photo frame, spreading energy into the room. The photo was beautifully captioned, 'Forests Are Necessary For Our Survival'. The wall behind Yashwant was adorned with three somber-looking photos—that of the President of India, the Prime Minister and Chandrashekharan, the President of Sriram's party.

"That's one of the most nicely done up offices of a minister, I have ever visited." Yashwant was quick to indulge Raju.

"The youngest minister ever, mind you. *Simbly the youngest.*" Raju corrected Yashwant.

"Oh, yes, Sriram. How can I forget that! The youngest minister with an independent charge."

"Oh, thank you Yash. You know, I must have spent around 40 lakh on furniture, upholstery, and the entire decor of the room." Raju did not miss the opportunity to boast before Yashwant. "The previous occupant had made a mess of it. Even *Vaastu*-wise it was not OK. That is why, perhaps, the Ministry never hit headlines. I had the necessary *puja* performed to rid the office air of all evils."

"You have an eye for the aesthetics, Sriram."

Sriram Raju was all of 33 and *simbly* (yes, his 'P' always sounded like a 'B') the Minister for Environment and Forest, all thanks to his political mentor and the President of Arm Twister Party of India (ATPI), Chandrashekharan, who, with his army of 11 MPs waited in the wings for three years for the right moment to strike. The opportunity came by when the Gate Crasher Party of India (GCPI), with a Big Iron Gate as its election symbol, pulled out from the Freedom Party of India (FPI)—popular among voters as Family Party of India—led UPDGA (United Parties for Democratic Governance by Alliance) alliance in New Delhi.

The GCPI subsequently brought a no confidence motion against the government during the coming monsoon session. The GCPI was egged on by a combined opposition. The UPDGA had, by now, become more popular as UPNDGA—

United Parties for Non-Democratic Governance by Alliance—given the FPI's penchant for taking important decisions without consulting its allies. A mid-term election was the most imminent prospect, a clear 18 months before schedule. Chandrashekharan, an arch rival of GCPI's Arvind Ramachandran, was quick to smell the political air and stepped in to fill the vaccum created by the exit of GCPI. The government was saved by a whisker. Though a small win, it took the winds out of the opposition sail. Chandrashekharan became the cynosure of FPI.

"See, Yash. I have a dream. I want to turn this Ministry around. I thought I should start from changing my office décor. What do you say?"

"Brilliant! That's a philosophy not many understand. Change always has to come from within," said Yashwant.

"My boss is a visionary. Only he knows the development potential of a Ministry. And thanks to good friends like you, I am here despite the Prime Minister's reservation on my name. But the way you broke the New Delhi ice, was *simbly* superb. The boss has a special place for you in his heart. He counts you as a friend."

"Tell him I will ever be an active partner in the construction of New India of his vision," said Yashwant.

"I have had a word with the Chief Minister Praveen Kumar early today. He is sending in his Chief Secretary, Mr John Fernandez. He shall be here any moment."

"Hope you have assured him we are his friends."

"Of course, yes, but he would like a personal assurance from you," said Yashwant.

Sriram Raju's intercom buzzed. The minister picked it up. "Send him in."

"Very good afternoon, sir!" Mr Fernandez stretched out his hands towards the minister as he took the seat right across from his desk.

"This is Mr Yashwant Thakur of the famous DNN."

"Oh, yes, the world knows him. He is a celebrity, an icon," said Mr Fernandez.

"Let's sit on the sofa there." Raju gestured his two guests towards the plush sofa as he got up from his swivel chair.

"This is of an imported leather from Italy," Raju said pointing out to the off-white sofa with unabashed pride as they all sank into it.

"Yes, Mr Fernandez, tell me."

"Sir, the situation is getting out of hand. The protests are rising by the day. We are made to look like thieves," said Fernandez.

"Well, did you not expect a single protest on the ground? Tell me frankly."

"We did, sir, but frankly it's swelling out of proportion," said Fernandez. "The court case has further compounded our problems," he added.

"I have studied the project documents. We have a way to get around the court." Raju didn't rush and oozed confidence.

"The court case only gets bolstered by the last report of your Ministry which expresses certain reservations against the project." Said Fernandez.

"There was a dissent note in that report. On that basis alone, I shall order another inquiry into the allegations of environmental impact." Raju laid out the strategy plan before Fernandez.

"Hope the court does not pronounce any unfavourable order by then." Fernandez replied.

"*Fait accompli*, Mr Fernandez. *Fait accompli*. We shall have proceeded to a significant stage in the project by then," said Raju with a chuckle.

Yashwant looked assuringly at Fernandez, whereas Fernandez looked quizzically at Raju.

"I will set up a new committee to look into the project. Meanwhile, tell Praveen Kumarji to write a letter to the Prime Minister." Sriram went on to dictate the draft of the proposed letter: "OK, here it is... Tell the Prime Minister that any delay from Delhi will adversely impact development of the state. The delay shall also jeopardise national interest. This is a test case for multinationals and NRIs who want to bring the money back to India. We cannot afford to reverse the process. The project shall generate direct & indirect employment for 400,000 people from across three states. A fresh environmental assessment study should be undertaken. The court should be taken into confidence over the efficacy of the last ministerial report. Post this letter ASAP and ask Pravinji to send a high-level delegation to New Delhi. Meanwhile, get another environmental impact study done and leave the rest to us," said Raju.

"Sir, we have another problem at hand. Mr Sidhartha Sawhney is visiting the area next week to show his solidarity with Bhambhuki tribals, who are also going to get displaced by the project," said Fernandez.

"So, let him go." Sriram said with a wave of his hand.

"Sir, but that will only lend credence to the protestations. What the Chief Minister sa'ab fears is that Sidhartha might just take the project back to square one. We are already behind schedule."

"If only Sidhartha could get his trip cancelled," said Yashwant. "And only you can persuade him since he is your friend," he added.

"Well, I don't meddle into his politics. I know he is your friend too, Yash. But let me share a secret with you if it does not travel outside the four walls of this room. I don't think Sidhartha understands politics. If he is trying to fish for a constituency among tribals, he is sorely mistaken. They behave differently in different states."

"But the general perception is that he favours the underdog," said Yashwant.

"He is no Super Dog. My boss is the Super Dog of this alliance." Yashwant had hit the bull's eye. It was so easy to provoke Sriram.

"Let him do whatever he wants. You go ahead with your exercise. Bring out a report and I promise New Delhi will give a stamp of approval," continued Raju, sounding pompous as expected.

Yashwant and Fernandez looked at each other. And then both of them turned their gaze at Sriram Raju.

"It's so *simble*. We have the people's mandate for development. Nothing could stand between development and nation-building. Put out advertisements across media publications in your state. I will take care of it from my end. This should take the sting out of Sidhartha's visit."

"Nilofar shall also be briefed." Yashwant assured the gentlemen.

"Don't worry! You will have your project through." Raju told Fernandez.

"My Chief Minister wants his state to be the number one state in the country," said Fernandez.

"You want your state to be number one, I want my Ministry to be number one , my boss wants ATPI to be the number one Arm-Twister Party of India, Yashwant wants DNN to be the number one news channel. We are all committed soldiers to our cause. India's future is secure in our hands." Yashwant and Fernandez listened with rapt attention to Raju's *simble* philosophy.

"Sir, I know there is a poet that resides in your heart. And a poet can never allow injustice," said Fernandez.

"*Arrey*, Fernandez sir, you don't know his poetic skills. He is also the chief slogan-writer for his party. He keeps doodling short poems on his BlackBerry," said Yashwant...and then turning to Raju, he muttered: "I think it's high time you came out with a book of your poems, Sriram."

"Oh, come on, Yash. I am a nobody."

"No, seriously. I have even thought of the name of your book, '*Simbly*, His Master's Voice'." Yashwant broke into laughter and stretched out his hands to Raju to seek his endorsement.

"No, no, I am a nobody. God has given me the opportunity to serve my guru and mentor. I am committed to give him *guru-dakshina*."

"Amen..." said Yashwant.

"Amen..." said Fernandez as he stood up from the sofa to take leave.

"Amen...!"

The echo could be heard across the hill ranges mounted on the photo frames on the office walls. Bhambhukis let out a exhausted smile. Chandrashekharan beamed at his prodigy from the photo frame.

With Fernandez gone, Sriram opened up before Yashwant: "I don't know how Nilu would react. Try to calm her if you get to talk to her. I told her I can't stop Sidhartha but I will ensure things don't go out of control."

"Don't worry. She is a clever lady. I will handle her." Yashwant assured, stretched out his hand and got ready to take leave.

But Sriram was not yet finished: "I have a message for you from my boss. He wants to gift you something unique."

"I did not get you?" Yashwant sank back in his chair.

"Come on, Yashwant. Time to give flight to your ambitions."

"Please don't talk in riddles, Sriram. What is it?"

"After what you have done for the party, boss was keen to return the favour. It's high time you got a Padma Award." Sriram Raju took Yashwant by pleasant surprise. For a brief moment, Yashwant's thoughts travelled all the way to the Rashtrapati Bhavan and imagined receiving the coveted Padma Shri from the honourable President of India. Yashwant could feel a thousand crackers burst inside him. *'It's going to be an extraordinary Diwali this time,'* thought Yashwant, but pretended to be normal before Sriram.

"I don't think the time is right," said Yashwant.

"Well, there could not be a more appropriate time than this," said Raju. "The boss has already directed Som Sundaram at the Ministry of Culture to do the needful. Yours shall be the strongest recommendation to the Home Ministry. I don't think even the FPI would have any reservation over your name. Hope Sidhartha does the rest."

Yashwant could not contain the excitement. "I really am thankful to this great motherland, that it has a special place in her heart for her worthy sons. I feel honoured, Sriram."

"Go back home and have a toast with Shalini. You deserve it." Sriram got up from his seat, came around his table and shook hands with Yashwant before taking him into warm embrace.

"Give my regards to Mr Chandrashekharan," said Yashwant.

"You already have his blessings. Amen...!"

Fear

In the rear view mirror, he could see a mass of light from the truck's high beam headlight that almost blinded him. On other days, he would not have grown suspicious. But, with his wife and his six year old son in the car, Satyendra was not just a hot shot reporter. He could see a truck trailing his car from the last twenty minutes. The father in him feared the worst. He cursed himself for having set out late from his brother-in-law's place, where they had gone to attend on his son's '*mundan*' ceremony.

What if the truck-borne men courted some dangerous intent? The lonely stretch of the highway only aggravated his fears. He knew that the villages were few and far between on that highway and even if he were to shout for help, the darkness will absorb his screams and would not let it travel afar. For the first time he realised that having a mobile phone is not reassuring. By the time any help would arrive, it would be too late. And sharing his fears with his wife would mean attending on her, rather than working on an escape route.

For the moment, his car was the only secure place. And the fastest he could enter the city periphery— and also the point where he would find a police check post—was a clean 30-minute drive from that stretch.

When he tried to slow down to check the reaction of the truck tailing him, the truck slowed down too. His fears were confirmed. He pressed on the accelerator. Ritika could feel the sudden uneasiness which had taken over her husband. He had suddenly gone silent and the car had picked up sudden spurt of speed. "What's wrong, Satya? Don't you think you are crossing a threshold?" Satyendra ignored her and kept driving, darting looks at the rear view mirror and the side view mirror like a sprinter who sneaks a furtive look behind as he inches close to the finish line, reassuring himself that his rivals are, at least, a pace or two behind.

"What is it, Satya? Why don't you say something? Why are you driving so fast? There's Saagar also with us, do you have any idea what you are upto?" Ritika was now losing patience with her husband.

"It's nothing, just that I am reminded of a task I was supposed to have completed and dispatched it to the headquarters by evening."

"Come on, you took an off today. It could be postponed for tomorrow as well." Ritika sounded pricky.

"I had promised I would deliver it by 7 pm. I thought we would return by 5.30-6.00 pm. We should have left early."

"So, what if we got late? It is not often that we visit my brother. When do you get time from your busy office schedule?" Ritika snapped.

Satyendra chose to remain silent. But Ritika continued, "At the moment, our safety is more important than your office assignment. Why don't you slow down? It's a highway, damn it! It's dark!"

"This is precisely why I am trying to get out of this place as soon as I can." Satyendra's pitch was a tad lower than a shout. Satyendra was a patient man. He didn't like to talk rudely with his wife because every time he did that, she would go into a deep sulk and getting her back from that recess was too taxing an exercise. But, this time around, he didn't mind taking the risk. His shriek scored an expected result; Ritika moved further into the corner of the seat, leaned towards the door, rested her elbow on the car window and stared blankly outside. Saagar had dozed off on the back seat.

The truck moved closer. He honked hard. There was no vehicle in front of him, but Satyendra honked incessantly. This was one of the ways to banish fears from his mind and feel reassured, or so he thought.

Ritika sat puzzled and chose to remain silent. Satyendra ceased honking, but his fears refused to die down.

He saw the silhouette of what could be a police beat box. When he saw the barricades, it opened the floodgates of happiness. '*Yes! Yes! I have made it. I have made it,*' he thought to himself. The police check post was now clearly visible in the high beam of his City. He could also see a constable loitering about, holding the ubiquitous *lathi*. He slowed down and manoeuvred his vehicle neatly through the barricades. The constable came up to the driver's side and tapped the window. Satyendra wound the window down. Even as the constable threw the torch beam inside the car, Satyendra's eyes groped for the truck in the rear view mirror. As far as his eyes could take him, there was pitch darkness on the road and not a trace of any moving vehicle. The two white masses of dazzling lights had disappeared.

But what triggered a fresh stab of worry was the thought: '*Why was that truck trailing me?*'

Late that night he wrote a quote by Mohandas Karamchand Gandhi in his blue diary:

There would be nothing to frighten you if you refuse to be afraid.

Part III

New India

Yuvraj

"I shall go there, irrespective of the pressure of alliance," said Sidhartha Sawhney, the young MP and General Secretary, FPI, as he worked on the treadmill.

"That should be a wise decision. You don't need to bow to any pressure." Yashwant was quick to add.

Loose Control gymnasium was their rendezvous point. Sidhartha was a fitness freak and worked out at the gym every alternate day. Yashwant was not as regular, but he looked forward to working out with Sidhartha if he had an important issue at hand.

"What could be the pros and cons of my visit to Ullasganj?" Sidhartha asked Yashwant, having slightly raised the speed on the treadmill.

"You must go ahead... you have nothing to lose."

"I believe Sriram is coming out with a favourable report on Tathaastu's environment impact," said Sidhartha.

"Even if Sriram okays the project, your visit to the tribal areas shall only enhance your image as the leader of the downtrodden," said Yashwant. "You are not a minister yet and, that's an advantage," he added as he tweaked his pace on the machine.

"You see, Yashwant, FPI (Sidhartha always referred to his party in the third person. This was a meticulously rehearsed stand to blunt the opposition sting that 'he used the party as his fiefdom') highly values its relationship with Mr Chandrashekharan. I know it's a one-man show. If you ask me, I find Sriram bright and intelligent. We debuted the same elections to enter Parliament. He's a friend. But I also know why Mr Chandrashekharan was desperate to get this Ministry for his man," said Sidhartha as he got down from the treadmill and wiped his sweat with the hand towel.

Yashwant could see the plain-clothed commandoes standing guard outside the huge glass wall—watching Sidhartha's each and every move—as he searched for a dry hand towel inside his kit.

"Probably, you are right! Mr Chandrashekharan's philosophy is no secret, but I guess this is just a small price for sustaining the coalition government."

"You guys seem to be ignoring the whole issue." Sidhartha changed the topic of discussion. "I have not seen one decent report on the Tathaastu project on news channels. I am utterly disappointed by media coverage."

"Well, there is so much happening around us these days that we have to become rather selective." Yashwant tried to evade a direct answer.

"I expected media to, at least, take up the issue of killing of farmers in that firing. But you guys had such a hands-off approach as if you were going to contact plague," Sidhartha put it bluntly.

"You see a vote bank among tribals and downtrodden, but those are not the people who constitute our viewer base," said Yashwant.

"Don't know what your viewer base is, but frankly I loved the Cash-For-Question Undercover Operation against members of the Parliament. That shook the system. But, that again seems like some other era. The media has re-discovered India suddenly. Like those *phirang* tourists, your idea of India does not transcend beyond babas, sadhus, *nag-nagin*, the weird and the exotic… Isn't it? So, things like Tathaastu fall off your radar, but I am sure if there is an X amount of returns on what you put on air, there must be a hidden agenda behind what you people don't show?" Sidhartha was unstoppable. "I always thought we politicians have been bequeathed a rather warped culture, devoid of morals and ethics, but I turn to media and find we run the risk of losing our monopoly." His sarcasms were unmistakable.

Yashwant put up a patient hearing, but desperately waited his turn. "Well, Sidhartha, you can forgo a berth in the cabinet because you know the crown shall be yours for the asking one day. You are the Yuvraj today and a king tomorrow. You hail from a political family. Those are beautiful constants in your life. Our lives are marred by vagaries of change. I would rather allow myself to be led by the market, than write my own epithet trying to be different." Sidhartha was in rapt attention. He always liked Yashwant for being brutally honest about his take on life.

"You don't encourage inner party democracy. Those who raise their voices are dumped forever, those who do business over farmers' dead bodies are invested with greater responsibilities by your party supremo," Yashwant said with a chuckle. "Half of your ministers have not delivered. And can you take any guarantee about the misdemeanours of your alliance partners? Balendu Rai, your oldest alliance partner, visited the most dreaded criminal Mujtaba Alam in jail to chalk out his party's election strategy. You hate Mr Chandrashekharan's politics, but your government is living off his support. One of your alliance partners is playing havoc with medical administration of the country. Despite the CAG reporting thousands of crores of scam in the Transport Ministry, you can't remove the Minister because you need even his crutches to run the government. The power snuff is too overwhelming, Sidhartha. The marriage of convenience is dictated by the same market forces. Market does not discriminate, it does not spare you either." Yashwant suddenly realised he had rather pushed the envelope. "I am sorry, I think I got carried away. Please don't mind my soliloquy," he said with a tentative smile on his face.

"Oh...come on, Yashwant," said Sidhartha. "You know I like people who speak their mind. By the way, that only strengthens my belief that you should be making such speeches in Parliament."

"Not my cup of tea." Yashwant responded.

"Get out of that mind-set, you are made for greater things in life."

Sidhartha's symbolism was not lost on Yashwant. "Well, thanks so much! But, I don't think I am cut out for that," said Yashwant. "Why do you want to drag me into this dirty world of politics?" Yashwant sounded humble.

"You are now also an entrepreneur. I see no reason why you can't wear another hat—that of a politician. Youngsters like you must come forward to participate actively in politics and help India stride the world stage like a true leader. Let me speak to FPI high command. You must give it a thought."

"Well, only if you insist. Let me discuss with Shalini and Rahul. In fact, Rahul is eighteen and shall be an eligible voter when the country goes to polls next." Yashwant doted on his teenage son, Rahul, who had qualified for IIM (A).

"Let the father son duo make history next year. While the father makes his debut in politics, the son debuts as country's enlightened voter." Sidhartha was developing the art of pitching it right.

"I can't say a 'yes' to you right away," said Yashwant in his vain effort to sound humble.

"I have high hopes from Rahul. I am sure he will catch the spirit of my thought," said Sidhartha.

"He is a big fan of yours," said Yashwant indulgently. "In fact, he requested me the other day if you could visit the IIM campus for a lecture soon."

"Sure, I will, if only they think I can deliver," said Sidhartha reassuringly.

"So when do you plan to leave for Ullasganj?"

"Next Thursday."

Boy O Boy...!

Himmatganj

"Sir, it's been ages since you treated me to some real stuff." Satyendra was polite but the complaint in his tone was unmistakable. He was referring to Prof. Misra's collection of imported scotch. He knew Professor Misra would not mind his informal tone. Their acquaintance went back to the days in the capital city of Himmatganj when fame had not touched either. Satyendra Mahto came from Singhbhum—then part of undivided Bihar—as a Bureau Chief working with a national daily, desperately trying to find his feet in the new terrain and Misra taught Political Science at the State University.

Misra wrote articles for the newspaper for which Satyendra worked. Satyendra remembered he had gone up to Misra once to get his opinion on a research series he had planned, on criminal-politician nexus in the mineral rich state. The story went on to become the talk of the town. *Satyendra had arrived.* Misra's writings drew the attention of the incumbent Chief Minister Praveen Kumar, who had taken over his father's political mantle after having stayed and taught in a college in Australia.

Misra's ten-point charter laid the foundation of Praveen Kumar's government. It became common knowledge that if Praveen Kumar was the face, Kanti Kumar Misra was the brain behind that face. He became the CM's mentor. It was said that the government was not run from 7 Mahatma Gandhi Marg, the official residence of the Chief Minister, but from 10 Kautilya Enclave, the official residence of Misra as the Political Advisor to the CM.

All policy decisions of Praveen Kumar government had the 'Misra touch'. Signing an MOU with the Aryan International for the Tathaastu Steel Project was one such. However, the bonhomie between the two began to wear thin as Praveen Kumar gave in to whisper campaign, launched by a section of his own partymen, who dubbed him as sissy and incapable of running a government without the 'Chanakya' Misra.

In the last six months, the CM had taken a string of decisions independent of Misra, in a bid to get out of his shadow. Misra maintained a discreet silence and took to his parliamentary work (he was nominated to the Rajya Sabha two years ago) rather seriously and spent more time in New Delhi. But he would keep coming back to Himmatganj. His Himmatganj visits no longer evoked media response. He was dumped by the media that realised Prof. Misra was no longer a TRP material.

Satyendra had an inkling that Prof. Misra was desperate to share some of the lesser known secrets about Praveen Kumar's style of governance and his recent moves on Tathaastu project, which, according to the Professor had skidded off the state's development highway.

Satyendra could read that Misra did not want to be seen as plotting a smear campaign against the CM, but it hurt his ego if he did not teach his former student a befitting lesson. He wanted the whole thing to look like a set-up. Satyendra wanted to make the most of Professor's dilemma.

"I am no longer useful to you guys. Why would anybody come to me now?" That was a voiced dipped in hurt, loneliness and disappointment. Satyendra had struck the right chord.

"You are the Tathaastu man, Professor. You brought the biggest development project to the state. When can I see you?" Satyendra indulged the Professor.

"Anytime! It's been longest since we met," he replied.

An appointment with the Professor meant a session of VAT 69, a raucous session over Professor's anecdotes recalling the 'fun-and-frolic' at the 'all-boys' nights at 7, Chanakya Avenue, juicy stories on Praveen Kumar's 'boyfriends' from Mumbai film industry, including the latest rage Riz Khan who was also signed in as the State's Brand Ambassador.

"The camera shall be fitted on your shirt button." Altamash was explaining the operation of spy camera to Satyendra. "It shall be part of you, so stay normal, stay cool," he assured.

"I don't want to cheat on Professor Misra, but can't help it. That's the demand of the profession. I hope I will be able to pull it off." The nervous excitement was writ large on Satyendra's face.

"Trust me. It shall be the world's cleanest sting. You will have a scoop tomorrow morning," Altamash reassured Satyendra.

"I believe he had had a fight with Riz when he came calling last month. They have not yet made up." Professor Misra rocked with laughter, his breath stinking of VAT 69 whisky.

"Come, I'll show you something." Professor Misra picked up his glass, led Satyendra along a deep aisle towards the back of the house and slipped into a dark room. Once Satyendra was inside, Prof. secured the door with a latch. When the lights came on, Satyendra could see a lineup of book shelves ranged against each other, each running almost up to the ceiling. In between two shelves to the left, a squarish wooden three feet by two feet plank thrust out of the wall. Prof. drew the chair in front of the wooden plank adorned with a flat panel Dell computer monitor, beckoned Satyendra to pull the red beanbag and sit next to him.

"You think I am joking." Prof. Misra sounded grave as if he will turn the student out of the class if caught mimicking behind his back the next time. He played around with the mouse for some time before clicking on a clip on the windows player. '*A picture speaks a thousand words,*' Satyendra could write a whole book on the visuals running in front of him on the damned computer screen. The pixels broke at points, but Satyendra could not miss the fast-paced movement of a human mouth, opening and closing on a taut muscle shaft of a penis.

The man with his back to the camera faintly resembled CM Praveen Kumar, while Anil Wilson smiled every time he released his mouth after a satisfying session.

In the next 12 minutes of the film, the silhouetted man got exposed by the camera as the two swap positions. The following 'spy cam shot clip' proved beyond doubt that the Chief Minister preferred to play the passive partner but dictated the moves with authority at his command.

"When was that? I can't believe it!" Satyendra was shocked beyond belief. He was so overtaken by the emotions running on the computer screen that he forgot the button camera was recording it all for him.

"You guys think Chief is one smart guy...*huh*...? You forget, I am his guru and shall ever remain so," said Prof. Misra. Satyendra could read confidence in Prof's voice and disdain for his former student. "Prraveeeeen Kumaaaarrrr can be beaten at his own game. I can destroy that man. The public that voted him to power will pull him down from his throne. They will not even wait for the next elections."

Satyendra had no reason to disbelieve Prof. Misra. "You took quite a risk there, Prof.?"

"Well, that's what I teach my students. That's what I taught Praveen. You have got to take risks in life."

'*This can be the biggest scoop in a journalist's career.*' Satyendra thought. '*What could be a better proof of a Chief Minister getting fucked regally by the PR manager of a multinational company?*' The visuals said it all.

"When these guys started out the project, there was a clear intention of paying off the farmers at 50 per cent more than the market rate," said Prof. Misra as he paused the windows player, freezing Praveen and Anil in a tight embrace and Anil taking stance to ride his VVIP partner.

"I had worked out a shareholding for the farmers and tribals in the project. But what Praveen is doing now is simply not what I had envisaged. He has Tathaastu up his arse now and he can't wriggle out of it." The swivel chair rocked with Professor's roaring laughter.

"So he messed up the whole project?"

"The farmers and villagers were to be properly rehabilitated in the neighbouring district. I had drawn up the rehabilitation and resettlement plan after speaking to local

NGOs and experts. Things were very smooth until this guy had a change of heart. He dumped me and took dictation straight from the Oswals."

"But why this change of heart?" Satyendra probed.

"He got greedy. He was misled by his advisors. His hold over the electorate has considerably slipped in the last 12 months. Results of two bye-elections and 12 corporation elections have only proved his declining popularity. So, he panicked and made some unworthy promises to the Oswals."

"The Oswals played carrot danglers?"

"A hefty amount of 200 crores in Indian currency was stashed in the Bank of Europe. Of the steel city the Oswals are supposed to build, a green patch of 100 acres will be developed as Golf Course and around that an enclave for the CM, his cronies, friends and relatives will be built."

Satyendra realised this was perhaps the only interview (or rather a covert operation) which did not require questions to be asked. Secrets tumbled out in free fall, like skeletons from the cupboard.

"Look at this," Prof. Misra opened his Gmail account to show a clutch of emails that passed between the CM's office and him on Tathaastu Steel Project. "I had clearly laid out that Oswals will distribute two per cent of company stocks to farmers and villagers, whose land would be eaten up by the project. Now, the promised two per cent is being gobbled up by Praveen and his cronies. I had laid out a detailed plan for employment for each displaced family, their generation and so on. It's all there in official noting. You can always crosscheck the official files."

"But the real trouble now seems to be New Delhi."

"Well, that too has been taken care of. Why do you think the ATPI got Forest and Environment Ministry? The FPI nominee and former Minister, Kuldeep Singh questioned the environmental impact and the violation of green laws by the Tathaastus. He had to pay the price for this. What Sriram Raju will do is anybody's guess," said the Professor.

"If you say Tathaastu was your baby, how come you planned to uproot the tribals?" Satyendra asked point-blank.

"Journalists never take pains to study the documents. The original MOU never mentioned about the villages inhabited by the Bhambhukis. The tribal villages were to remain untouched. But Oswals laid claim to Nilamata Parvat too and they got Praveen to sign a fresh MOU."

"Could RTI help solve the mystery in this regard?"

"Try your luck in New Delhi. You know fairly well that the state does not have an Information Commissioner yet."

"Why don't you come out in public and expose the CM?"

"I can't. He will have me killed. His table courts the most anti-social elements of the society. They are the ones who are most likely to get tickets for the next year's Vidhan Sabha elections," said Misra. "You should launch an extensive probe into it."

"So, the poor farmers and forest-dwellers shall never get justice, either by the State or by the Centre?"

"Expecting any justice from the State Government is like looking for a needle in a hay stack. And you must not forget, Satyendra it's a non-democratic governance by alliance at the Centre." The Professor laughed at his own intended pun.

Satyendra only hoped his button-eye caught the entire action in 70 mm.

Haldi Shows His Colours

Sir, we have got them," Haldi was on phone at his breakfast table.

"Who are these gentlemen?"

"Deshraj Deenbandhu and Ram Charan Misra, the leader of opposition."

"I am delighted! Deenbandhu is not only Praveen Kumar's younger brother, but also his finance manager." Yashwant sounded as excited.

"Ram Charan Misra is the leader of the opposition in the State Assembly." Haldi showed off his knowledge.

"Are they quoting any price?" Yashwant asked.

"No and yes. The offers are interesting and for everyone to hear."

"I hope the audio-visual quality is not choppy."

"The visuals are sharp for a spy cam, the sound, too, is crisp."

"That's wonderful!"

"The second undercover is a real scoop," Jagat was unable to hold his excitement. "Imagine the CM giving a blowjob to Tathaastu chap Wilson. It is proved beyond doubt that Praveen Kumar is gay," added Jagat.

"Satyendra hit the bull's-eye two times in a row!!"

"Operation Deep Woods has been a super success." Haldi replied in a self-congratulatory tone.

"Superb! Get the recording in your charge." Yashwant directed on the phone.

"It's already in my possession, every bit of it," said Jagat gleefully.

"But, remember, the stories are not to be aired unless I give the go ahead," Yashwant coached.

"Satyendra is getting impatient with the story, he is trying for a few more documents from his sources. You know how meticulous he is," Jagat replied.

"We should have these goddamned politicians by their balls. Having said that, my old brief stands. I shall take the final call."

"Yes boss, don't you worry." Jagat replied in endorsement.

"Be discreet about it with Satyendra. He is an emotional guy."

"Sure, don't worry…will handle that."

"Well, best of luck to you guys! Before I forget, please mail me the coverage plan of Sidhartha's Ullasganj visit." Yashwant instructed.

"Sure, you shall have that by evening," said Jagat. "By the way, Nilofar called to ask me about our coverage plan. I told her we are covering it LIVE." Jagat added.

"Don't worry. Will speak to her on the issue, you go ahead with your plans." Yashwant was unequivocal.

"Got it, sir."

"Do remind her that she has to update me on Narottambhai Oswal's itinerary, so we can work out our dates for New India Achievers Awards."

"Sure, will do."

Stop Sidhartha!

"Good morning, Yash. Hope I did not disturb you," Nilofar Goradia's early morning call did not surprise Yashwant.

"Oh, not, Nilu. I was about to leave for office," said Yashwant matter-of-factly.

"Narottam bhai has sent his good wishes to you," said Nilofar.

"How is he doing?" There was perceptible warmth in Yashwant's voice.

"He was delighted to hear the progress in the case. He told me Yashwant can never compromise on national interest."

"Well, that's very nice of Narottam bhai."

"He is of the firm view that the Tathaastu Steel Project will not only brighten up lives of farmers, but shall also boost the growth of the country. When it comes to the nation, he is touchy and sentimental. You know him."

"I know. He has had a humble upbringing. He is a grounded person." Yashwant was a tad generous with his praise for Mr Narottam Oswal.

"I am hearing about Sidhartha going to Ullasganj," Nilofar was talking business now.

"Well, that is right," Yashwant responded.

"I just spoke to Sriram and he confirmed the news to me. This is bad news for us. This does not augur well for our project." Nilofar could not hide her anger.

"Those are two separate things," Yashwant maintained his cool.

"No, the two issues are intrinsically interlinked. Those farmers and tribals haven't had enough or what? Six of them died in the last firing. We, I mean Mr Praveen Kumar and I thought that will deter them from taking up cudgels against us. How much more blood do they want to shed?" Nilofar's statement was followed by a pregnant silence.

Though he did nothing for their cause blanking out bit coverage from his channel, those chilling words coming from a ruthless corporate lobbyist gnawed at the remnants of Yashwant's conscience.

"You can't silence them by guns," Yashwant snapped.

"My client only wants peace. If the price of peace is violence, then so be it," Nilofar spoke like a pugnacious lawyer tearing the opposition apart in the court.

"Sidhartha shall not do anything that shall stoke violence, I suppose," said Yashwant.

"But, don't you see Sidhartha's visit acting as a cannon fodder for those staunchly opposing the project?" Nilofar's tone pitched low this time.

"Your fears are unfounded. I told you…keep the two things separately. Sidhartha does not represent your client," Yashwant almost failed in keeping his emotions in check.

"It shall be good for my client if Sidhartha changed his plan. I banked on both you and Sriram…you would be able to stop him in his tracks."

"Tribals and farmers are Sidhartha's constituency, he has been raising his voice for their cause. Praveen Kumar is a part of the opposition coalition. You can't stop anyone from pursuing his or her political agenda. We are living in a democracy." Yashwant was unequivocal.

"I am only concerned about Tathaastu, that's it." Nilofar shot back.

"As far as Tathaastu is concerned, Sriram is doing his bit. His mentor Mr Swamy and Praveenji were once part of the same coalition. They share a good rapport. Remember, Nilofar, we had won the Tathaastu battle the day Sriram took over the Ministry," Yashwant poured out his take on real politik.

"But, Sidhartha might just need Praveenji's support after the next general elections." It was Nilofar's turn to surprise Yashwant.

"What do you mean?"

"Vishy is not doing well on his political turf and you know that well. He desperately needs this project to lift his image and party coffers. Must tell you, he is not averse to hopping sides if that suits his interest," Nilofar almost echoed Yashwant's political calculations about Praveen Kumar, which he never shared in public. He knew a shrewd politician like Praveen Kumar would pull every string to stay in power. Yashwant knew that Praveen Kumar worked on a very fundamental premise: *everything had a price.*

"I still don't get you," Yashwant feigned cluelessness.

"You have heard me, Yashwant. Sidhartha has to think long-term," Nilofar persisted.

"I am not running the FPI, ma'am. These are things beyond my control," Yashwant shot back.

"So what happens to our project?"

"We have taken care of that!"

"I heard you guys are covering Sidhartha's visit LIVE."

"That's what we plan to do," Yashwant said matter-of-factly.

"I thought the issue will not figure on DNN's agenda. I trusted you for that!"

"Sidhartha is adamant. He is a young leader and a Prime Minister in waiting. We must not forget that. The press follows him everywhere, we have to beat the competition. Can't help it!" Yashwant argued.

"My only concern is Tathaastu," Nilofar was not willing to be put down by argument.

"Don't worry. The LIVE coverage shall be a touch and go."

"That's enough to dash our hopes. I thought Sriram and you will work out things to our mutual advantage," Nilofar was adamant.

"Nothing untoward is going to happen. Unless, of course, Sidhartha decides to sit on a fast unto death."

"You are scaring me," Nilofar's voiced frustration and panic.

"No need not be scared. That's what I told Praveenji as well. The script has already been worked out," Yashwant reassured Nilofar.

"Hope you are serious."

"As serious as your one-night flings," Yashwant teased her playfully wrong. She could hear him break into a mighty laugh. "How is your new boyfriend doing? All of twenty-two, I heard, dear mommy."

"Why do I get these funny names?" She feigned annoyance at being called a 'mommy' by Yashwant.

"He must be less than half your age, isn't it?" Yashwant rubbed it in.

"Oh, come on, Yash. You know how boys are. But this one is such a cutie pie. He is the most obedient."

"Obedient, hey...wait a second, so you are playing his teacher?"

"Well, Karan is such an adorable baby," Nilofar was willing to play along. She sounded as if she was dying to tom-tom her latest possession like one of those gowns she picked up from Harrods at London last summer. "He is such a darling. He is an ace jockey. You should come and watch him at the Mahalaxmi Race Course sometime."

"*Aah*! Best of luck with the horse, mommy. Have a beautiful ride!" Yashwant said playfully.

"Hope the plan works out to our collective advantage," Nilofar was back to business.

"It will," Yashwant replied.

"Let's hope for the best."

"Hope Narottam bhai does not reschedule his visit..." Yashwant changed the topic.

"Unlikely. You will have his itinerary in your mailbox by tonight," said Nilofar.

"We are running against time, will have to be quick with our invites for the New India Achievers Award," said Yashwant sounding a trifle exasperated.

"He is a true 'Son Of The Soil'. He can never betray his '*maati*', his own motherland," Nilofar hung up with those reassuring words.

Wedding

Paagalvaani.blogspot.com

A recent survey by a news channel shows that trivia sells. The animal kingdom of the fabled Panchatantra has now come to life on news channels and is on track to becoming the new national icon. The *nag-nagin* is the most voted 'made-for-each-other' couple on prime time, their revenge stories beating Salim-Javed's most celebrated film scripts by a mile. The nation has awakened to a new conscience dictated by news channels, peddling the most ridiculous and the most banal.

What does the future hold?

If you are still not among those blessed by the coveted national nag-nagin couple, you have another opportunity knocking your TV sets tonight. The number one claimant—Visphot—is showing you the grand wedding of nag-nagin at 9 pm. Do attend the ceremony and bless the newlyweds.

RSVP: The entire Visphot team and the rival channels (who sure will retrieve library footage on their innumerable nag-nagin fables to counter Visphot's mega TRP offering).

Mata Karuneshwari

Raman and Binny were the firsts to contribute for the weekend office party.

Tanya came up to Sabir with a notebook tucked under her arm, "Your contribution, sir..."

"What contribution...?"

"For the party, sir!"

"What party? Are you getting married?"

"No no... I hate this marriage-*sharriage*. I want your contribution for the weekend bash."

"How much do you want to fleece from me this time?"

"Just 500..."

"OK if I pay you in installments?" Sabir said playfully as he winked at Binny and Raman.

"Come on, sir. You don't mean that, you're just pulling my leg. Please give me the money and I shall disappear. I have a story to edit."

Sabir fished out his wallet and took out a 1000 rupee note. "Can I have the change, please?"

"Yeah," Tanya seized the note from his hand. She plucked a pen from around her ear and noted down Sabir's name in the little notebook she carried.

"You are a darling!" Tanya's parting words turned Ranvir and Baba green with envy.

"She is a promising girl," Binny quipped as Tanya hopped on to the Output Desk. "Probably the best among the new breed of journos we have."

"I thought it was Anushka," Sabir teased her.

"*Hmmm*... Well...in the eyes of the bosses, yes."

"Does that also mean Tanya is not the best."

"She is, in my eyes, the best ever."

"So you see things from your eyes as well?" Sabir said tongue firmly in cheek.

"I know what you are getting at, Sabir," said Binny even as she playfully slapped Sabir on his arms twice.

"I was just joking! *Achcha,* tell me what's the party for?"

"As if you don't know," Binny said with a chuckle as she pulled her chair close to Pushkar, Sabir and Raman.

The foursome went into a huddle with their heads bowed down at a malicious angle. "The party is to celebrate the end of election season. But, frankly speaking, it is being organised for Mata Karuneshwari and her stupid show, *HHRS* which has completed two years," Binny finally got to blurt her heart out.

HHRS was born *Rote Rote Hansna Seekho (RRHS)*. But Binny worked overtime to ensure everyone referred to it in its derisive *avtaar—Hanste Hanste Rona Seekho.* Drama queen Mata Karuneshwari only added grist to the whole campaign by producing one tear-jerker after another.

"I thought the party was being thrown for the unprecedented success of election coverage," Sabir expressed his surprise. Sabir's thoughts meandered to the exchange of official mails on the election coverage of the four states that concluded last week. He remembered how Prithvi and Hemendra wrote back-to-back congratulatory messages for everyone in the election team, doggedly omitting to acknowledge Sabir's role. Yashwant's brief response to the mail, especially mentioning Sabir for 'leading the team from the front', was sent to all recipients.

"I am on for any party, yaar," said Ranvir.

"This party must be Hemendra's doing?" asked Pushkar.

Sabir nudged him to shut up. It was a sign for Pushkar to avoid saying nasty things about Hemendra in Binny's presence. She was close to Hemendra more than she showed, but she hated Karuna alias Mamtamayi Ma Karuneshwari and reserved her most rabid remarks for her show, *Hanste Hanste Rona Seekho*.

But Binny did not seem to mind Pushkar's remark. "I don't know what Hemendra sees in that bitch," her vitriol poured out.

"You know what? Bhoomi told me that she was in PCR two the other day while the *HHRS* recording was on and she saw what the teleprompter read for our show host Ma Karuneshwari. It read something like: '*Yahan aap ko rukna hai... mahila ko gale lagana hai...aur rona hai...*'" Binny doubled over in laughter hardly able to stand, but her laughs kept coming.

"I had heard *HHRS* is scripted to the last tear; now, it is proved beyond doubt," Pushkar quipped.

"So much for pegging Mamtamayi Ma Karuneshwari as India's answer to Oprah," Raman said with a sigh.

"She is not even a speck of dirt on Oprah's slippers. *Kameeni...! Bloody bitch...!*" Binny was caustic and gave a hard look at Raman.

"Are we all just wasting our time on this? Anybody interested in Mamu's Secular?" Sabir got up from the chair and walked briskly ahead, while Pushkar and Raman followed suit.

Nag-Nagin & Gulab Jamun

Hemendra was surprised to see Satyendra's name flashing on his mobile. Satyendra mostly interacted with Jagat Singh and called up Hemendra only in emergency.

"Yes, Satyendra. What's up?"

"Sir, I have some exclusive on Tathaastu that can embarrass the State Government."

"What is it that you have got?"

"I launched an undercover operation and I succeeded. The Tathaastu project is steeped in corruption."

"*Hmmm,* all big projects ride on the corruption element, what's new about it?"

"I have an audio-visual proof that shows ruling party politicians offering bribes to the movement leaders to back off."

"What proof?"

"It's an undercover sting operation. It shows MLAs of the ruling and opposition parties discussing the project and offering bribe to the anti-Tathaastu movement leader on a spy-cam."

"Are they offering cash?"

"There is a proposal for an offer of bribe," said Satyendra.

"You mean visuals of someone being offered cash and someone receiving it?"

"Well...not exactly. But as I said the offer is being made and the entire conversation has been captured on our spy-cam. It's a watertight undercover operation." Satyendra hastened to add.

"But some within the coalition at the Centre, including the FPI, are opposed to the project. It may not be that easy for the Union Ministry to make a case against Tathaastu."

"The vagaries of coalition politics place irreverent demands on partners. At times, those can only be ignored at the peril of losing power," said Satyendra.

"What do you mean?"

"I think, the cabinet reshuffle and Sriram Raju's bargain for Climate and Forest Ministry is a pointer at things to come," Satyendra explained.

"And your Chief Minister?"

"Sir, the Chief Minister has an election to fight next year. His popularity is at an all time low. Is there a reason why the Chief Minister is floating around as the biggest mascot for the Aryan International? He knows Tathaastu could be his milch cow."

"You never told us about the assignment. Who approved it?"

"I have been working on the story for some months now."

"But who asked you to do it?"

"I had a go ahead from Haldi sir."

"Then go to him. Get your instructions from him. If the Input Head has cleared it, where is the need to brief the Output Head?" Hemendra sounded agitated. His disliking for Haldi was all well known. "As far as I am concerned, these stories are not expected of you. Who cares about a bunch of farmers in a far off jungle? Any viewership, any takers? *Nah...* Have been longest since I am telling you guys to work hard on stories which can get eyeballs rolling."

"I am trying my best."

"Best is not enough. I want the kind of stuff that Visphot does. Why do you think it is the number one channel? By the way, let me break good news to you. We have surged ahead of our most immediate rival, Angaar this week."

"Congratulations! But there's always scope to offer something different to our viewers, isn't it?"

"We have tried to be different with our one hour special show on debt-ridden Vidarbha farmer's suicides," explained Hemendra. "We got below par TRPs. So, I had to offset the loss the next day with that cobra couple which feasts on *gulab jamun*." Hemendra argued.

"Yes, sir, I remember the story." Satyendra replied.

"The entire village seeks blessings from the *nag-nagin*, with offerings of best *gulab jamuns*. You have a sweetmeat shop in every household in the village now. The village economy, *boom*; the human interest angle, *kaboom*!!"

"Sir, there have been six cases of death by snake bite in that particular village in the last three months," Satyendra said in a matter-of-fact tone.

"Now that is what I call negative thinking," Hemendra snapped. "Do you know we fetched a TRP of 35 on that *nag-nagin* story? Almost three times our average TRPs. People may accuse me of glorifying superstition, but I can feel the nation's pulse," he bragged.

"Isn't Tathaastu's a story etched in national interest? The rights of farmers and tribals are at stake. Somebody is out to steal their resources, to usurp their land for a pittance." Satyendra argued aggressively.

"What is the contribution of 'your farmers' to 'our' economy? Do you understand the erratic way stock markets are behaving the world over? Look, Satyendra, I don't want to get into any argument with you on this. Why don't you go back to Jagat and sort out your problem?" Hemendra was in no mood to listen to Satyendra.

"OK, sir, I am sorry to bother." Satyendra had no idea why his efforts to apologise fell on deaf ears. His labours met with silence for five seconds and then the line went dead.

Satyendra made this entry in his blue diary that night, originally written by Milan Kundera:

Kitsch is the inability to admit that shit exists.

Party Time

The rookie reporters, Tanya and Chandan were the first to arrive at the Blue Ocean. It was 7.30 pm already, the time they had put out on the mail for the party to roll.

It was close to 8 pm when the first batch—girls from the Output Desk who worked on the day shift—streamed in. They quietly took the far end of the sofa, under the dim beam of disco light.

Suddenly, there was a loud and lusty cheer from those girls. Gaurang had appeared! A ladies' man and a killer on the dance floor, he stood well over six feet. He darted a look across the hall. He could see the cute, Kilol, the charming Farhat, the beautiful Tavleen and the beauty with no brains, Deepshikha on the far-end sofa, across from the dance floor. He paced across to the floor and joined the girls on the sofa.

The foursome had nothing in common, except for their love for dance on occasions like these. Tavleen was an expert at cabaret moves, with the typical *filmi jhatkas* to boot. Kilol had to be persuaded every time. Once in her element, she would edge out others from the dance floor with her electrifying moves. Farhat would join in, no doubt, but always took time to get into the groove. Deepshikha thought she was born to dance.

"The DJ mixed the tracks quite decently and had more than made up the mood. "Come, let's hit the dance floor," Tavleen grabbed Gaurang's hand.

"The floor is inviting us. Come before these *buddhas* join us and spoil the fun with their weird dance forms."

They looked at the DJ and shouted in unison, "*Rock On...!!!*" Deepshikha also pulled Tanya on the dance floor, who was playing party manager for the second time. The last party was marred by spats and fisticuffs between colleagues and bartenders. '*Hope everything goes alright tonight,*' Tanya mumbled to herself as she took the first tentative gyration on the dance floor.

The haryali kebabs, chicken lollipops and paneer tikkas were doing rounds in small platters. Colleagues in small packs, in ones and twos and threes, started pouring in. Within the next half an hour, the place had enough footfalls to declare the party a mega hit.

Haldi was first among the bosses to join the party and he hit straight for the bar, his two *chelas*—Pankaj and Dharmesh—in tow.

The DJ rocked with his Punjabi and Indi-pop remixes. And in between, Alice would drive out in the limousine, giving no chance to Smokie who can't get used to not living next door to Alice. But, who was Alice? Yes, that was for those on the dance floor to ask as they would raise their hands in a fist and shout in unison—*Alice, Who the fuck is Alice?*

Minutes later, in walked '*The Gang*' minus Pushkar. The gang lacked the coherence, though and its identity was in tatters. Pushkar was the soul of the gang. Uday could not have replaced Pushkar, but he had now jelled well with the senior members of the gang. They headed straight to the bar.

"These motherfuckers are not to be seen anywhere," said Ranvir as he lit the cigarette and placed a request for his favourite scotch at the bar.

Sabir nudged Ranvir before leaning over him and speaking into his ears: "Haldi *madarchod* has already hit the bar. He is sitting there on far left."

"Look, who is here," Baba tapped Sabir's shoulders as he held the whisky glass in his other hand.

All eyes riveted to the bar door on the extreme right. Hemendra walked in with Karuna.

"The host couple is here," said Uday as the gang broke into another round of laughter. The DJ raced to a chartbuster from the year's biggest hit, *Race*. The sexy female voice delighted the hearts of the young as they foot-tapped and raised a lusty '*Dam-Dadam-Dadam*' in tune with the singer.

Raman had joined the gang by now. He tugged at Uday and threw a glance at Hemendra and Karuna. Uday could read what was running in Raman's mind at that precise moment. He recalled what Raman had told him on candid camera, admitting to his kitchen escapades, '*Ek haq ki ladai, doosri* fuck *ki ladai*'. He could see Raman smiling away mischievously.

Uday went up to him. "Do you think the crotch-scratcher will succeed with Karuna bhabhi?" Uday asked playfully.

"You know what, Uday, Hemendra has got his both hands full. Whether it's *haq ki ladai* or fuck *ki ladai,* he's a winner all the way. Give it to him, man. Such a lucky bastard he is..." said Raman.

"Has Hemendra changed his partner for the *nagin* dance number?" asked Ranvir.

"I hope not! I think Psycho and crotch-scratcher still make for interesting *nagin-sapera* couple," said Sabir.

Muskan spotted the gang and hopped out of the dance floor. She came whirling up to Sabir and caught his hand, "What sirs, you are needed on the dance floor."

"*Arrey*, why to drag old men like us?"

The DJ changed the track and the 'Singh' came back as the 'King'. Tanya would not take a 'No' for an answer as she tugged at Sabir. "Sir, you remember *'Beedee'*? You danced like a *mast* Bipasha last time." Sabir and Baba would not budge.

Uday spotted Sudhanshu on the dance floor. Touching 40, Sudhanshu always got thumbs down from female colleagues—they kept him at an arm's length at office parties. They could never excuse Sudhanshu after the Rati episode. Led by Muskan, the woman power had got together and ostracised Sudhanshu in the newsroom, the office canteen and even at the Mamu's.

The incident had rubbed off on Mamu also and he only prayed for Sudhanshu's absence at his stall. His table for six would go unoccupied if Sudhanshu took one.

'Tanya wouldn't have gone up to Sudhanshu for the contribution,' Uday thought. Tanya had once told him how she "feels like puking" every time Sudhanshu passed by in the newsroom. *'Sudhanshu must have invited himself over,'* thought Uday... *'Free booze and food and infinite voyeurism.'* What more he could ask for.

Tanya was firm that she would not let Sudhanshu have his way at this party.

Uday watched Gauri and Anubha step out of the dance floor the moment Sudhanshu stepped in. Deepshikha, Nigar, Kilol and Tavleen danced in one group with Gaurang. They had Muskan to give them company. Nidheesh, Irfan, Dhananjay and Manpreet sweated out on the other corner of the disco floor. Khyati and

Safia—recruit to the Graphics Team—had taken the centre stage. And Uday could see Sudhanshu eying his potential prey.

Uday saw Sudhanshu getting close to Khyati and Ritika and suddenly, as if in a flash, he somersaulted to the dance floor. In a filmy way, he now stood between Sudhanshu and the girls like a wall. Tanya was impressed, she prayed this does not turn ugly.

Sudhanshu smiled and force-jigged with Uday on another chartbuster, *'Mauja Hi Mauja'*. Tanya let out a smile when she saw Sudhanshu giving up and leaving the dance floor to head straight to the bar. She stepped in on the dance floor and gave Uday a tight hug.

The Revenge

A big "HI" from Anushka drew Tanya's attention, as they both hugged and kissed each other on the cheek. "I came with Prithvi sir," Anushka said. Prithvi stood next to her, grinning from ear to ear. "Why should I be deprived of a similar exchange of pleasantries," he asked Tanya.

"Sir, Anushka is a dear friend."

"Am I your enemy?"

"No, sir, you are not. But...sir, that is how we girls greet each other," Tanya giggled.

"Why a discrimination against the boys?"

"Sir, you are not just any boy. You are the boss," Tanya was direct.

"*Soch lo*, you have to come back to the newsroom and I am the boss there too," Prithvi said that in mock anger, but she could feel that he took her disapproval with a pinch of salt.

"As the party manager, I welcome you with folded hands," Tanya did a quick *namaste* as a mischievous smile crossed her face. *'But Pappu Can't Dance Saala,'* the giant speakers swooshed out the sound like a torrent.

"Poor Psycho! It was double jeopardy for him. He must have lost it, seeing you and I locked in a hug," Tanya told Uday as Prithvi turned towards the bar.

"Let's tease him further," Uday locked his arms around her waist and dragged her on to the dance floor.

Ernesto and Amitabh followed Prithvi to the sofa as the latter got busy playing with his BlackBerry. On the sofa across from them, Hemendra was 'pro-active' with Karuna as he slung his arms around her, while she held a huge glass of a sea-green mixture of a mocktail.

She came dressed in a chiffon sari as if she were attending a wedding ceremony in the family. "I prefer a quiet evening, not this *shor-sharaba*," she had told Muskan and Ritwik at one such office party. "Ma'am, you should be sitting at home listening to Kewat Bhai's religious *pravachan* on Hare Rama Hare Krishna channel." She could never excuse Ritwik for his cheekiness and reported the incident to Hemendra. Ritwik was clueless that he had laid the foundation of his own demise at Diamond News Network. His showdown with Sudhanshu proved to be the proverbial Last Straw on the Camel's Back.

"This girl is too good, Prithvi." Hemendra would always refer to Karuna as a 'girl', in spite of the fact that she was a mother of two and despite those unmitigating office rumours—after colleagues in office saw her younger baby intermittently reach out to his pubic area with his small hands—that the baby carried Hemendra's genes.

"She carries the entire show on her shoulders." When it came to praising Karuna, Hemendra did not know where to stop.

"Her silken voice does wonders to our show, no doubt about that," said Prithvi.

"She is a show stealer! She established the brand in just three months, while some people take years," said Hemendra, making a slanting reference to *Nexus* and *Om*, the two shows that were unceremoniously killed. In latter's case, almost killing the producer too. Well, almost.

"Absolutely! Nobody can make people cry and emotionally energise the audience the way she does. Kudos!" Prithvi dittoed.

"I have set her a new target. I have asked her to get me two more TRP points in the next four weeks. I promise to throw a bigger party at my own expense," Hemendra boasted.

"They make a perfect couple," Sabir pointed out to the occupants of the sofa across the floor.

"Who... Hemendra and Prithvi? Or Hemendra and Ma Karuneshwari?" Pushkar quipped triggering an uproarious laughter among the foursome.

Suddenly, the whole atmosphere seemed supercharged. The crowd was ecstatic. A lusty voice wafted from the hi-fidelity speakers, which throbbed and threatened to tear apart the boxes that encased them. People were seen lip-synching and simulating flying the kite. The crowd shouted full throated and in unison, *'Jigar Maa Badi Aag Hai!'*

'Beedee...' Hemendra started humming the number and threw a look at Karuna. She gave him a constipated look in return. Hemendra soon realised that the quilt was not warm enough and he had better borrowed some fire from the crowd on the dance floor, particularly from Anushka.

Anushka and Muskan exchanged greetings on the dance floor as Hemendra jumped into the crowd. Soon, he was surrounded by Shahid, Nidheesh and Amitabh. Sudhanshu tried to saunter in, but was elbowed out.

The gang spotted Rajkishore sitting at the far end of the bar. He appeared to be by himself, shut out to the noise around. Baba raised his glass to him. Rajkishore looked around—as if making sure nobody was watching—before raising his glass. A wry smile crossed his face, but he did not utter a word.

"Do you know about Rajkishoreji's tragedy?" Baba lobbed the question to Sabir and Ranvir.

"What? No, I don't," said Ranvir.

"His wife passed away recently. She had cervical cancer," Baba told.

"*Tch…Tch…* I used to wonder why Rajkishore bhai had become so quiet and withdrawn. The man must have gone through hell," said Sabir.

"Frankly, I have always thought he was a spineless character who never took a stand in meetings," Ranvir said as if admitting his guilt.

"Strange, we know so little about people we work with. Sometimes I feel one is always so lonely in this 'dhandha.'" Sabir said sipping his Black Label.

It was getting past 11.30 pm when Tanya announced on DJ's mic that "the bar shall close in another 30 minutes". There was another mad scramble for that "one last" at the bar.

Prithvi's eyes desperately looked for Anushka, but she had long melted into the crowd; soon almost in Hemendra's arms keeping with the spirit of the ball-dance number, '*Teri Ore*' from *Singh is King*. Hemendra made those hopping motions he mistook for amazing dance.

'Man Dole...' Ernesto screamed his lungs out looking towards the DJ. Realising that Ernesto's voice would not quite reach the DJ, Amitabh paced up at the console and requested the special number. As the*'Man Dole'* remix wafted through the air, the crowd watched Prithvi go down on his knees. Soon, he was rotating his head as if possessed. Hemendra flashed out a kerchief from his trouser pocket as he complemented the perfect *sapera.*

The kerchief had an immediate effect on the *'nag'*. Prithvi stretched out his palms over his head, denoting the hood of a snake and swayed more frantically.

Sudhanshu watched his colleagues dance to the excitement of the closing number, but did not quite have the energy to pull himself in to join them on the floor. The alcohol had taken its toll. He got up from his table and staggered away towards the loo, his whisky glass still in his hand.

He wasn't wholly conscious that two pairs of discerning eyes keenly watched his movement. Muskan pressed Tanya's hand and the two girls exchanged glances. Uday joined them from nowhere. He also pulled out Gaurang, Nigar and Tavleen from the dance floor.

Six of them then took firm and steady steps towards the direction Sudhanshu had headed. Keeping enough distance to not arouse suspicion, they saw their prey zig-zaging his way up to the loo, spilling the alcohol all over.

"He has no idea he shall meet his waterloo in the loo here," said Muskan as Tanya clasped her hands tightly.

Sudhanshu reached out his hand on the doorknob when he felt a huge weight push him into the loo and down on the floor. He could hear footsteps around him as the door shut with a 'click' sound. It was Sudhanshu's turn to black out.

Uday and Gaurang, who were standing guard outside heard the girls scream cuss words inside the loo. Tavleen's 'Bastard' and Muskan's '*bencho*' came regularly for about 90 seconds. Uday and Gaurang celebrated the moment with a dozen of mighty 'give me fives'.

The door opened and the four girls walked out, their hair dishevelled, breath coming out in short spurts and faces sprinkled with sweat. Muskan, who was carrying sandals in her hands was the last girl to emerge out of the loo. Uday and Gaurang clasped the girls in a big hug. Then, almost with the speed of lightning, Muskan turned around and landed a mighty kick on the loo door: "*Man Dole*...! *Tan Dole*...! My foot...! Here's a girl's *sholays*...! *Bencho*...!"

An Ode To Krutika Kolhatkar

Paagalvaani.blogspot.com
November 7, 2008

The entertainment industry shall ever love your attitude, but we—in the world of TV news—are equally indebted to your sense of enterprise. You made us believe there is more to news than getting to report the stark reality of poverty, underdevelopment, malnourishment and injustice that confronts those living in villages and remote towns of India.

You made us believe entertainment is news. The entertainment genre of news is now celebrated in the TRP *bazaar*. You gave a boost to our falling esteem as Hindi TV journalists. Viewers watched your soaps religiously, but we in TV newsroom tried to ape your style unabashedly, thought by thought, frame by frame, edit point by edit point, dissolve by dissolve, by the hour and late into our prime-time. And lo and behold, we got excellent returns! Those news channels who glossed over your formula of achieving climax through unadulterated melodramatic and absurd kitsch, fell by the wayside on the TRP index. We got into people's living rooms, bedrooms, their love life, sex life—and all that which makes a man a social animal (why only humans, we never once shied away from depicting the animal kingdom in all its beastly and horny glory). You led us to believe even the dead can talk and we barged into funeral processions unannounced, just for that veritable sound byte.

You left a lasting mark on the psyche of a lay news follower. All thanks to you, the discerning viewer switches on a news channel today only to watch his favourite soap opera's highlights and we think our viewer has evolved, that he has come of age. If penicillin was touted as one of the greatest medical discoveries, you shall have a place no less venerable than that of Alexander Fleming. You developed an antibiotic resistant to news. Penicillin proved to be a miracle drug in the 20th century and saved millions of lives, but you sustained many brilliant TV News Managers through your K-pill. Thank you, for giving us our daily bread.

On a day when your most venerable and authentic soap opera, *Kyunki Bahu Bhi Ek Din Saas Banegi* goes off air after eight years of uninterrupted run we, TV Managing Editors Inc., take a bow.

Paid News

Paid news is the biggest blot to journalism. It robs off the element of fearlessness and integrity from our profession. Leaders of our freedom movement won many a socio-political battle with the moral power of their pen. The menace of paid news does no good to their memories. It's a type of cancer that has come to threaten the very existence of free press. This has to be fought with all the moral power at our command."

"Yashwant boss is too good, yaar. Did you read his piece today?" Shahid asked Priyam while working on the rundown.

"No, sir, you don't get the time to read newspapers in the morning shift," Priyam said without looking away from his screen.

"You must read it. It's an excellent piece," said Shahid.

"Must be! After all it is Boss's article," he acknowledged.

"*Ha-ha!*" Shahid could catch the intended pun. "The way he has woven the freedom movement into his piece is commendable."

Shahid went back to his terminal and logged on to *sharebazar.com*. Soon, he was finished and it was time for personal chores. Paying online for his mobile and credit card use, paying off electricity bills, searching for the latest car models, socialising on the Facebook, an account he had recently opened. It shall be lunch break when he would be through with all these important businesses, including time to stretch his legs and take co-ordinated *sutta* breaks. He will pick up his tiffin and accompany Hemendra, Prithvi and Haldi to the canteen.

"Sir, what do you say about this interview?" Priyam pointed to the Narottam Oswal interview on air.

Shahid turned around to watch the interview. "He's said one beautiful thing in his interview: 'You can take the country away from a person, but you cannot take the person away from the country'. That's the spirit of a successful entrepreneur," said Shahid. "He knows he has to win over people before he hopes to get his business going."

"Is it true that we are giving away the 'Son Of The Soil' Award to Narottam Oswal?" The question caught Shahid off guard.

"Frankly, I have no clue. But, he sure deserves it. He has spawned a new model of development and I am amazed at the string of philanthropic works behind him." Shahid was always good with diplomacy.

"That is the longest way of saying a yes to my question," Priyam was sarcastic.

Shahid laughed aloud. "Well, I have nothing to add to what I have already said."

"By giving away the award are we not in effect pitching for the Tathaastu project?"

"We are pitching for development," Shahid was terse.

"Oh, yes, how can I forget that? After all, we are running four minutes advertorials put out by Tathaastu and Aryan

International. Obviously, if Tathaastu is pro-development, we cannot be anti-development," Priyam rubbed it in.

"But your great 'Son Of The Soil' is getting severe resistance from the original sons of the soil. There is a huge resentment against the project on the ground," Uday jumped into the conversation voluntarily.

"There are always hurdles to development. As channels, we are responsible to educate our viewers, remove their mental blocks. Don't you think so?" said Shahid.

"Is that why we are blocking out anti-Tathaastu protests on our channel?" said Uday in an accusing tone as he crossed his arms across his chest.

"Every channel pursues its own agenda; they have their niche viewership," Shahid sounded like a teacher caught amid protesting students.

"What is our agenda? Pro-poor or pro-rich?" Uday asked point blank.

"We are pro-development, that's that!" said Shahid.

"The Tathaastu group is known for ruthless corporatisation of natural resources which impacts the biodiversity and the indigenous people dependant on it," said Uday. "And sir, the group is a known history-sheeter in flouting environmental and forest laws. They went to Malaysia, but were turned out for defying green laws. I wonder what kind of a development model they would create in India," Uday argued.

"*Arrey* bhai, why are you guys after my life? I am not working for Tathaastu," Shahid was clearly on the back foot.

"You know, Shahid sir, Dushyant wrote a beautiful couplet for such an occasion. Here it goes:

"Ub Yahan Par Nazar Aati Nahi Koi Darar,
Ghar Ki Deewar Par Chipke Hain Itne Ishtehaar."

Before the impact of the couplet could sink in, Uday disappeared from the scene and got back into his edit suite, leaving Shahid with his decisive moments.

"So, all set to give Narottam Oswal a red carpet welcome?" Sachin asked Priyam while leaving, at the lounge downstairs.

"Do you have a light?" Priyam asked without caring to answer back.

"No wonder he has flown all the way from London and is coming straight down to sit in the lap of the government and their media *dalals*," said Sachin as he lit Priyam's cigarette.

"It does not stop at that, brother. I heard the Chief Minister, Bajrang Prasad is getting the Achievers Award for Law and Order. It's like patting the butcher on his back for delivering the freshest produce."

"People like Oswal and Bajrang Prasad are the channel's new bridegrooms. You and I and countless others in the newsroom are destined to prepare the *mandap*. Give the best slugs, dig in research and adorn with some over the top packaging."

"I am aghast that a panel of such distinguished experts—comprising of former judges, ex-bureaucrats and some of the country's who's who would choose names like Oswal and Bajrang Prasad to earn such awards," Priyam said.

"Everything is fixed! Yashwant has paid them to pick the nominations of his choice," said Sachin as he blew out a big gust of smoke.

"Sometimes I wonder why nobody has thought about an exclusive PNC." Priyam took a deep drag at his cigarette, as a playful smile crossed his face.

"PNC? What's that," asked Sachin.

"Paid News Channel," Priyam replied and they both laughed their hearts out.

"You and I are already part of one such channel." Sachin laughed out hysterically at his own repartee.

"Don't you remember how Uday's investigative piece on Ranjit Diwakar's alleged role in the mysterious murder of two employees of his distillery industry was spiked?" Sachin tried to explain his point.

"Yes, I do. I was designated Producer-In-Charge for that special story," said Priyam. "The seniors first cited lack of documentary evidence. After all, Diwakar was an MLA and a FPI Chief Minister's son and the only political heir. When Uday fished out more evidence, they said the facts must be crosschecked. Uday crossed this hurdle as well, but the story was given a quiet burial after a word came over from none other than Sidhartha Sawhney. End of the matter." Priyam rattled off the entire incident.

"So, while Sidhartha and Ranjeet enjoyed a game of squash at the High and Mighty Club, seniors here decided to play poker with Uday." Sachin concluded.

"Precisely," Priyam took a deep drag at his India Kings.

"I heard Super Boss wants to expand further and set up a channel, exclusively for NRIs, headquartered in Toronto, Canada. He cannot afford to upset his business prospect for a cheeky little story." Priyam added.

"There is someone out there who has the capacity to tag us for a price." Sachin said philosophically.

"Not us... It's them!" Priyam chided Sachin.

"The line that separates us from them is very thin. I always fear crossing over," a shiver ran down Priyam as Sachin spoke those words. "Was he not equally vulnerable?" He blew the last gush of smoke and flicked the cigarette butt away.

"*Chalo,* I will take leave. The vultures on the fourth floor must be timing my entry," he shook hands and took leave of Priyam.

Aryan Go Back

"You can make a difference to the life of thousands of poor by one small step. It is indeed heartening to note that the philanthropic arm of Aryan International—Shubhichcha Institute—has already taken a giant step towards this." Anushka was moderating a small presentation ceremony on behalf of Shubhichcha Institute with confidence and panache. DNN was TV partner of this ceremony. Prithvi, in consultation with Hemendra and Jagat, had decided to put Anushka's moderating skills to good use.

"Let me take this opportunity to introduce you to Kanta Kumari. Kanta was barely 15 when her mother died. Tragedy struck her again, when her father lost his battle to cancer. Kanta was left to tend to her younger brother. A sudden darkness befell in Kanta's life, but, as they say, there is always light at the end of the tunnel. The Shubhichcha Institute came as a beacon of hope for Kanta and her younger brother. Kanta Kumari was adopted by the Institute, which took to financing her further studies and helped her stand on her feet. Today, Kanta is a graduate and she teaches in a local girl's school. She is now Kanta *'behenji'* and every villager feels proud of her. May I invite Ms Kanta Kumari to come on stage and receive a token of appreciation for her courage and determination.

I would request Mr Arvind Patel, head of the India chapter, Shubhichcha Institute, to give away a plaque and a cheque of Rs 1 lakh to Ms Kanta Kumari."

"I want all the information on Shubhichcha on air, one after the other," Sudhanshu was screaming from the PCR.

"Just stick to Patel and Kanta," Prithvi shouted for everyone to hear as he walked out of his cabin.

"I would appreciate if the distinguished audience could raise both their hands as a resolve to end poverty and help shape a new India." Anushka's voice blared from the 26-inch LCD panel mounted across the wall, leading to the Production Control Room.

"This girl carries it with aplomb. What do you say, Dheeraj?" Prithvi posed a direct one at Ernesto.

"She is the right choice to anchor such a prestigious show, sir." Ernesto was quick on the uptake.

"Time to play Super Boss's recorded message!" Prithvi pressed the talk-back microphone on Ernesto's desk to relay his fresh instructions to Sudhanshu in the PCR.

In a flash, Yashwant Thakur was all over the screen on DNN channel, LIVE: "Poverty is the biggest scourge that beset our country 60 years after independence. It is indeed ironical we are still fighting over *mandir-masjid* when the real danger lies elsewhere. Let's take a pledge today to eradicate poverty, not only from this country but from the face of the Earth. The only way we can do it is by empowering the last man on the socio-economic ladder. And empowerment can only come through education." Yashwant Thakur looked down from the TV panel in tight close up as he went on to describe the India of his dreams.

"Time for you to sit for LIVE chat after the Super Boss's recorded message," Sudhanshu replied from the talk-back inside the PCR.

Prithvi quickly darted across the floor and took the seat in front of the camera—placed at the far end of the newsroom—for his LIVE chat, while the screen showed visuals from the Shubhichcha presentation ceremony LIVE.

Suddenly, a slogan got pasted on the screen:

GO BACK, TATHAASTU.

In a matter of seconds came another:

TATHAASTU, DOWN DOWN.

Prithvi could hear a violent slogan rent the sober ambience of the newsroom.

"Tathaastu Ki Dadagiri, Nahi Chalegi Nahi Chalegi...
Aryan, Go Back, Tathaastu, Go Back..."

"Some anti-Tathaastu protestors have barged into the function," Sudhanshu screamed into Prithvi's earpiece. "Seems a bunch of tribals," he added.

"Tathaastu, Down Down... Aryan, Go Back..." the slogan kept booming across the newsroom. The sound engineer got caught in the sudden rush of events and forgot to minimise the impact by pushing the 'fader' down on the control panel.

"Take a break. Take a break!" Prithvi unplugged the earpiece, threw it across the floor and darted across the PCR.

Son Of The Soil

Delhi, November 23, 2008

"Yes boss, almost all guests have confirmed our invitations except the I&B Minister, Mrs Kavita Nagpal. The Secretary is coming. We have six Chief Ministers, eight Union Ministers, the Deputy Leader of the opposition and 12 MPs across party lines who have confirmed their participation." Prithvi was floating around on the floor, his BlackBerry plugged to his ears.

"What about Sriram Raju?"

"He, too, has agreed. Your intervention did help."

"The rundown looks impressive now. Let's hope everything turns out fine tomorrow. Hope there is no coordination hassle with our print partners *New India Times*."

"Absolutely not! They have delivered their bit." Prithvi assured Yashwant.

"The final forty-eight hours, Prithvi. We must not leave any stone unturned."

"You will get a top class show," Prithvi slipped into his glass cabin.

"Boss, it's been a good day. Your interview did it all!" Shahid announced to Prithvi excitedly as he barged into his cabin.

"What happened? You never sounded so happy before," said Prithvi.

"Sir, it's been a windfall," Shahid announced ecstatically. "Aryan International closed on an all-time high," he added.

"How much did you make?" Prithvi was curious.

"A clean fifty!"

"The Oswals' can move markets," said Prithvi.

"You bet. Until last week, the scenario did not look encouraging. But, I think the news of Narottam Oswal's visit and your interview impacted the stock market directly. I owe my windfall to you."

"That calls for a party, Shahid bhai." Prithvi indulged Shahid.

"Sir, did you invest in Aryan International?"

"No yaar, I don't invest in stocks...you know that."

"I know. You are a man of gold. You invest in real estate."

"A small penthouse will make me more than happy," said Psycho rubbing his hands in nervous excitement.

"*Inshallah*... You will have it sooner than later. Haven't you booked one in India Heights yet?"

"I am being offered a good deal by the builders."

"Good Luck to you, sir. I was thinking of taking my family for a vacation to Manali."

"*Arrey*...you should not think of staying anywhere else except my hill-top bungalow. It's just three kilometres uphill from the last bus stop. You can drive further up if you have your own vehicle. It's a beautiful place! I will get everything arranged for you. When do you plan to leave?"

"Next week. This is the right time to visit Himachal."

"Yes, you don't have to stuff too many woolens."

"That means you are confirming my leave in principle... *He he he...*"

"*Achcha,* what's the update on New India Achievers Award preparations?"

"The promo is already on air. The graphics are ready. The packages shall be ready by tomorrow. The technical team should be taking over the venue by tomorrow midnight. OBs are on standby. You can see the rehearsal day after at noon. We'll have a top class show. Dheeraj has already got into the groove along with Priyam and Sachin."

"That's great! I want hourly updates for the next forty-eight hours. Let's catch up again tomorrow morning."

Himmatganj, November 24, 2008

"Do you think our story will ever see the light of the day?" The resigned tone in Altamash's voice was not to be missed.

"I am not the one to give it up so easily," Satyendra sounded optimistic.

"I know, but it's been three weeks since you sent all your stories to the headquarters and there has been no official response as yet."

"Haldi sir never said it will not be aired," Satyendra tried to pacify Altamash, but he did not sound confident.

"My gut feeling is they are not going to run it." Altamash found Satyendra's optimism misplaced.

"Haldi sir said they were looking into pros and cons of the entire story." Satyendra replied tentatively.

"Oh, really? Pros and cons of running the story or stalling it for now?"

"We will have to believe them. We have no other option."

"I allowed them the benefit of doubt until three days ago. Ever since I have come to know of the 'Son Of The Soil' Award, my blood is on the boil. I feel cheated. Now, I do suspect their intentions." Altamash was ballistic.

"Patience is a virtue," Satyendra was getting philosophical, a hint that even he has resigned himself to fate.

"This is not virtue, but foolhardiness. We cannot afford to sit on this story for long. Does the office know the anonymous threatening calls you have been getting? Do they know they tried to kill you, push you under the wheels of a running truck? Do they know there was an attempt to kidnap Saagar from school?"

"You know if I tell them, they will get an excuse to drop the story. If they don't run the story, I shall be in further danger of being exposed to those vultures who would continue to hound me and my family, and, maybe, even you," Satyendra appeared defensive.

Satyendra's logic cut no ice with Altamash. "I have sent my wife and kids away to her native place. I will advise you too to do the same. Those vultures are following us. These fellows don't have any scruples. I don't want my family to look for me in a morgue." Altamash's paranoia was not an overexaggeration.

"Ritika's paranoia is tearing me apart. She refused to send Saagar alone to school. Now, I drop him to school and pick him up after it gets over."

"Time is of essence, Satyendra. Why don't you understand that? The world has to see our story or we are doomed. We cannot put our families at risk at the altar of one goddamned story." For the first time in the last three months, Altamash showed signs of cracking up. "Who will take care of our families after we are gone?" Satyendra could see tears welling up in Altamash's eyes.

"Don't lose hope, Altamash bhai. You have been my strength. I promise I will talk to Prithvi sir as soon as this award function gets over."

New India

November 25, 2008; Delhi: 7 pm

From the sidelines Yashwant could see the country's who's who filling into the banquet hall of The Centurian Plaza, a 7-star hotel in the heart of Delhi. His channel, Diamond News Network had instituted this award—New India Achievers Award—only this year. It was a proud moment for Yashwant.

Karuna and Anushka were rehearsing their scripts behind the stage; Karuna in red chiffon, Anushka in fiery orange. For Yashwant, these two colours had ascendancy and that is why these were also DNN's predominant on-screen colours.

Prithvi and Hemendra decided to play the usherers themselves—escorting Union Ministers and Chief Ministers—along with Binny in blue *chanderi*. *'Prithvi selected two dresses of his choice—one for Anushka and the other one for me,'* Binny could not help sharing the secret with Raman during a 'quicky' in the office's unisex washroom last evening.

Sabir and Ranvir were responsible for ushering in other ministers and top secretaries. Thethar was seen floating around in the hotel corridors; his chest was puffed up as if he was one of the award prospects. His task was cutout already. He would usher in the 'Son Of The Soil', Narottam Oswal.

Bajrang Prasad was among the first to arrive. His work uniform was as clichéd as corporate India's work uniform. Immaculately outfitted but more boring for his lack of experimentation. A starched white *kurta, churidar,* an ethnic jacket and black boots. Prithvi jumped the protocol by stepping forward to greet him at the portico, than waiting in the lounge. Hemendra and Binny followed suit. Raman, along with Muskan, Bhoomi and Uday was responsible for ushering the rest of the guests to the hall, including women MPs, entrepreneurs and others from the intellectual diasporas.

Jagat Singh Haldi was seen holding animated talks with Pankaj and Dharmesh even as he flicked a comb over his heavy mop of hair every now and then, just to check not a strand was out of place. Shahid, Dheeraj and Sudhanshu took turns to coordinate between editorial and technical duties. Upretiji, who had the camera holstered to his waist kept climbing up and down the stage mock-shooting. In between, he was also seen giving directions to his colleagues over the talk-back system clipped to his ears.

This was a special day for Yashwant mainly because of two reasons. First, DNN was going to be in an all new avatar after midnight. And second, for managing another coup of sorts. He had succeeded in persuading the distinguished selection panel to nominate Prime Minister Chintamani for Best Visionary category. When this came about, he approached the Prime Minister himself, who accepted the honour but refused to share the dias with Narottam Oswal.

When Chintamani refused, he drew out another ace. He had the PM record a congratulatory message, which was to be played out during the course of the awards night.

A victorious smile flashed across Yashwant's face. His life was taking a turn for the better with three companies under his wings, an entertainment company in the pipeline, an offer to enter the August portals of the Parliament from the country's future Prime Minister and a Padma Shri in waiting. He was on top of the world!

'*It seems like yesterday,*' Yashwant thought. He remembered the hot sultry afternoon of May 1988 when, armed with a Masters degree in Political Science from Patna University, he knocked at the office door of *Leading Light*—one of the country's prestigious English language dailies published from New Delhi. His first big moment came when he was assigned to report on an ailing Raj Kapoor, the much-celebrated Bollywood director, who had been admitted to Delhi's All India Institute of Medical Sciences (AIIMS). In another two years, Yashwant was seen covering the assassination of a former Chief Minister, Arul Raj followed by a scoop on the assassination plot.

By mid-nineties, Yashwant switched to electronic media when the country witnessed the boom of private TV production houses. In 1998, he set up his own production house—Diamond Productions—and was seen producing a couple of current affairs shows for Doordarshan's various regional channels. His production house's popularity grew by the day, his dreams multiplied by the night. He yearned to own a 24×7 news channel. The big day came in 2002. Yashwant had arrived! Diamond News Network (DNN) had now over 300 employees on its rolls. Yashwant Thakur had the world at his beck and call today. Even the redoubtable Chief Minister Bajrang Prasad graced the occasion to receive the New India Achievers Award for the Best-Administered

State in terms of Law and Order. The presence of the VVIPs and the VIPs was a salute to Yashwant's standing in the media world.

November 25, 2008; Himmatganj: 9 .30 pm

"Why don't you take the office transport?" Altamash asked Satyendra.

"No, I am driving my own car today. Actually, I have to join Ritika and Saagar at my cousin's house. We might have to stay the night there. I thought I'll get my own vehicle." Satyendra replied.

"OK! Drive safe." Altamash appeared concerned.

"Ya, don't worry. See you! I hope that we will take up our cause afresh tomorrow with New Delhi." Satyendra's words triggered a fresh wave of hope in Altamash's heart.

It was a seven-kilometre drive past a desolate stretch of about a kilometre, slightly off the city's populous area where his cousin, Saurabh had got his new house built. Saurabh had promised to throw a party exclusively for friends once his parents were gone. Tonight was the night!

Satyendra was looking forward to such an evening with his family. He desperately wanted to spend more time with Ritika, assuage her fears, comfort her and bring back normalcy into her life. Poor Saagar had spent more time crying, than playing in the last three weeks. His mother refused to let him go out of sight once he was back from school.

Satyendra crossed the city area and negotiated the last lap towards his cousin's residence. The streetlights refused to come on; the darkness of the night only accentuated the loneliness of his drive through the desolate patch. His heart pounded in his chest as snatches of memory of the drive back home with Ritika and Saagar came back at full force. Suddenly, his car was filled with pale yellow luminous light giving some comfort to the cold darkness, but spreading a yellow mist that enveloped his vision. The source was finally visible. Fighting to stay in its lane, a huge, heavy vehicle rose into view, its high beams blinding Satyendra.

New Delhi, The Centurian Plaza, 10:45 pm

Prithvi's phone buzzed on the silent mode from the jetted inner pocket of his chocolate-brown jacket. He was standing on the dais, helping Yashwant welcome the guests on to the stage. He held a cordless gun-microphone in his hand, which he passed on to the awardees when they received their award. This was the hour of power and pride for Prithvi as well.

Karuna announced the next award category. A man rose from the circle of chairs in the centre of the first row of tables. He was a man in his mid-fifties, a salt and pepper mop covering half of his broad forehead. The bald patch on the back of his round head only betrayed the number of scheming summers he spent appeasing the governments he did businesses with, or ever intended to. While his black tuxedo enhanced the air of luxurious lifestyle he was accustomed to, a silk handkerchief stuck out neatly in a triangular fold from his breast pocket. He confidently walked up to the stage amidst thunderous applause.

"Ladies and Gentleman, The 'Son Of The Soil'...may I call upon stage Mr Narottam..."

Haldi's mobile phone buzzed inside his jacket pocket as he passed the microphone from one guest to another for some LIVE question-answer session.

Himmatganj, Saurabh's house, 10.15 pm

Ritika got another call from Satyendra's mobile at five past ten. She had put the handset in her bag after receiving the last call from Satyendra at 9.30 pm. A little later, she dug into her bag for the mobile and saw it ringing.

"Where are you? It's almost half an hour since you last called. You should have been here by now." Ritika hurled a volley of questions into the speaker. She was greeted by a strange voice on the phone: "Ma'am, do you know Satyendra?"

"Who are you?" Ritika's voice dropped.

Ritika rushed to the spot along with Saurabh. She could see Satyendra's white Honda City lying upside down on the street, its tyres hanging in the air. She let out a scream as she rushed towards the car. "He is stuck inside...we can't get him out. We have sent for some help. We need iron-cutters to get him out." A constable was heard shouting.

"How did you call from his number?" asked Saurabh.

"We were doing the rounds of the area when we heard a massage from our Control Room. When we reached here, we found the smashed car. We found the mobile lying on the road close to the car." One of the two constables explained to Saurabh. He continued in the same vein: Fortunately, it was in a working condition. "I tried last three numbers on the 'dialled' list on his phone. One was to someone called Prithvi and another one was to some Jagat. The third one was Ritika. Is this Ritikaji?" The constable pointed to the woman crying herself hoarse. "Is she his wife?"

Saurabh did not bother to answer the constable. He had so many questions running in his mind.

"Looks like some heavy vehicle, most probably a truck, hit his car." The constable stated matter-of-factly.

Saurabh took in the impact of the accident. *'The front of the car has borne the maximum brunt, the tyres appear to jut out of the metallic chasis; it seems like a head-on collision,'* he thought to himself. Ritika was on her knees crying inconsolably, trying to peep through the window. She could touch Satyendra, but could not pull him out.

"Will somebody get him out? He is asthmatic. I need a puff. Will somebody get me a puff? Please, Saurabh *bhaiyya*, please, get him a puff, he will die without it." Ritika was getting hysteric.

"Sir, why don't you take care of ma'am. We have called the ambulance." The constable screamed.

"Let's first turn the vehicle over." Saurabh screamed back. Nobody had quite realised there were enough hands to get the vehicle back on its four tyres.

"We should get him out of this mangled heap first, only then we'll be able to save him. He seems to have lost a lot of blood." Saurabh tried to control his emotions on seeing a drop of blood dribbling down the adjacent window.

It took some time to cut the iron before Satyendra could be pulled out from behind the wheels. Satyendra was unconscious and bleeding profusely. It seemed his skull had taken the hit; shards of glasses were stuck all over his face and body, a thick trickle oozing out of his right temple. The twisted steering wheel seemed to have used its momentum and hit him full-thrust into his chest.

At the hospital, the doctors put him on oxygen. Suspecting it to be a case of multiple fracture, since much blood had flown out of his body as he was been wheeled into minor O.T, they looked for the pulse. It was not found. They tried to pump his chest. The body lay cold. Those attending on him feared precious time was lost getting him out of the car, they knew the steering wheel had thrust deep into his vitals. They feared the worst. Their fears were proved right when a doctor gestured Saurabh in the O.T that things were beyond him now.

Altamash replied to Satyendra's call on the third ring. "We would never get to hear Satyendra again." Saurabh's voice shook in between muffled sobs.

It was past midnight when Altamash dialled Prithvi on his mobile. Prithvi did not take the call. He then dialled office. He broke the news to Farhat, who was on the night shift.

The Centurian Plaza, 00.10 am

The guests had gone. In the dining area, they had all gathered in a huge circle. Yashwant was holding forth, his arms casually flung around Prithvi's shoulders. He held a glass of scotch in his right hand. Everyone else held a glass of their favourite drink. Binny was yapping away about the humongous success of the show, her arms locked into Raman's. Everyone seemed to be praising everyone.

"Here's raising the toast to LAVA LIVE." Prithvi raised his glass.

"I told you, it shall be a hit." Jagat Singh Haldi raised the toast to Yashwant.

"Sir, the channel's new name is too good. It sounds true to our character of aggression." Hemendra raised his glass and clinked it against Prithvi's.

"We are a channel with an 'L', two 'L's to be precise. We will fuck the trip of our rivals." Ernesto appeared sozzled.

"It's a coup of sorts," Shahid chipped in.

"Three cheers for Amitabh. Only he could have come up with such a terrific name for the channel." Prithvi's statement sent a mild aflutter among the crowd. "Amitabh's truly a genius. He has made history today." Prithvi added much to the envy of Shahid.

"Cheers..." Yashwant raised the toast to Amitabh, Prithvi and the rest of the team.

"Nobody can stop us from being number one. That's a promise, Yashwant boss." Prithvi boasted to the loud cheers of the court attendants.

Delhi, November 26, LAVA LIVE HQ. 10.30 am

"He was the tireless worker and the ace investigative reporter. Who would know fate will be the so cruel," said Prithvi, addressing a condolence meeting held for Satyendra. He had so much in him to contribute for the even greater success of the LAVA LIVE. We have not just lost the good reporter, but also the very nice human being. Satyendra always worked silently without any protest. Now, the God has silenced him for the ever. Let's stand up everybody as a mark of respect to the memory of our most beloved, brave and the fearless comrade." Prithvi did not tell anyone he ignored two calls from Satyendra's mobile last night. Neither did he tell anyone he was sitting over Satyendra's most sensational investigative story on Tathaastu's deal, for the past six weeks.

"Let's run an obituary. Ask Amitabh to write the script. Ernesto, you help him with the script." Prithvi instructed.

"Sir, how long should it be?" Ernesto asked in a whisper.

"Not more than 90 seconds. Put it in the rundown for *Hila Ke Rakh Denge,* post 9.30 pm. Make sure you use his shots holding the gun-microphone with the channel ID. People should know he did some great stories for DNN." Prithvi turned to Hemendra: "Hope we are running the band that says 'DNN is now LAVA LIVE'. It shall run 24×7. Don't remove the band when we are showing the obituary."

Mamu's Tea Stall

Mamu thundered orders to Nandu interspersed with expletives and looked in a foul mood.

"Nobody is attending Satya bhai's funeral?" Mamu walked up to Sabir. Ranvir accompanied him at the table.

"They've sent Jagat Haldi there," Sabir stood up to match Mamu's towering presence. Mamu appeared concerned and dejected.

"His enemy would have waited for him for ever to make a mistake. Was he working on his toughest investigation as a 'khoji'?" Mamu seemed overwhelmed with emotion.

'How could Mamu read somebody's mind,' thought Sabir.

"Can't say any thing for now. But he was hit by a heavy vehicle. The police is still clueless," Sabir responded.

"Who all are there in his family?" Mamu lobbed one question after another.

"He has a six-year-old son," said Sabir.

"Hope the office adequately compensates the family." Mamu turned back and walked up to his seat without waiting for an answer. Ranvir and Sabir did not know what to say.

"Mamu may be right. I suspect Satyendra has been bumped off." Sabir broke the silence.

"I won't rule that out. He has shaped shocking stories with national impact, he'd made enemies along the bumpy way." Ranvir threw a big ring of smoke into the air.

"I spoke to him only yesterday. He sounded dejected that his latest investigative story was put in cold storage." Sabir recounted the conversation.

"The only way to pay homage to such a braveheart is to run his story," said Ranvir. "But I don't think these buggers have the spine to run it," he added.

"I will raise the issue if I can. Satyendra will have to rise from the ashes," said Sabir as his voice choked with emotion.

Delhi, LAVA LIVE HQ, 9.35 pm...

"True to his name, he never shied away from speaking 'Satya'..." Prithvi was reading out the Anchor Lead during the flagship show at 9 pm, *Hila Ke Rakh Denge*. "Satyendra Mahto is no longer with us. But the..."

"Prithvi, there are reports of some firing at Mumbai's Chhatrapati Shivaji Terminus. We are going LIVE with Himanshu's phone-in from Mumbai," Prithvi's earpiece crackled. Hemendra never sounded so excited.

The breaking news band popped up: *'Firing at CST. Terrorists strike Mumbai again.'*

In the next three minutes, reports of suspected terror attack was confirmed. *'Terrorists have struck at ten places across Mumbai, including two five-star hotels, with coordinated shooting and bomb explosions.'*

LAVA LIVE along with their competitors were LIVE with the news for the next three days. So did other channels. The nation was denied sleep until the terrorists were killed and the hotels secured. At the end of the operation, 173 people lay dead, all victims of Pakistan sponsored terrorism.

Tathaastu

Paagalvaani.blogspot.com

Today I am reminded of Mohandas Karamchand Gandhi. The journalist Gandhi. Gandhiji used to say, "I believe in soul communication."

Satyendra Mahto was among the few who represented *soul* in news business—which, today, is fast slumping into a bottomless pit of greed and perversity. He upheld highest tenets of journalism and gave up his life for a cause.

Our system either keeps whistle-blowers on the fringes or decimates them. The latter being an option increasingly adopted and put to practice by forces that are co-opted by the system, purely for its lethal strike rate. So whether it was Satyendra Dubey, who blew the whistle on corruption in the Golden Quadrilateral project, an ambitious venture to link India through highways or Manjunath, the Indian Oil executive who threatened to expose the oil adulteration racket, they had to pay a terrible price for their testimony.

The story of media's Satyendra was no different. Incidentally, the very forces corporate media is out to woo targeted him.

Media's Satyendra, however, suffered from a comparative disadvantage. While Satyendra Dubey and Manjunath were lapped up as icons of post-mortem ostentatious media chivalry, Satyendra Mahto had to vie for space in a media that outrightly refuses to be shown the mirror.

The media that is entrusted to act as a watchdog and act without fear or favour tucked its tail between its legs, its power to bark blunted to a whimper. The Electronic Media (Mass Media for some) has gone under the corporate hammer for a song.

In fact, the emerging Corporate Media is setting itself ambitious targets. It does not mind shedding the scruples and is not ridden with guilt. The market has discovered the potential of multi-tasking journalists, who fancy the flight to superstardom of stinking riches. They now aspire to be 'power-brokers-cum-corporate-lobbyists-cum-contractors-cum-film-producers-cum-parliamentarians-cum-miners-cum-members' of a government commission; everything a journalist ought not to have dreamt to stay true to the rulebook.

The prime time of typical Corporate Media Journalists does not begin at 8 pm and end at 11 pm. It transcends time barriers. They stalk communication network in the hush of the night, at page three circuits, during a political crisis, during vacations abroad, at the time of launch of an IPO, post its launch, pre-cabinet reshuffle and post it, before a story is aired and after it has been aired. It's a 24×7 job. For them, a losing proposition is also a cause for a celebration.

Let's ask all the Media Managers out there: "*Apko kaisa lag raha hai?* How does it feel to strike at the very foundation of the edifice called the fourth estate?" Like so many beautiful precedents—the ones we have mastered the art to sidestep instead of following them—that Mohandas K. Gandhi set before our society, we shall atleast circumvent the need to communicate with the soul. Or we can proudly say, "We don't have one now."

Prime Minister Sidhartha

Superpower News Network HQ, 9.30 am. November 2015

"I am all set to leave, bhai sa'ab... I had a word with the pilot. I shall be there before the function rolls. And yes, thanks once again for lending me your *udan khatola*," Ritwik's tone was almost obsequious.

"Oh, come on...you are like my younger brother. In fact, you are like a son but you prefer to call me bhai sa'ab, so be it." Vikramjit Tulsania was honey dipped.

"*Arrey*...bhai sa'ab..."

"OK. Have a safe journey! Driver Ram Subhag will come at the airport to pick you up," said senior Tulsania.

"That name sounds familiar."

"Ya, he's the one who went to jail for Veer," Vikramjit Tulsania was remorseful. "I have got him back on parole. He shall recognise you."

"Thank you, see you then!" Ritwik was talking to Vikramjit Singh Tulsania, Rajya Sabha MP, Chairman and MD of the Super Power Group of Companies. The Tulsanias had consolidated their empire over the last few years and now branched into power and petro chemicals. Son Veer had expanded the empire to software and breweries. It was his coronation today.

The Mercedes Series 10 was waiting for Ritwik below the portico at his Gulmohar Park residence. He had bought this house for 18 crores two years ago and pumped in another two crores on its decor before moving in. After all, he was not just an employee of the Super Power Group, but also a five per cent partner stake-holder in the brewery trade.

The car was a birthday gift from Vikram 'bhai sa'ab' on his last birthday. "I still remember the first time I asked you what you want," Rikwik remembered what he was told. "And you said you just need my blessings. Here are my blessings, son." Ritwik couldn't muster up the courage to say no.

The Tulsanias were indebted to Ritwik for the way he saved Veer from a veritable ignominy eight years ago. Ritwik had become family ever since. So when it came to launching Super Power News Network (SPNN), Veer was clear who would be its Director.

The SPNN channel had created a news window dedicated to the Super Power Enterprise with a team of reporters and producers working exclusively on the hand-over ceremony, ever since Vikramjit Singh Tulsania pronounced to pass over the baton to his son. It was Anushka who came up with the slug: *Raajtilak.*

On way to the airport, Ritwik fished out his latest iPad and tweeted: '*flying out to Suryavanshpuram for Veer Tulsania's Rajtilak.*' He paged Anushka to set up video-conferencing with the editorial team. '*Two minutes,*' Anushka paged him back. He switched on the dish, a palm-sized screen swooshed out of the head rest whirring to a stop after it had settled in its place; the screen now facing Ritwik, "HI Anushka! How's you, baby?"

"*Aww...* I am fine. Just read your tweet, baby."

"What's up on the agenda today?" Ritwik asked in a matter-of-fact tone.

"Sidhartha is leaving on a three-day trip to Brazil tonight," said Anushka. "This is the biggest ever delegation in recent years led by a Prime Minister," she added.

"Must get Sidhartha's brief interview." Ritwik appeared on the 47" plasma plastered at the other end of the conference room. "Mr Tulsania has already spoken to Mr Lavania...he is heading the business delegation. Get in touch with Mr Lavania, he will fix an interview with Sidhartha." Ritwik could see a set of hands writing furiously on their notebooks. "Mind you," Ritwik continued, "this is Prime Minister Sidhartha's first foreign trip after the multi-crore food grain scam that hit his government last month. Sidhartha wants to give the impression that Delhi is not a corruption capital that it is falsely made out to be and that his government means business with those probable investors."

"Ritwik, this is the right time to take up the cause of those affected by Sumangalam Power project," Uday spoke from the far end of the table in the conference room. His pepper-grey hair stretched his age by atleast ten years. "The protestors are sitting on fast-unto-death at Jantar Mantar. They are demanding the scrapping of the power project because it overrides environmental concerns. About 600 families, spread over sixteen villages, are going to be affected."

"Do they still stage sit-ins at Jantar Mantar? The people of this country have no better things to do? They think if they can make Tathaastu go down on its knees, they can make anyone cringe before them. I tell you..."

"Those people at Jantar Mantar are the same people who voted Sidhartha to power. They feel cheated now." Uday was polite but firm in his reply to Ritwik.

"You must be crazy, Uday," Ritwik shot back. "Do you want me to close shop? I have the responsibility of over 1200 people on my head. I am not paid to take care of the interest of those goddamned tribals. Anushka, I don't want those goddamned tribals on my channel for fuck's sake."

"But the country wants to know why Prime Minister Sidhartha is reneging on his poll promises? We need to investigate why the young Prime Minister has changed colours, in just about a year he has been in office. Is he under too much pressure from international quarters?" Uday insisted there was more to the new government's ad hoc policies than what meets the eye.

"Sidhartha is just trying to get the wheels of the economy back on track by endorsing Sumangalam. And as a channel, we ought to support that. I don't want any roadblocks. Hope I am clear." The words rang across the SPNN conference room. They could see Ritwik's face go red on screen.

"You ought to know that Muskan is leading that tribal delegation." Uday drew out the ace.

"Send the camera and archive the visuals if you so wish," Ritwik's tone dropped a couple of notches. "Next," he thundered putting a full stop to any further discussion on the Sumangalam subject.

"The Old Boys Association of the Thousand Galaxy Public School is donating Rs 2000 crores to their Alma mater," said Anushka. "The Thousand Galaxy is now expanding into a University and the Old Boys Association is organising the biggest cultural show at India Gate tonight. The singing sensation PK is going to sing at the concert LIVE under the baton of Aftab–Danish. Union HRD Minister, Mr Mukut Behari is the Chief Guest."

"Great! Hope we are covering it LIVE. Remember we are also its media partners." Ritwik instructed. "What else?"

"Rinki Raspberry's split up with Sweety Strawberry. It's official! Rocky has just tweeted it," said Anushka. "I feel sad for both of them. They made such a lovely pair on screen," continued Anushka.

"Does she love someone else now?" Ritwik seemed anxious.

"Yes, there is a *woh* factor...but I know Sweety, she is not up to Raspberry. She is so bitchy," informed Anushka.

"We should break the news and play it big," Ritwik pronounced.

"We already are on the news. Just check your screen," Ritwik pressed on the remote in the car and Raspberry came alive.

'*She made life hell for me. She is extremely suspicious of my friendship with other girls. It's impossible to live with her. She is a bloody bitch,*' said Raspberry. Ritwik switched back to the conference room. More people had joined in.

"Anu, just tell Sweety to behave on screen. I don't want the goddamned pensioners in the Broadcasting Council to get another opportunity to pounce on us."

"Sure, in a second."

"Is that all? Shall I switch off then?" Ritwik asked.

"No, there's an important judgement in Federal Court today. The Court is likely to re-define guidelines of what constitutes harassment at work place."

"A kind of an anti-management ruling? None of our concern..." Ritwik snapped.

"But it's anti-LAVA also, Ritwik." Uday knew what would make Ritwik pause for a rethink.

"Mandakini *bhabhi* had also raised the issue that due to persistent and continuous harassment of her husband at workplace, the couple suffered a loss of libido and self-confidence. The court is set to pronounce its ruling on this aspect as well. It's going to be a water-shed judgement," explained Uday.

Uday's entry into SPNN was under interesting circumstances. After the Tathaastu fiasco, Yashwant was under intense pressure to own up. He chose the easy way out. The trio of Prithvi, Hemendra and Jagat Pratap Haldi had to go. LAVA LIVE put up a brave face. The official word that went around was that global economic slowdown needed a fresh look at the market strategies and so the channel needed somebody young to head its content. In those circumstances, Sabir would have been seen as the natural successor, but he had already put in his papers and was all set to take over as Executive Editor of new Hindi daily, *Naya Sawera,* to be published from Noida.

Baba was the new kid on the block. But the post of Managing Editor sat heavy on his head. He was a changed man overnight. From an affable personality, he was now a quintessential authoritarian leader, with no appetite for disagreement. He was vulnerable to every whisper in the newsroom and one day he crossed swords with Uday over a trivial matter. Uday stood his ground, but decided the time was up for him in LAVA LIVE. He closed ranks with Ritwik, who was set to launch a new channel for Superpower Group of Companies with Anushka on board. '*Do dreams turn out to be true? Will Anushka again lord over him, throw him before the lions and let him die a bloody death?*' Uday watched his predicament right before his eyes. He owed it to the random combinations of thoughts he'd had and things he may have seen or heard back then. But he also realised he was ready to put up with that snooty 'whore', than work with a dysfunctional leader.

"Go ahead! Time to embarrass LAVA LIVE!" Ritwik's voice boomed through the plasma screen in the conference room. "Hope the judgement comes exactly on the lines we have anticipated." Anushka darted a look at Uday and smirked.

Uday felt relieved. The world did not know he was a silent crusader in this legal battle, rubbing shoulders with Mandakini bhabhi and also part-sharing the litigation cost.

"Cut Tulsanias LIVE for *Raajtilak*. Keep shuttling between Tulsania and Raspberry in the afternoon and you already have the prime time booked for the musical evening and the Tulsanias' special. The court stuff should not disturb our editorial line. I hope that's fine!" Ritwik dictated.

"Yes! Don't worry, baby," Anushka reassured him.

"OK then guys, see you in the evening. Chow..."

"Chow baby..." Anushka sounded happy. Soon after, her phone rang. It was Ritwik. "Hold on a sec," she got up from her chair and moved towards the door.

"Don't get worked up over Uday," Ritwik tried to comfort Anushka.

"I don't know why he always insists on stories which do not jell with the channel's line. It's not happening with him. Let's throw away this utter tripe." She flared up.

"No, no. We cannot do that," Ritwik cut her short. "At least, he is not scared of speaking the truth. I have respect for such people. In an age where conscience is all but dead, he is the only one who has kept it alive. I also do know, though, that too much of goodness is dangerous for our channel's health. Discuss that later, gotta go!"

Ritwik was cruising past Vasant Vihar when he sensed something fly past over his head. He looked out of the car window and saw the Delhi Metro. The Metro silently overtook

Mercedes Series 10 from the right. He remembered how he had covered its trial run, from Shahadra to Tees Hazari, as a young reporter for a local TV channel in the winters of 2002. This was Delhi Metro's 14th year of smooth run in the capital city. *'A miracle of sorts in a country that is still waist deep in governmental red-tapism and inefficiency,'* thought Ritwik.

Delhi: November 2015. HQ of LAVA LIVE, Morning Editorial Meeting in Progress...

"Get Thethar to put us through Yashwant sir. This business delegation is important for Sidhartha's international image. We must get his interview." Baba greeted colleagues at the LAVA LIVE conference room with his stern voice and took his chair at the head of the oval table.

Padma Shri and Rajya Sabha MP, Yashwant Thakur now worked out of the Prime Minister, Sidhartha Sawhney's office as State Minister. For Sidhartha, this was one of the foremost decisions after he took office as Prime Minister and leader of the redrawn UPNDGA. With Yashwant, Thethar too had moved into the PMO as Yashwant's Personal Secretary.

"Thethar has already confirmed the time. It is 2 pm at Vigyan Bhawan, after Sidhartha's meeting with State Director Generals of Police on tackling the spread of naxalism. Yashwant sir said he will put out the press handout later in the evening." Ranvir explained.

"We should also attempt a story on tribals, who are protesting outside Jantar Mantar against Sumangalam power projects coming up in Arunanchal." Gaurang butted in.

"What new on Sumangalam project? It's rather best avoided." Baba disapproved the idea with the wave of his hand.

"No, the protestors are angry that the environmental concerns are given a go by. They are also angry with the PM, saying that Sidhartha Sawhney has turned a deaf ear to their demands," Gaurang replied. They feel cheated that the person who stood rock solid behind Ullasganj tribals at the height of anti-Tathaastu agitation is now eating out of the hands of corporates," said Gaurang in a protesting tone.

"Sidhartha showed genuine concern for the tribals then. But nothing is static. India is on a super highway to progress and he is regarded as the new beacon of hope. We must all strengthen his hands," said Baba undercutting Gaurang's point.

"But," Gaurang persisted, "Sidhartha is showing his colours rather too soon. Just a year in office and he is already behaving like a typical politician who reneges on his promises."

"He is a new age leader. He is pro-technology, pro-development. The press has this penchant for hanging the accused even before he is pronounced guilty. I cannot allow that any longer." Baba snapped.

"But the new PM must realise that his government is still on crutches. He is heading a coalition government and cannot arrogate all powers to himself." Gaurang dug in much to the discomfort of Baba.

"No arguments. Next item, please." Baba was dismissive.

"It is Satyendra bhai's death anniversary. Ritika has come down to join the protest, along with her son Saagar. This shall be a great opportunity to meet her. After all, Satyendra bhai died for a similar cause." Gaurang provoked Ranvir and Baba. Baba was losing patience.

"Please send a camera there. Let's move on to our next agenda." Baba was dismissive.

"There is this musical evening lined up tonight. It's organised by the Old Boys Association of Thousand Galaxy Public School. The HRD minister is the Chief Guest." Shahid said excitedly.

"Great! Must go LIVE." Baba directed. "What else...?"

"The split between Rinki Raspberry and Sweety Strawberry is now confirmed," Ranvir announced.

"Now that's big!" Baba gasped in surprise.

Rinki and Sweety clicked as lesbian couple in a regional film. The new-wave Hindi film director, Prabhakar smelled a lot of potential in the duo and signed them for a remake of the south blockbuster, *'Rock Baby, Rock'*. In an effort to make them distinctive, he made them play almost identical characters, named them Raspberry and Strawberry and picturised two appealing songs on them. The songs proved a rage on music sites across the Internet even before the film's release and catapulted Rinki and Sweety to instant stardom. Raspberry and Strawberry were the new national icons of freedom and liberty within weeks of the film's release. They took the nation by storm when they decided to tie the nuptial knot last year. Theirs was the first celebrated lesbian marriage that openly challenged laws of the land.

"What happened? Why the split," asked Baba.

"Raspberry has a new love in her life." Ranvir broke the news.

"That's what I call *Exclusive*," Baba banged the oval table with excitement. "Paint the town red and pink and queer and whatever," he proclaimed.

"We broke the news. In fact, we were the first to go LIVE with their photos. We beat SPNN hands down." Binny expected a pat on the back from Baba.

"This is our top news since morning, Baba." Shahid chipped in. He picked up the TV remote and reluctantly changed the channel from Stock Today to LAVA LIVE.

Sunidhi was LIVE on phone with Sweety Strawberry.

'*I will sue Raspberry for domestic violence. I am not going to divorce her so easily. I know she will never be able to adjust with that whore called Chikni Tikli.*' Strawberry thundered over the phone from Mumbai.

"Are we not doing the court judgement on employee harassment?" Gaurang asked Baba.

"We are party to the dispute. Don't forget, the case is against us. Can't touch it even with a barge pole." Baba was dismissive.

"Not even for Pushkar bhai? This was Mandakiniji's do-or-die battle." Gaurang insisted.

"There is no room for emotions in business," Baba warned, got up from his chair and started walking towards the door.

Uday sat upright and his three-year-old daughter, Udita played in his lap. Tanya moved into the room with two tea mugs and a stack of newspapers tucked under her left arm. The front-page headline of *Naya Sawera* screamed '*Exclusive*'. Uday picked up the newspaper and started reading it. Nilofar Goradia's role in the Sumangalam deal was under suspicion for some time. *Naya Sawera* ran the transcript of the audio tapes in its possession, which had Nilofar Goradia, Chairman and MD of Vistaar Communications pushing the Sumangalam Power Project deal with the Joint Secretary, Ministry of Power. Nilofar's deputy,

Jagat Singh Haldi shared the space with his boss. The newspaper claimed Haldi's brief was to work on two media bigwigs—Farzana Patel, Managing Editor of *The New Post* and Raghuvir Anand, Co-owner and Publisher of *Modern India Chronicle*—to convince them to use their influence in different ministries to get the Sumanglam deal through for their clients, the Randhawas.

Naya Sawera also reproduced Haldi and Farzana's transcript in a separate box.

"Sabir bhai has done it again. The newspaper has gone from strength to strength under his stewardship." Uday told Tanya as he read excerpts of the story to her.

"And you know Tanya, the proud Allahabadi that he is, Sabir bhai is soon going to launch *Naya Sawera* edition from his home town as well. He was really excited when he broke the news to me yesterday."

More than Yashwant and Prithvi, Uday's dislike for Haldi grew manifold after Satyendra's death. Though, he also knew that Haldi only executed a script written by Yashwant.

His thoughts meandered to the night of November 25, 2008 when Satyendra met a brutal death and the events that soon followed. The public and political pressure against Tathaastu was building up. The controversy was pushed into a vortex of another storm when police investigations revealed that Satyendra's fatal accident had been planned to a fault. All fingers were pointed out towards Aryan International's Publicity Manager, Anil Wilson.

Uday recalled how, despite the public furore over Satyendra's murder, Yashwant Thakur shamelessly stuck to his guns and did not air Satyendra's investigative story on Tathaastu. The spy-cam visuals of CM's sexual promiscuity with Tathaastu's PR man, Anil Wilson were traded with FPI, which used it against the CM much to their advantage in the next elections.

But Satyendra's gutsy wife, Ritika decided to take on LAVA LIVE. She played out the CDs of Satyendra's sting—Operation Deep Woods—at a press conference organised by the Press Club of India in Delhi.

Snatches of Ritika bhabhi's press conference remained frozen in Uday's memory. Even in death, Satyendra had stung the very people who conspired to kill his story. In that press conference, Ritika read out an entry Satyendra made in his blue diary on November 24, 2008, a day before he was killed:

Strength does not come from physical capacity. It comes from an indomitable will.

– Mahatma Gundhi.

Uday was flooded with memories. He remembered how rival channels had lapped up the CD's content. Yashwant washed his hands off the entire episode, blaming it all on the Managing Editor, Prithvi for sitting on Satyendra's "brilliant piece of investigation".

It was an indication for Prithvi to own up moral responsibility and quit. But he hung on. Prithvi's forced exit from LAVA LIVE happened on a fateful Friday, a day when the channel vacated its number three spot, which it loosely hung on to for the last six weeks and dangerously slipped to number five. Uday still remembered an excerpt from *Paagalvaani* that celebrated Prithvi's exit from LAVA LIVE. It read: *At the height of his glory in Diamond News Network (now LAVA LIVE), Prithvi was convinced that the flash floods in the Indian border town of Rimrola was caused by chemical clouds sent by China. I wonder if he would still blame India's mighty neighbour for sending across three-legged dragon called TRP to eliminate him.*

Prithvi's luck had finally run out. Media houses were not willing to bet on a lame horse. But he knew well that one man would never fail him. In the end, it was Chief Minister Bajrang Prasad, who came as Prithvi's saviour and offered him the post of Media Advisor.

Bajrang Prasad's stature grew in the party. Midway through his third term, he was called upon to take up the mantle of his party—The Hindoosthaan Party—in Delhi. Prithvi also moved back with him to Delhi. Bajrang Prasad had his eyes set on 7 Racecourse Road, the official residence of the country's Prime Minister. But allies played spoil sport and refused to endorse Bajrang Prasad's name for Prime Ministership. Bajrang's umbrella coalition of nine parties—All Party Nationalist Alliance (APNA)—was defeated at the hustings last year. The Freedom Party of India (FPI) emerged as the single largest party; though, far short of majority, in a fractured verdict yet again. Sidhartha Sawhney emerged as the 'consensus' candidate to lead the coalition government of United Parties for 'Non'-Democratic Governance by Alliance or UP(N)DGA.

Uday remembered every bit of it distinctly. Suddenly, his eyes panned across to a four-column six-inch deep advertisement on the seventh page of *Naya Sawera*. The advertisement solicited investors for buying 2 BR and 3 BR flats in multi-storeyed Karuna Towers in Kasauli. The advertisement was put out by Nautiyal Real Estate Developers, the real estate company run by Hemendra. After the roaring success of his tourist resort in Uttarakhand, Hemendra had decided to expand his business to neighbouring hill state of Himachal Pradesh. Hemendra parachuted from Fourth Estate to Real Estate in an almost perfect landing with Mata Karuneshwari in tow. Karuna's husband, now ex-husband, had filed for a divorce after their second child charged her with infidelity. Hemendra sent his first wife back to his village before marrying Karuna. Both Hemendra and Karuna were now Uday's Facebook friends. Mata Karuneshwari read each and every word from Hemendra's script without the aid of a teleprompter, Uday would think. Her countenance (the photo she made her Facebook profile picture) was the only constant—she still wore the look of a woman wronged.

Three-year-old Udita offered a stiff competition to his father, Uday, showing promise of being a voracious reader herself. Something had caught her fancy and she was trying to point that out to Uday, who carefully followed her. It was a photo spread five columns above the fold on page 1. Udita was trying to recognise Sia and Sidhi in the photo. She had made friends with them, particularly Sidhi. Uday wanted to give his daughter the first lesson in photo journalism—*A photo is worth a thousand words*. And this was one such photo. A photo of Mandakini bhabhi flashing a victory sign. She was flanked by two young girls. Sia, the eldest, stood holding the push bar behind a wheel chair and Sidhi had her arms draped around her father. The wheel-chair occupant seemed to be staring blankly, but Uday knew that the man was happy inside. Uday was with him in the afternoon yesterday, when the Federal Court delivered its judgement. The Federal Court not only upheld the High Court's judgement of granting monetary compensation to Pushkar's family, but ruled that the harassment of an employee by his seniors or by the employer affects not only the employee, but his entire family and the organisation should compensate adequately for the emotional stress and trauma suffered by the family. The court also asked the media industry to frame transparent guidelines regarding appraisal and promotion of employees.

Sabir bhai had captioned it beautifully, with a couplet from Pushkar's favourite poet, Dushyant:

> *"Sirf Hungama Khada Karna Mera Maqsad Nahi,*
> *Meri Koshish Hai Ki Ye Soorat Badalni Chahiye."*

Uday's eyes grew moist. A lump grew right in the middle of his neck as his eyes narrowed down yet again on the photo—Pushkar bhai was diligently aping his gritty wife in the photo, his hands raised a little over his head, triumphantly frozen in a 'V.'

Acknowledgements

My deepest debt to colleagues in the newsrooms since my days in *BiTV*. Especially camerapersons, VT editors, fleet assistants, drivers, producers, graphic artists, PCR producers, sound engineers, guest coordinators, reporters, librarians and researchers.

Special thanks to Rudra—my sounding board who travelled with me through the manuscript's journey.

To Prasanna for his sustained counsel at a crucial stage of the project.

To Parvez bhai for being such a support and Sufiya ji for being the perfect host always.

To Sunanda, Sandeep, Swati and Prashant for their sustained encouragement.

To Chhote and Manish—whose friendship I take for granted.

To Kanwaldeep—my 'Guru bhai' and a friend.

To Sangeeta Menon Malhan for diligently working on the translations of the couplets. Now, a writer and a poetess herself.

To Sumit, Sukesh, Darain, Sandeep, Aloka, Ipshita and Abhishek—for being such a ready audience always.

To Shailendra, who has left behind fond memories.

To Anil Vats for his optimism.

To Papa, who has taught me never to give up.

To my affectionate brother Prashant, his caring wife Ruchika and their daughter, Pari—my bundle of joy.

I also wish to thank all my relatives and cousins for showering their love and affection on me, from time to time.

A special word of thanks to Ajay Mago, Publisher, Om Books International for reposing faith in me. After two back-to-back rejections, he came as a beacon of hope.

Thank you Dipa Chaudhuri, Editor-in-Chief, Om Books International, for all those amazing discussions on the state of media.

To Nitin Abbey for all the pains he took to edit the language bloopers in the manuscript, his honest suggestions, (much of which I considered and accommodated some too) and his reassuring way of putting things across as if it was the greatest manuscript ever, that passed through his hands.

To Neeraj Tyagi, who is for ever so eager with ideas for the book's publicity.

Thanks also to:

Arif bhai (my *sangeet* guru) NP Singh, Sumant bhai, Aparna, Abhishek Upadhyaya, Samrendra, Sabir Hussain, Rubaiyat Ali, Anurag Vats, Mukesh Yadav, Sandeep Shukla, Dilip Mandal, Amitaabh, Girijesh, Anant, Sharat, Ratna, Saroj, Amitabh Gautam, Prasil, Sanjay Chowdhary, Satyendra Negi, Pankaj Mehta, Sunil Sagar, Gauri ji, Anu Rizvi and Kakul, Ehtesham and Tabassum.

And to Sangita for being there.

A very special thanks to the batch of '85, St. Joseph's College, Allahabad. Pankaj Bhola has left a void which can never be filled.

My deepest gratitude to Late Dushyant Kumar ji, whose ghazals and poems have inspired newsroom youngsters and elders alike.

Sudha Madhavan is a writer, artist and educator based in Bengaluru, India. She specializes in travel writing, children's stories and poetry as well as opinion pieces, all of which are imbued with her deep interest and research in history, civilizations and diverse cultures. Sudha has been published in leading print and digital publications since 2003 and her stories for children are featured in the anthology *100 Greatest Stories for Young Children* (Hachette India, 2020).

Sudha's oil-on-canvas artworks are part of several private collections and have been exhibited in Mumbai and Bengaluru. She has been an educator and consultant with leading NGOs such as Maya Organic, a livelihood development initiative involved with artisans, self-help groups (SHGs) and micro-entrepreneurs, and Shishu Mandir, a children's welfare institution founded by Hella Mundhra. Sudha attended St. Thomas School, Shimla, and has degrees in English Literature and Education from Isabella Thoburn College and Lucknow University respectively.

When not writing or painting, Sudha loves gardening, yoga and sharing her love for old movie songs with her little grandson, Rishi.